D0053079

*No writer captures the seasons of
our lives better than Judy Blume. Now, from
the internationally bestselling author of* Wifey *and*
Smart Women, *comes an extraordinary novel of
reminiscence and awakening—an unforgettable story of
two women, two families, and the friendships
that shape a lifetime.*

SUMMER SISTERS

"An entertaining adult fairy tale . . . with engaging
characters, an intriguing plot and plenty of sex."
—*San Francisco Examiner & Chronicle*

"She catches perfectly the well-armored love between
longtime female friends. Blume's characters still tend to
hover after the book is set aside, proving that this
talented realist continues to do what she does best."
—*The Seattle Times*

"You don't have to be a Blume fan to enjoy *Summer
Sisters,* but if you are, you'll remember why you loved her
books as a child and read them again and again."
—*San Antonio Express-News*

"*Summer Sisters* is a fictional fountain of youth sure to
make the reader young all over again."
—*Newsday*

"Blume tells a good story, creates memorable
characters . . . and demonstrates an ear for up-to-the-
minute vernacular. . . . Many readers of *Summer Sisters*
who traveled with Blume in their youth will welcome this
new opportunity to visit with a writer who now spins
provocative tales for them and other grown-ups to read."
—*The Tampa Tribune*

Please turn the page for more extraordinary acclaim. . . .

"A relentlessly readable book . . . The strength of this novel is its vivid portrait of teens in the 1980s. Interspersed viewpoints of various characters add interest and depth."
—*Library Journal*

"*Summer Sisters* is not for kids. It is Blume's third book for adults, coming 10 years after *Smart Women* and *Wifey*, both of which were best-sellers. . . . [And] it's pretty darn good."
—*The Philadelphia Inquirer*

"Engaging . . . sympathetic characters and realistic situations."
—*The Oakland Tribune*

"A healthy mix of drama and wry humor . . . An effortless, enjoyable read . . . [Judy Blume] is a woman for all seasons."
—*Bookpage*

"A book for all readers . . . an adult book with universal appeal."
—*Seventeen*

"Blume keeps her story moving . . . her portrait of an unlikely yet enduring friendship as it changes over time will remind readers why they read Blume's books when they were young: she finds a provocative theme and spins an involving story."
—*Publishers Weekly*

JUDY BLUME'S BOOKS

For Adult Readers
Wifey
Smart Women

For Young Adults
Tiger Eyes
Forever . . .
Letters to Judy: What Kids Wish They Could Tell You

For Younger Readers, the "Fudge" books
Tales of a Fourth Grade Nothing
Superfudge
Fudge-a-mania
Otherwise Known as Sheila the Great

For Middle Grade Readers
Iggie's House
Blubber
Are You There God? It's Me, Margaret.
Then Again, Maybe I Won't
It's Not the End of the World
Starring Sally J. Freedman as Herself
Deenie
Just As Long As We're Together
Here's to You, Rachel Robinson

Picture Books
The One in the Middle Is the Green Kangaroo
The Pain and the Great One
Freckle Juice

SUMMER
SISTERS

A Novel

JUDY BLUME

A DELL BOOK

Published by
Dell Publishing
a division of
Random House, Inc.
1540 Broadway
New York, New York 10036

ISBN: 0-440-22643-0

Reprinted by arrangement with Delacorte Press

Printed in the United States of America

Published simultaneously in Canada

May 1999

10   9   8   7   6   5   4

OPM

To Mary Weaver
my "summer sister"

WITH MANY THANKS to Randy Blume, Larry Blume, Amanda Cooper, and their friends for talking with me about music and memories during long, leisurely Vineyard dinners on the porch. Special thanks to Kate Schaum, dedicated early reader, and to Gloria DeAngelis, Kaethe Fine, and Robin Standefer. Also, to my Harvard connections, Nicky Weinstock, Ted Rose, and Seng Dao Yang (my unofficial guide to Weld South).

Contents

Summer Sisters

Prologue

THE CITY IS BROILING in an early summer heat wave and for the third day in a row Victoria buys a salad from the Korean market around the corner and has lunch at her desk. Her roommate, Maia, tells her she's risking her life eating from a salad bar. If the bacteria don't get you, the preservatives will. Victoria considers this as she chomps on a carrot and scribbles notes to herself on an upcoming meeting with a client who's looking for a PR firm with an edge. Everyone wants edge these days. You tell them it's edgy, they love it.

When the phone rings she grabs it, expecting a call from the segment producer at *Regis and Kathie Lee*. "This is Victoria Leonard," she says, sounding solid and professional.

"Vix?"

She's surprised to hear Caitlin's voice on the other end and worries for a minute it's bad news, because Caitlin calls only at night, usually late, often waking her from a deep sleep. Besides, it's been a couple of months since they've talked at all.

"You have to come up," Caitlin says. She's using her breathy princess voice, the one she's picked up in Europe, halfway between Jackie O's and Princess Di's. "I'm getting married at Lamb's house on the Vineyard."

"Married?"

"Yes. And you have to be my Maid of Honor. It's only appropriate, don't you think?"

"I guess that depends on who you're marrying."

"Bru," Caitlin answers, and suddenly she sounds like herself again. "I'm marrying Bru. I thought you knew."

Victoria forces herself to swallow, to breathe, but she feels clammy and weak anyway. She grabs the cold can of diet Coke from the corner of her desk and holds it against her forehead, then moves it to her neck, as she jots down the date and time of the wedding. She doodles all around it while Caitlin chats, until the whole page is filled with arrows, crescent moons, and triangles, as if she's back in sixth grade.

"Vix?" Caitlin says. "Are you still there? Do we have a bad connection or what?"

"No, it's okay."

"So you'll come?"

"Yes." The second she hangs up she makes a mad dash for the women's room where she pukes her guts out in the stall. She has to call Caitlin back, tell her there's no way she can do this. What can Caitlin be thinking? What was *she* thinking when she agreed?

Four weeks later Caitlin, her hair flying in the wind, meets Victoria at the tiny Vineyard airport. Victoria is the last one to step out of the commuter from LaGuardia. She'd spotted Caitlin from her window as soon as they'd landed but felt glued to her seat. It's been more than two years since they've seen each other, and three since Victoria graduated from college and got caught up in real life—a job, with just two weeks vacation a year. No money to fly around. *Bummer*, as Lamb would say when they were kids.

"Going on to Nantucket with us?" the flight attendant asks and suddenly Victoria realizes she's the only passenger still on the plane. Embarrassed, she grabs her bag and hustles down the steps onto the tarmac. Caitlin finds her in the crowd and waves frantically. Victoria heads toward her, shaking her head because Caitlin is wearing a T-shirt that says *simplify, simplify, simplify*. She's barefoot as usual and Victoria is betting her feet will be as dirty as they were that first summer.

Caitlin holds her at arm's length for a minute. "God, Vix . . ." she says, "you look so . . . grownup!" They both laugh, then Caitlin hugs her. She smells of seawater, suntan lotion, and something else. Victoria closes her eyes, breathing in the familiar scent, and for a moment it's as if they've never been apart. They're still Vixen and Cassandra, summer sisters forever. The rest is a mistake, a crazy joke.

PART ONE

Dancing Queen
1977–1980

1

VICTORIA'S WORLD SHOOK for the first time on the day Caitlin Somers sashayed up to her desk, plunked herself down on the edge, and said, "Vix . . ." It came out sounding like the name of a beautiful flower, velvety and smooth, not like a decongestant. Caitlin had transferred to Acequia Madre Elementary School just after Christmas, having moved to Santa Fe from Aspen over the holidays. Everyone in Vix's sixth-grade class fell instantly in love with her. And it wasn't just the way she looked, with her pale, wavy hair, her satin skin and deep-set, almost navy blue eyes. She was scrappy, fearless, and had a smart mouth. She was the first to say *fuck* in class and get away with it. No teacher, no adult, would have believed the words that rolled so easily off Caitlin's pretty pink tongue. And then there was that smile, that laugh.

Vix was too shy, too quiet to even speak her name. She sat back and worshiped from afar as the others fought over who would get to be her partner, who would share desks with her. So she thought she'd heard wrong when Caitlin asked, "Want to come away with me this summer?"

Vix was wearing worn bell-bottoms and a juice-stained purple T-shirt, her dark hair pulled back into a sloppy ponytail. She had a pencil smudge on her left cheek. As Caitlin spoke Vix could swear she heard Abba playing in the background. "Dancing Queen" . . . She missed most of what Caitlin said except it had to do with some island in the middle of the ocean. The *ocean*, for God's sake, which she had never seen. She was unable to answer, sure this was a trick, a joke. She expected the rest of the class to start laughing, even though the last bell had just rung and the other kids were rushing past them toward the door.

"Vix . . ." Caitlin tilted her head to one side and the corners of her mouth turned up. "My dad gets me for the whole summer. July first until Labor Day."

The whole summer. The whole goddamned summer! The music swelled. *You're a teaser, you turn 'em on, Leave them burning and then you're gone* . . . "I've never even seen the ocean." She could not believe how stupid she sounded, as if she had no control over the words that were coming out of her mouth.

"But how is it possible in this day and age that you've never seen the ocean?" Caitlin asked. She was genuinely interested, genuinely surprised that a person could have lived almost twelve years without ever having seen it.

All Vix could do was shrug and then smile. She wondered if Caitlin heard the music, too, if music followed her wherever she went. From then on whenever Vix heard "Dancing Queen" she was back in sixth grade on a sunny afternoon in June. The afternoon some fairy godmother waved her magic wand over Vix's head and changed her life forever.

At home, Vix asked her mother, "How is it possible, in this day and age, that I've never seen the ocean?"

Her mother, who was bathing her youngest brother, Nathan, looked at her as if she were nuts. Nathan had muscular dystrophy. His body was small and misshapen. They had a contraption that allowed him to sit in the bathtub but he couldn't be left alone. He was seven, sassy and smart, a lot brighter than her other brother Lewis, who was nine, or her sister, Lanie, who was ten.

"What kind of question is that?" her mother said. "We live in New Mexico. Hundreds of miles from one ocean and thousands from the other."

"I know, but so do plenty of other people and *they've* been to the ocean." She knew damn well why they'd never been to either coast. Still, she sat on the closed toilet seat, arms folded defiantly across her chest, as she watched Nathan sailing his boats around in the tub, stirring up waves with his arms.

"This is *my* ocean," he said. His speech was garbled, making it difficult for some people to understand him, but not Vix.

"Besides, you've been to Tulsa," her mother said, as if that had anything to do with what they were talking about.

Yes, she'd been to Tulsa, but only once, when her grandmother, a grandmother she'd never known she had until then, lay dying. "Open your eyes, Darlene," her mother had said to the stranger in the hospital bed. "Open your eyes and have a look at your grandchildren." The three of them were lined up in front of their

mother, while Nathan slept in his stroller. This grandmother person looked Vix, Lewis, and Lanie up and
down without moving her head. Then she said, "Well,
Tawny, I can see you've been busy." And that was it.

Tawny didn't cry when Darlene died the next day. Vix
got to help her clean out Darlene's trailer, the trailer
where Tawny had grown up. Tawny took some old
photos, an unopened bottle of Scotch, and a couple of
Indian baskets she thought could be worth something. It
turned out they weren't.

She couldn't sit still. She'd never wanted anything so
badly in her life. And she was determined. One way or
another she was going away with Caitlin Somers.

"Stop squirming," Tawny said, tossing Vix a towel.
"Get Nathan dried and ready for supper. I've got to help
Lewis with his homework."

"So, can I go?" Vix called as Tawny left the bathroom
and headed down the hall.

"Your father and I will discuss it, Victoria," Tawny
called back, letting her know it wasn't a done deal.

Tawny never called her *Vix* like everyone else. *If I'd
wanted to name my daughter after a cold remedy, I would
have.* You'd have thought a person named *Tawny* would
have been more flexible.

She'd been to Caitlin's house, an old walled-in place on
the Camino, just once, in March, when Caitlin had invited the whole class to her twelfth birthday party.
They'd had live music and a pizza wagon with a dozen

different toppings. Caitlin's mother, Phoebe, dressed in faux Indian clothes—long skirt, western boots, ropes of turquoise around her neck. Her hair hung down her back in one glossy braid. Some of Phoebe's friends were there, too, including her boyfriend of the moment, a guy with long, silvery hair, a concha belt, and hand-tooled leather boots. Vix had never been to a party like that, in a house like that, with grownups like that.

She'd brought Caitlin a blank book for her birthday, covered in blue denim, with a silver chain as a page marker. She only hoped it was worthy of Caitlin's thoughts and feelings. She dreamed about touching her hair, her sun-kissed skin.

She wrote her parents a letter, making a case for letting her go, not the least being Caitlin's promise that it wouldn't cost them a penny.

But Tawny didn't buy it. She claimed Caitlin came from an unstable family. "Just one look at that mother . . ."

"But we won't be with her mother," Vix countered, "we'll be with her father and he's very stable."

"How do you know?"

"Everybody knows. He's going to call you. You can ask him yourself."

In the end, it was *her* father who convinced Tawny to let her go. Her father, a man who looked surprised when he opened their front door to find he had four noisy children inside. A man of so few words he could spend a whole weekend without speaking, but if he did, his voice dropped way low on the last part of every sentence and

someone was always asking, *What? What'd you say, Dad?*
But he was never unkind.

She imagined jumping into his arms, hugging him as
hard as she could to show how thankful she was, but that
would have embarrassed both of them so she said,
"Thanks, Dad." And he mumbled something, something she didn't get, while he rested his hand on top of
her head.

Until then the highlight of her childhood had been
the weekend her father installed a molded laminate
shower in the half-bath in her parents' room. When it
was hooked up and working Vix, Lewis, and Lanie all
begged to be first to try it out. Her father looked right
at her and said, "We'll do it in age order. Vix gets to
go first."

How proud she was that day! How grateful to her
father for recognizing her as having a special place in the
family. First daughter. Eldest child. A yellow shower
with its own glass door. She'd wanted to stand under the
warm water forever. Only later did she realize how
crowded their house was, with small, high, north-facing
windows, making it dark and cold year-round, even in
relentlessly sunny Santa Fe.

She knew next to nothing about her parents' early
lives. Whenever Vix asked her mother a personal question Tawny answered, "We don't wash our linen in
public."

"I'm not public," Vix argued. "I'm family. I'm your
daughter."

"You know enough," Tawny told her. "You know
what's important. Besides, curiosity killed the cat."

But satisfaction brought her back again, Vix thought,

not that she'd dare say it out loud. If she did, Tawny would shout, *That's enough, Victoria!* So she quit asking questions. What was the point?

Sometimes she tried to imagine Tawny on the day she graduated from high school, boarding the first bus out of Tulsa and traveling as far as her money would take her, all the way to Albuquerque, where, thanks to her typing and shorthand skills, which Tawny reminded them of regularly, she found a job working for a young lawyer. Seven years later she was still working for him. By then she was engaged to Ed Leonard, a Sioux City boy, polite and nice-enough looking, whom she'd met at a dance at Kirtland Air Force Base.

They were married by a justice of the peace when Ed got out of the service. The young lawyer, who wasn't that young anymore, threw a party for them in his back-yard. Tawny didn't invite Darlene. Didn't even tell Ed her mother was living.

Then came the dead babies, three in five years, born before they were old enough to breathe on their own. Vix and Lanie used to play The Dead Baby Game the way other kids played A, My Name is Alice, reciting the names Tawny and Ed had chosen for their babies. *William Edward, Bonnie Karen, James Howard.* They'd just about given up hope when Vix was born, strong and healthy, a survivor. Lanie and Lewis followed. They moved to Santa Fe where Ed landed a job selling insurance. And then they had Nathan.

Her father used to joke about making the Million-aire's Club, selling a million dollars' worth of insurance in one year. Then he might win a vacation to some exotic resort, maybe even to Hawaii. If he did, he promised he'd take all of them. Vix dreamed about that vacation until the insurance company went under and her father was out of work for close to a year. Tawny was lucky to find a job working for the Countess. Even after Ed found a new job as the night manager at La Fonda, the old hotel on the Plaza, Tawny kept hers. "It's hard enough to make do on both our salaries," she'd say.

The Countess wore suede jodhpurs, blue nail polish, and exotic jewelry. She had five dogs. Nobody knew her exact age. Tawny had to take her to AA meetings. Sometimes, when the Countess fell off the wagon, Tawny would get really mean at home.

Vix lay in bed in the room she shared with Lanie, dreaming of the summer to come. She envisioned palm trees swaying in the breeze. She could almost feel the long, sultry nights, hear the beat of reggae music. Fantasy Island or, at the very least, Gilligan's. She had to pinch herself to make sure it was real, that she was really going away with Caitlin Somers, that she hadn't invented the whole thing.

Lanie didn't like the idea. "It's so unfair!" she cried. "You get to do everything."

Lanie was probably wondering why Caitlin Somers, the biggest deal in the whole school, had invited her to spend the summer. She was wondering the same thing herself. She tried to console Lanie. "Look at it this way . . . you can have our room all to yourself for the whole summer. You can have friends stay overnight and everything."

"Can I have your Barbies?"

"Have? No way."

"Use?"

"Use . . . okay . . . if you promise you'll keep them exactly the way they belong. And Barbie's Dream House is off limits."

"No fair . . . that's the best."

"Then no deal."

Lanie pouted. She and Vix shared Tawny's dark eyes and high cheekbones, a gift from some Cherokee ancestor. But Lanie was the best looking of all of them, with Ed's auburn hair and fair skin. "Okay . . . I won't touch Barbie's Dream House."

Vix was almost asleep when Lanie whispered, "If you go away you'll miss your birthday."

"No, I won't. I'll just be in a different place."

Phoebe never drove to Albuquerque, even when she was flying somewhere herself, so Caitlin rode down with Vix and her family in the RV, fitted for Nathan's chair. At the airport, when Vix bent down to hug Nathan goodbye, he said, "Don't worry . . . I won't forget you," and he gave her his lopsided smile.

"I won't forget you either," she promised. As she stood up she noticed a woman staring at Nathan. She was used to the way people looked at him, with a mixture of curiosity, pity, and revulsion. They'd look away if she happened to catch their eye.

Once they were on the plane, seated and buckled in, Vix pulled a lunch bag out of her backpack. Tawny had packed two bologna sandwiches, several juice cartons, and bags of pretzels and potato chips, as if Vix were going on a camping trip. She unfolded a note scribbled on lined paper.

In case you don't like the airline food. Mother

She wasn't sure if she was going to laugh or cry.

"What's that?" Caitlin asked.

"A note from my mother."

"She wrote to you already?"

Vix nodded.

"Phoebe loves having summers off from being a mother," Caitlin said proudly. "She's going to the south of France. She'll send a postcard and bring me back something great to wear."

Vix was thinking her mother would give anything to go to France. But the Countess never missed opera season in Santa Fe. She'd throw huge parties and Tawny would be responsible for everything.

The plane was taxiing down the runway now, picking up speed, faster and faster until they lifted into the air. As they did Vix closed her eyes, said a prayer, and clutched the arms of her seat.

"Wait . . ." Caitlin said. "Let me guess . . . this is your first flight."

"Right. And don't ask, *How is it possible in this day and age*."

Caitlin laughed. "You're totally different," she said, squeezing Vix's arm. "I like that about you."

Tawny

WHAT WAS SHE THINKING, packing a lunch for Victoria? It's not like her to fuss over her children. They have to be prepared for life and life is hard, full of disappointments. She shouldn't have listened to Ed, shouldn't have agreed to let Victoria go to an island, of all places, when she can't even swim. And telling *her* not to worry. Worry? She's too tired to worry. She can't remember what it's like not to be tired. She closes her eyes and prays to God to protect her daughter. To keep her safe. But it will never be the same. Once Victoria gets a taste of another way of life, once she spends a summer with a girl like Caitlin Somers, she'll be lost to them, sure as a dog chews a bone. She knows it even if Ed doesn't.

And now the other children are pulling on her, begging for money for the gumball machine. Only Nathan is still thinking of Victoria. She can see it on his face. She's surprised herself that Victoria just up and left him. She counts on Victoria to help out over the summer. The other two are useless, cut from a different piece of cloth. But Victoria is more like her. She does what needs to be done.

Ed

TAWNY EXPECTS TOO MUCH of the girl. Gives her too much responsibility. She's still a kid, just turning twelve. The same age he was when his father died. For three years his mother's neediness nearly suffocated him. *My little man*, she'd called him. Hell, he was no man. Never mind how hard he tried. And then one day, with no warning, she announces she'll be getting married over the weekend, to a man he's never met, a man he's never even heard of, a widower with three children, all younger than him. Just like that.

His stepfather hated his guts. *That's a useless kid you've got there, Maddy.* And the kids, taking his lead, took pleasure in tormenting him.

Is he shy?

Nah, he's just stupid.

Cat got your tongue, Eddie?

Nah, cat's got his dick!

For a while he quit talking at home.

His mother said, *We need him, Eddie. Try to understand. He's got a good job. He'll take care of us. You'll see . . .*

But she was the one who took care of him and his three brats and the twins she had with him seven months after they were married. Worked herself into the grave before she hit fifty.

Not that he'd hung around to watch. He'd enlisted at eighteen. *Join Up . . . See the World.* Sounded good to him. Anything to get away.

All he wanted was a decent job, a family of his own, kids to love. He'd be a real father, not that he'd ever seen one in action, but he'd figure it out. Then he met Tawny, a woman who knew her mind. He liked that about her. She was no wish-wash like his mother.

Now . . . hell, it's all different. And it's made Tawny hard. Nobody's fault. Just the way it is.

2

CAITLIN DIDN'T ALWAYS tell the truth. She left things out. Sometimes, important things. She had a brother. A brother and a dog. The brother was puny for fourteen with a sad face framed by shaggy brown hair. He didn't look anything like Caitlin, didn't even live with her, but she swore they were from the same mother and father. She called him Sharkey.

The father had already told Vix to call him *Lamb*. "As in baby sheep," Caitlin added. "As in *baaa baaa* . . ." Maybe they had some kind of animal fixation.

"Lamb," Vix said, trying it out. It felt weird to call a grownup, somebody's father, *Lamb*. He was tall and lean, wearing Birkenstocks, jeans with an iron-on patch, and a black pocket tee. He had the same toothy smile as Caitlin, and when he held out his hand to welcome her she saw that his arms were covered in pale fuzz, lighter than the hair on his head, which was mixed with gray even though he wasn't *old*-old, not that his age meant a thing to Vix. Parents were parents. They were all about the same.

In the baggage area at Logan she identified her bag and Lamb grabbed it from the carousel. She wished she had a canvas duffel like Caitlin's instead of her mother's old Black Watch plaid suitcase held together by duct tape, with her name printed across it in Magic Marker.

The dog, a black lab with a bandanna around its neck, was in the back seat of a beat-up gray Volvo wagon. The brother was in the front. "They both live with Lamb in Cambridge," Caitlin told her, before dashing across the street, making the driver of a Toyota slam on his brakes. But Lamb didn't say anything. He just smiled and shook his head. Tawny would have shouted, *Watch where you're going, Victoria! Do you want to get killed? Do you have any idea how much a funeral costs these days?*

"Sweetie, you old thing!" Caitlin cooed, kissing the dog on the mouth. "Hey, Vix, this is Sweetie . . . she's older than Lamb in dog years. Give Vix a sniff," she told the dog, who did exactly that, starting with her crotch. Vix felt her face redden. She shooed the dog away and crossed her legs.

When Caitlin introduced Vix to Sharkey she said, "You better treat her right!"

"I treat all your friends right unless they don't get it," Sharkey said.

Vix vowed then and there not to be a person who didn't *get it.* Whatever *it* was.

The drive seemed to take forever. Lamb tapped the steering wheel, keeping time to the music on the tape deck. "Hey, Jude." They came to a bridge with a sign that read, *Feeling desperate? Call the Samaritans.* It gave a phone number. Did that mean desperate enough to jump? Suddenly, a wave of homesickness washed over her. What was she doing here? Who was Caitlin, really?

It was almost sunset as they pulled onto the ferry,

another first for Vix. She'd never seen so much water in one place but Caitlin assured her this was *not* the ocean. Seabirds circled the boat as the ferry glided along and Caitlin warned Vix to stay alert because when they let out their stuff it went flying.

Forty-five minutes later, when they docked, Vix sensed that this would not be the tropical island she'd conjured up in her fantasies. The night air was far from sultry, there was no reggae music, and the trees were pines and oaks, not palms.

The phone was ringing as Lamb unlocked the door to the house. He ran for it, then handed it to Vix. "For you, kiddo."

"You were supposed to call," her mother said.

"I know, but—"

She didn't give Vix a chance to explain that they'd just arrived. "I expect you to do what you're told, Victoria."

"I will, it's just that . . ." Lamb turned on a light and Vix saw they were in the kitchen. There was an old stove, shelves but no cabinets, red linoleum on the floor, a table whose yellow paint had cracked and peeled.

"How was the plane trip?" her mother asked.

Caitlin was motioning for her to hurry. She pointed across the room to eerie-looking shadows dancing across the windows.

"The plane?" Vix asked.

"Yes, the plane," her mother repeated.

Caitlin threw a towel over her head and walked toward Vix, arms outstretched like a zombie. Sweetie started barking, excited by Caitlin's antics. "The plane was okay," she told her mother. Already, it felt like ages ago. Her first trip on a plane. She wondered if all the firsts in her life would go by so quickly, and be forgotten just as quickly.

Phoebe

SHE SINGS ALONG with Paul Simon as she packs her bags. *Just slip out the back, Jack, Make a new plan, Stan* . . . She twirls over to the dresser, grabs an armload of lingerie—lace bras with matching bikinis, long satin nightgowns, teddies. She dumps everything onto her Habitat, a sleek, white, four-sided bed topped by a Mylar mirror.

She's always had wanderlust. Not like Caity, who never wants to go anywhere unless it's to be with Lamb. She's beginning to think it was a mistake to take her away from him all those years ago. Of course, if Caity wanted, she could live with Lamb. All she'd have to do is ask. *She* won't be hurt. *Really.* She knows she's not a bad mother, just not a very good one. But she and Caity get along.

Sharkey, on the other hand, is à complete mystery. Grown men she can understand, she knows what they want, what they expect, but this is something else. Maybe they're all odd at fourteen. She's sure he'll appreciate her when he's older. He'll be glad then to have a live wire for a mother. They both will be.

Funny about this girl Caity took away for the summer. Another of her impulsive decisions? Last year's friend lasted just ten days. Ten days and she'd flown home, and as far as *she* knew Caity hadn't given her a second thought. After the summer, when she'd asked What happened? Caity told her, *She just didn't get it.*

Get what, Caity?

Come on, Phoeb . . . you know.

But she didn't. Ah well, it wasn't her problem, was it? Let Lamb work it out. Ten months a year is enough to be a parent. Everyone needs time off to rejuvenate.

Tonight she'll be in New York, tomorrow night, Paris.

3

IT WAS THE KIND OF SUMMER you don't write home about. Vix didn't exactly lie, but like Caitlin, she began to practice selective truth telling. What her family didn't know wouldn't hurt them.

The house was dark and messy, a place where nobody cared how much sand was on the floor or in your bed. Caitlin called it Psycho House. Vix could see why. Their room had unpainted wooden walls, twin beds with squeaky springs, faded red bedspreads, and pillows that smelled worse than the damp sponge used to clean off the lunch tables at school. The shelves were crammed full of headless Barbies, Legos, board games with missing pieces, tennis racquets with broken strings, starfish, hermit crab shells, jars of dead insects, pyramids of rocks.

The bathroom was down the hall. They shared it with Sharkey. When Vix sat in the claw-footed tub she could look out over Tashmoo Pond, which was a mile long. It opened into the Sound, allowing boats to come and go.

In the pond things floated, brown things that looked like turds. Caitlin swore they weren't but Vix wasn't so sure. Caitlin swam every day in her purple tank suit. Vix's suit was blue and white with red stars. She hated it. Her mother said there was no point in buying a new one if she didn't plan on getting it wet. And she didn't. She'd be like Sharkey. He never went anywhere near the water. He never even wore a bathing suit.

Another thing about him and Caitlin, they hardly ever changed their clothes. But the really disgusting part was Caitlin didn't change her underpants. Sometimes she didn't even wear underpants. She hadn't taken a bath or shower since they'd arrived. Her hair needed shampooing. She and Sharkey were both starting to smell of unwashed feet and something else, something Vix couldn't identify. But it wasn't good. If Lamb noticed, he didn't say anything. He was so laid back he was practically horizontal.

"He was a hippie for a while," Caitlin told Vix. "He lived up island with all the other hippies. Some of them are famous now. Some of them are rich."

Vix was dying to ask the obvious but she didn't. Nobody was going to accuse her of being a person who didn't get it. Sometimes at the end of the day Lamb took them fishing. If they caught a blue or a bass he'd cook it on the grill, wrapped in foil, with tomatoes, green peppers, and onions. *One fish, two fish, red fish, blue fish*. At first Vix wouldn't even taste Lamb's concoction. The closest she'd come to eating fish was tuna from a can. Lamb didn't mind. He'd say, "No problem, kiddo . . . make yourself a peanut butter sandwich instead." After all, Sharkey didn't eat fish either. He ate only Cheerios.

But after a while the fish started to smell good and Vix discovered it didn't taste that bad except for the bones. She marveled at the way Caitlin pulled them out of her mouth and lined them up on her plate, while she sometimes had to spit a chewed-up mouthful into her napkin.

Caitlin taught her to play jacks. She shook baby powder on the floor so their hands would slide easily across the old pine boards of the living room. Caitlin was a whiz, running through three fancies before Vix could finish sevensies.

There was no TV in the house. In Vix's house in Santa Fe the TV was on all the time. Lewis and Lanie watched re-runs of sitcoms before supper and Tawny never missed *Laverne and Shirley* or *Charlie's Angels*.

This place was filled with old books. They smelled musty. One rainy day while she and Caitlin were browsing they came upon *Ideal Marriage* and *Love Without Fear*. That night in their room they took turns reading aloud to one another, breaking up over the language, but disappointed neither book had pictures. Caitlin said *coitus interruptus* sounded like something you ordered in a French restaurant.

They used the dictionary in Lamb's study to look up *cunnilingus, fellatio, dingleberry*. The last was their favorite. *Dingleberry: a small clot of dung, as clinging to the hindquarters of an animal*. Vix told Caitlin if she didn't start wearing clean underpants she was going to get the Dingleberry Award. Caitlin took this seriously for a few days, then returned to her old ways.

The first time Caitlin led Vix through the woods with Sweetie following, along the secret pine needle path that led to the north beach and Vineyard Sound, they clasped hands, closed their eyes, and vowed they would never be ordinary. Phoebe had told Caitlin that to be ordinary was a fate worse than death. Caitlin called this the NBO pact. "NBO or die!" she sang into the wind. "Agreed?"

"Agreed." At that moment Vix felt like the luckiest person on earth. She was the chosen one, chosen for reasons beyond her comprehension to be Caitlin's friend, so if Caitlin wanted her to swear she would never be ordinary, fine, she'd do it. She made her mark in the sand, a heart with a V inside, while Caitlin drew an elaborate lightning bolt around her initials.

Caitlin was impressed by how dark Vix's skin turned in just a few weeks. "It's my Native American gene," Vix explained. "I'm one-sixteenth Cherokee on my mother's side." She wasn't sure of the exact fraction. She just knew it was something to be proud of.

"God, that is so interesting! I wish I had unusual genes."

"I'm sure you do," Vix said, thinking of Phoebe and Lamb.

When Caitlin swam Vix watched over her until she was just a dot, bobbing in the sea like a lobsterman's buoy. "I can't swim," Vix confessed to Sweetie. "So you'll have to save her if she needs saving. Okay?"

Sweetie didn't seem concerned. She cocked her head as if listening carefully, then ran off to find something to roll in, something dead or decaying. Whatever it was, it would leave her fur smelling like old fish.

Caitlin shook herself off like a dog when she came out of the water, then wrapped a beach towel around her waist so it dragged in the sand like a long skirt. "Did I ever tell you that in my former life I was a mermaid?"

"But in this life you're a human," Vix reminded her, just in case she forgot. "And I wish you wouldn't go out so far." She drizzled turrets of wet sand onto their elaborate castle.

"I like the way you worry about me," Caitlin said.

"Somebody has to."

In their room at night they played Mermaids, using the makeup Caitlin bought on Lamb's charge at Leslie's Pharmacy to paint their lips dark red and outline their eyes in coal black. The mirror on the wall above the bathroom sink was as old as the house, with a crack that stretched diagonally across it, making them look as if they had scars running across their faces.

They vamped and sang to Abba, the Eagles, Shaun Cassidy—"Da Doo Ron Ron"—socks stuffed into the tops of their bathing suits to see how they'd look with big breasts. Caitlin was still totally flat but Vix had tiny mounds, the beginning of something.

Caitlin was fascinated by Vix's pubic hairs. "Lay down," she said, "and I'll count them for you."

"What for?"

"Aren't you curious? Don't you want to know how many you have?"

"Curiosity killed the cat," Vix said.

Caitlin looked at her as if she were beyond hope. "A person without curiosity may as well be dead."

Vix wished somebody would explain that to her mother. To prove she was far from dead she lay on her bed with her underpants pulled down, laughing hysterically as Caitlin lifted one strand at a time, counting out loud. "Sixteen," Caitlin said, announcing the grand total. "You're so lucky!"

"I don't see what's lucky about having sixteen pubic hairs."

"You would if all you had was this!" Caitlin pulled down her shorts to show Vix her tiny patch of pale fuzz. Not that Vix hadn't seen it before.

Sharkey barged in on them like that and they shrieked so loud he took off, a terrified look on his face. From then on they shoved a chair in front of their bedroom door because there were no locks in the house.

When they grew bored with Mermaids they invented a better game. Vixen and Cassandra, Summer Sisters, the two sexiest girls on the Vineyard, maybe anywhere. They had The Power. The Power was inside their pants, between their legs. They'd just discovered that if they rubbed it in a certain way it was like an electrical current buzzing through them.

> *Dear Folks,*
> *Having a great time.*
> *Love, Vix*

And then there was Von, the most gorgeous guy Vix had ever seen. He was maybe sixteen, with a long sunstreaked ponytail, muscles in his arms, and a pack of Marlboros tucked into the sleeve of his T-shirt. His lips were full and so soft looking Caitlin said she could suck on them all night. Until then Vix had never thought of sucking on anyone's lips.

Von worked at the Flying Horses, which was supposed to be the oldest carousel in the country, one of those national treasures people on the Vineyard were always raving about. He collected tickets and fed the rings back into the machine as the carousel spun round and round. Vix thought Von should be declared the National Treasure. Every time Lamb headed for Oak Bluffs they'd beg to come along. He'd give them a couple of dollars and while he ran errands they'd ride until they were so dizzy they could hardly stand.

Von called them *Double Trouble*. He groaned when he saw them coming, pretending they were a real pain. Caitlin punched him in the arm when he acted that way. She loved to tease him, pulling his ponytail, jumping from horse to horse, daring him to stop her. She broke all the rules but he never kicked her off the carousel. Vix knew he never would have noticed *her* if it hadn't been for Caitlin. But she didn't mind. She was proud to be Caitlin's friend.

One night the National Treasure introduced them to his cousin, Bru. Bru was taller than Von with sinewy arms. He didn't say much. Vix could tell he considered them *children*, not worth his trouble.

Another night Lamb took them to the movies to see *Annie Hall*, and after, when Caitlin begged for just one ride on the Flying Horses, Lamb said, "Okay, but just one." He and Sharkey headed up Circuit Avenue to get a slice at Papa John's.

But Von wasn't on the carousel that night. Instead, Caitlin swore she saw him with some girl in the dark alley next to the Flying Horses, with his hands inside her shirt and her hand on his—Vix couldn't say it. She couldn't say *dick* or *pecker* or even *penis*—not when it came to Von. So Caitlin gave it a new name. *The Package*. She said this girl's hand was wrapped around Von's *Package*.

That night they came up with a new game. Vixen and Cassandra Meet Von. When they played they took turns pretending to be Von, lying on top of one another, rubbing The Power against the other's Power until the electrical current buzzed through their bodies.

They vowed never to tell anyone about Vixen and Cassandra. Caitlin said they weren't necessarily lesbos because they always pretended to be doing it with a boy. On the other hand, they might be.

Lamb

HE SWEARS, on the night she was born, when they put her in his arms, she looked directly into his eyes and smiled. He touched the tiny rosebud mouth and fell head over heels in love. His daughter. His little girl. He never imagined he'd lose her. And he hasn't, he keeps telling himself. She's never missed a summer, never asks to spend the holidays with anyone but him.

He and Phoebe were fools, thinking it would be easy. Sure, they'd divorced without rancor. He can't even remember if it was Phoebe's idea or his. All that open marriage business. Someone was bound to get hurt. But separating the kids just to be fair? *A girl for you, a boy for me* . . . How was he supposed to know Phoebe would take Caitlin to live halfway across the country? Regrets? Sure, he has regrets.

He watches her on the Flying Horses. He can't believe she won't always be this young, this innocent.

4

IT'S HARD TO REMAIN in awe of someone you're as tight with as Vix was with Caitlin that summer, someone with dirty feet, feet that smelled like the muck on the bottom of the pond, someone who spread her legs and rubbed her Power against yours.

"God, I love that feeling!" Caitlin said. "You're turning out to be a lot different than I thought."

"What'd you think?"

Caitlin picked up two small, red flannel squares and began to toss them from hand to hand. Maybe she was going to ignore Vix's question. She did that when someone asked her something she didn't want to answer. She'd just act as if she hadn't heard a word.

But after a while, Caitlin said, "I knew you were smart but quiet." She caught the squares and checked out the next exercise in *Juggling for the Complete Klutz*. "I knew you wouldn't ask a million questions and get in the way." She began again, this time with three squares. "And I liked the way you smiled . . . and that purple T-shirt you always wore." She didn't take her eyes off those red squares, not for a second.

Those were her reasons? But what had Vix expected?

After all, she hadn't known Caitlin any better than Caitlin had known her.

Caitlin tossed all three squares into the air at once, then dove onto Vix's bed, knocking her flat. "I just wasn't sure you'd know how to have fun!"

Vix took that as a compliment. She knew Caitlin liked her. The kind of *like* that had nothing to do with their secret games. Sometimes, when they were in town, Vix would notice people staring and she'd remember Caitlin was beautiful, but for the most part it didn't matter anymore. It didn't get in the way.

One night at dinner Lamb asked if she was having a good time. *A good time?* Vix couldn't believe what a time she was having. It was the best time of her life! Sometimes she wished summer would never end. Sometimes she wished she'd never have to go home.

She looked down at her plate filled with a heaping portion of bluefish, new potatoes, and green beans, and answered Lamb's question in a small, quiet voice. "Yes, thank you, I'm having a good time." Caitlin kicked her under the table and Vix was scared she might laugh.

Then Lamb said, "Do you miss your family?"

Suddenly Vix was filled with guilt because she didn't miss her family. She hardly ever thought about them. Well, maybe Nathan, but that was it. She wrote to him every week, sending a small Tupperware container of sand, a plastic jar filled with water from Tashmoo, a piece of blue beach glass Caitlin had found and given to her for him. "It looks like cobalt, doesn't it?" she'd asked Vix.

"Yeah, really . . . ." Vix had answered, whatever co-balt was.

They'd laid it on a bed of cotton in a jewelry box, then wrapped the box in bubble wrap, after Caitlin finished popping the bubbles with her bare feet.

"You can call whenever you want," Lamb continued. "Don't worry about the charges."

"Lamb . . ." Caitlin said, "let it go."

"It's just that Vix is so quiet," Lamb told her, as if she weren't sitting at the same table, as if Sharkey weren't, too. Sharkey, who never said a word at dinner but who made a strange, humming sound as he ate his cereal, as if he had a motor somewhere inside his body.

Vix was curious about why Sharkey didn't bring a friend for the summer, too. When she asked, using up her question of the week, Caitlin said, "I don't think he has any friends."

"That's so sad."

"Pathetic," Caitlin agreed.

"I guess Vix is the shy, quiet type," Lamb said, still on her case. "Like Sharkey."

"She's not anything like Sharkey," Caitlin told him.

Suddenly, Sharkey spoke. "How would you know?" he asked Caitlin. "How would any of you know?"

Sharkey

IT'S ALL SO EASY for them, yakety-yakking all day and half the night! Do they think he doesn't hear them, doesn't know they think he's weird? *Jesus!* His life is none of their goddamn business. He doesn't need friends. There's a difference between lonely and alone. Not that they would know. Alien creatures, if you want his opinion. *Beam me up, Scottie* . . .

ANYTHING SHE WANTED to see or do on the island was hers for the asking. *Your wish is my command*, Lamb told her, like in some fairy tale. So she said, *I'd like to see the real ocean*. And *abracadabra*, the next day they were off to the ocean, making a quick stop in Menemsha, an old fishing village, with almost as many boats in the harbor as tourists snapping pictures. Sharkey had opted to skip their outing and stay at home, probably to drive Lamb's old truck up and down the dirt driveway, or bury himself under the hood of the Volvo, or slide around on his back on the body-size skateboard he'd constructed to get underneath the cars.

She and Caitlin followed Lamb way out onto the dock until they came to a rundown wooden sailboat, *Island Girl*, where Lamb called, "Trisha . . . hey, Trish . . ."

A deeply tanned woman with a tangle of brown curls, wearing cutoffs and a work shirt, came out from inside the boat, shading her eyes from the sun. She jumped up onto the dock and threw her arms around Lamb, then Caitlin.

"Meet my friend Vix," Caitlin said.

Trisha gave her a high five.

"We're on our way out to Gay Head," Lamb said. "Want to join us?"

Vix had just found out that *gay* and *head* had meanings she hadn't known about before, and hearing Lamb say those words aloud made her feel funny.

"Be with you in two seconds," Trisha said. "Just let

me grab my stuff." She jumped down onto her boat and ducked inside the cabin. Lamb followed.

"They're just friends," Caitlin said, while she and Vix waited. "From the old days . . . when Lamb lived up here. They might still have sex though. I'm almost sure they do. I wouldn't mind if they got married. She's a flake but she loves us."

They picked up lunch along the way—clam dogs and lobster rolls. Vix had never heard of either and ordered french fries with ketchup. By the time they got going again Vix was more interested in Trisha than the ocean, and wondered if she and Lamb had been doing those things to one another, those things she and Caitlin had read about, while they were inside the cabin of the boat. She didn't think so because they weren't gone that long, not that she had any idea how long it would take.

The ocean was exactly as she'd imagined it, exactly the way she'd seen it in a million movies. The only surprise was the smell, salty and fresh, and the roar as the waves crashed against the shore. They followed Lamb and Trisha to a place sheltered by a high clay cliff, but even so the wind whipped their hair, and when they tried to talk, sand blew into their mouths.

As soon as they dropped their bags on the beach Trisha started taking off her clothes. First she unbuttoned and slipped off her shirt, revealing humongous breasts, with nipples the size of vanilla wafers. Vix had never seen anything like them. She tried to look away but she couldn't. Despite the wind, she felt her face grow hot.

Trisha could tell from the expression on her face something wasn't right. "Oh, honey . . ." she said, "is this going to be embarrassing for you . . . because I don't have to undress." She had to shout to make herself heard. She looked over at Lamb for guidance.

"I think it would be better . . ." Lamb began.

"Gotcha," Trisha said, pulling on her shirt.

"It's a nude beach," Caitlin told Vix, "but you don't *have* to take off your clothes. I never do."

Only then did Vix shade her eyes and look around. It was true! Most of the people on the beach were totally naked. Lamb stepped out of his jeans and for a second Vix held her breath because no way did she want to see his Package, but it was okay, he was wearing a tiny Speedo, the kind Mark Spitz wore at the Olympics when he won all those medals, when she was just in second grade. She could not believe the way they were all acting, as if a beach full of nudists was no big deal.

"So, Vix . . ." Lamb said, "what do you think?"

"Think?"

"Of the ocean."

"Oh, the ocean." She tried to think of something interesting to say but the ocean wasn't number one on her mind. When she didn't respond, Lamb laughed. "Pretty overwhelming, huh, kiddo?" Then he and Trisha grabbed hands and headed for the waves.

She imagined telling her mother that Lamb had taken her to a nude beach. *Indecent*, her mother would say. *Lewd and indecent and I want you on the next boat out of there!* Her parents did not walk around without their clothes. Her mother was, after all, a Lapsed Catholic.

Trisha

SHE'D FUCKED UP TODAY, big time, taking her clothes off that way in front of the kid. No common sense. On the other hand, it was a nude beach. Why'd he take them to a nude beach if she wasn't supposed to take off her clothes? What kind of sense did that make?

No matter how hard she tries, she never gets it right with him. Fifteen years ago he'd chosen Phoebe instead of her. The money thing, she's always thought. The family thing. She could have told him back then it would never work. Phoebe was used to getting whatever she wanted whenever she wanted it. Oh sure, she'd played at their way of life, but she hadn't really believed it would create a better world. Not that *she* believed it anymore either. But back then . . . She'd arrived on island at eighteen, fresh out of Bridgeport, and she'd never left. Not like Phoebe, who'd dropped in for a summer, hooked Lamb, and took him away.

After he'd split with Phoebe he'd come back and she'd cared for his little boy as if he were her own. *Lambsey-Divey*, she'd called him. Now they called him Sharkey and she was lucky if she saw him a couple of times every summer.

She's waited all these years for Lamb to get it through his head that they belong together, that she loves his kids as much as she loves him. But he has a new woman in his life, a woman he's *serious* about. As if what they've had for all these years isn't serious. She cried when he told her, cried and threatened to slit her wrists,

but he'd held her, promised he'd always be her friend
. . . always be there for her.

And he'd set her up in business, hadn't he? Encouraged her to go out on her own with Trisha's Melt-in-
Your-Mouth Muffins, fresh-baked daily. Light. Fluffy.
Not like those lead balls they sell at the Dog. All the
best restaurants and shops in town are after *her* muffins
now.

She's in her prime he told her. She'll find someone
else, someone to make her happy, someone to share her
island life. So she hasn't slit her wrists. She's too busy
baking. But, oh, she misses their lovemaking. How long
since they've been together? Four months, two weeks,
three days. Ever since he met the new woman.

Fifteen years ago she'd thought they'd be together
forever. Fifteen years ago she'd woven ribbons through
her hair.

5

VIX HAD NEVER KNOWN anyone like Lamb. All he asked of her was that she learn the lyrics to the Beatles songs, which wasn't exactly a hardship. So during the second week in August, when he told them he had to go to Boston for the day, she didn't mind. He promised to be back in time for dinner. "You okay with that, kiddo?" he asked her.

"Sure," Vix said, "no problem."

But at six P.M. he called from Boston. Logan was fogged in. *A real bummer.* He wouldn't be able to get back until morning. Vix couldn't believe he would leave them alone overnight in Psycho House.

"I'm not afraid of the dark," Caitlin said. "I don't believe in ghosts."

Neither did Vix, exactly.

After an early supper, Sharkey offered to take them for a drive in the truck. At fourteen he had no license, not even a learner's permit, but he was a careful driver—two hands on the wheel at all times, always under the speed limit. He drove them up island and down, but he wouldn't stop, not even for ice cream. Something about the battery. By the time they got back it was after nine and there were flashes of lightning in the distance. Twenty minutes later all the lights in the house went out. Caitlin tried the phone. "Dead," she said, striking a match and lighting a candle.

A violent storm followed. Sweetie trembled and hid beneath Caitlin's bed. Sharkey dragged a sleeping bag into their room and camped out on the floor. Vix huddled next to Caitlin, in Caitlin's bed, covering her eyes as each bolt of lightning lit up the sky. Trees went down in the woods and the rain turned to hail, pelting the house like a machine gun. "It's just a storm," Caitlin said. "I don't know why you're both acting like Sweetie."

In the morning Lamb called to say he'd be home by noon and he was bringing a friend.

"A friend?" Caitlin said.

"Probably Abby," Sharkey told her, grabbing a handful of Cheerios from the box, dribbling them into his mouth.

"Abby?" Caitlin said. "Who's Abby?"

"Some woman," Sharkey told her.

"Woman?" Caitlin said. "You mean woman as in *girlfriend*?"

Sharkey shrugged.

"Lamb has a girlfriend and he didn't tell me?" Caitlin asked.

He shrugged again.

"I'm his daughter. I should be told these things."

"He's not a monk, you know," Sharkey told her, "any more than Phoebe's a nun."

"But he's never brought anyone *here*! The Vineyard's always been just for us."

———

They arrived in time for lunch—Lamb, the woman named Abby and her son, Daniel Baum, who was Sharkey's age. Abby greeted Sharkey as if they'd met before but it was clear the two boys hadn't and neither one was thrilled. Daniel was two heads taller than Sharkey, preppy, with Top-Siders and an alligator shirt. He acted bored.

Abby was almost as tall as Lamb, rail thin, pale, with baby-fine brown hair hanging to her shoulders and bangs drifting toward her eyes. She wore jeans, a *terrific* T-shirt, and wavy-soled shoes that made her seem even taller. Abby smiled at Caitlin, told her how happy she was to meet her, how much she'd heard about her. Daniel yawned, really loud, without covering his mouth. Caitlin looked like she was going to throw up.

They came into the house through the kitchen door and were hit by last night's mess—the macaroni and cheese pot on the floor, licked clean by Sweetie, their gooey plates still on the table, together with boxes of breakfast cereals, banana skins, and a half-eaten piece of toast smeared with grape jelly. Abby's face registered surprise, then disgust. Vix spied the milk carton on the counter and tried sneaking it into the fridge, but Abby didn't miss that either.

Sweetie, who'd been resting under the table, began to bark and when Daniel kneeled down to pet her she growled at him. "Jesus . . . what kind of dog is this anyway?" Daniel asked, jumping out of the way.

"A lab," Lamb said. "She's usually very friendly." He opened the door and shooed Sweetie outside.

"Well . . ." Abby said, trying to be positive. "This house has a lot of . . . possibilities."

They went on an island tour, all six of them crammed into the Volvo, the two boys in the back seat, one staring out the left window, one staring out the right, and Caitlin and Vix on the floor in the *way-back* with Sweetie. Lamb opened the rear window so they wouldn't suffocate. In the front, Abby and Lamb were just *la-ti-da*, as if this were even better than the *Brady Bunch*. While they were gone the cleaning service would be trying to whip the house into shape. They'd told Lamb it would take all day, maybe two days. Lamb promised a bonus if they finished in one.

They didn't visit Trisha's boat this time, or go to the nude beach. Instead of clam dogs and french fries, lunch was a dreary affair at a harborside restaurant, with Daniel sulking and Sharkey's inner motor running on high. Caitlin moved her food around on her plate but didn't eat a bite.

Vix tried her best, pretending to be fascinated by *The Story of Abby and Lamb*, and how they'd met and how they'd instantly been attracted and blah blah blah . . . who cared? "He couldn't believe I was a student at The B-School," Abby said, laughing.

"Still can't," Lamb added, nuzzling her.

Vix didn't have a clue what The B-School was but it didn't matter. Nobody noticed.

"I came to Boston after the divorce, after living my entire life in Chicago," Abby said. "I'd hoped Daniel would come, but you know how it is, he didn't want to leave his friends or his school." She tried to tousle Daniel's hair but he pulled away angrily. "So, for now, Daniel's living with his dad."

Vix kept nodding, the way reporters do on TV when they're conducting an interview, to prove they're really listening.

"And when I get my MBA, next summer," Abby continued, "I'll decide whether to go back to Chicago or look for a job in the East." She smiled at Lamb, a private kind of smile.

Vix wondered if she knew about Trisha.

Lamb

SHE'S WONDERFUL, isn't she? He can't believe his luck, how she came into his life out of nowhere, when he least expected it. And this one's a keeper. It's not just the sex. Everything about her makes him happy. She's so bright, so sweet. The kids are going to be crazy about her. He can't believe he's thinking this way. Thinking about a future with this woman. But he is.

———————

EVERY DAY LAMB SANG in the outdoor shower. "All You Need Is Love," "Come Together," "We Can Work It Out." He was happy. He was in love. The happier he was over Abby, the unhappier Caitlin grew. And he didn't seem to notice.

One day Vix overheard Daniel telling Abby, "This place is a dump. They don't even have a TV or a dishwasher."

You didn't have to be a genius to see that Lamb had as hard a time making do as her parents. All you had to do was look around at the shabby furniture, the beat-up cars, the clothes they wore. They even ate poor. No meat, not even hamburgers.

"I'd like you to remember you're a guest in this house," Abby told Daniel. "And I expect you to behave in a way that doesn't embarrass any of us."

"I don't see why you had to drag me here," Daniel said. "This is supposed to be my vacation."

"You've been at camp all summer," Abby told him. "You've had plenty of vacation, but I've got just these two weeks."

"Dad says your whole life is a vacation."

"Don't start, Daniel . . ."

"If you'd let Gus come I'd get off your back."

Abby sighed. "We've already been through this. Two weeks without a friend won't kill you."

"It might," Daniel said.

Vix was embarrassed for eavesdropping. She decided not to tell Caitlin what she'd overheard. It was too . . . personal.

That night they played mini golf. Daniel held his club like a pro, one hand over the other, thumbs locked. He checked his feet to make sure they were lined up properly. He took two practice swings on each shot. Caitlin and Vix hooted. Daniel told them to shut up. He was trying to concentrate. He took the game seriously. His father played. His father had an eight handicap, whatever that meant.

They'd played mini golf to celebrate Vix's twelfth birthday, on the last day of July. Sharkey had shot a hole in one that night, winning them a free game. Nobody won a free game this time.

After, over ice cream at Mad Martha's, Daniel started in on Abby about inviting a friend. Abby said no as if she meant it, but Daniel didn't give up. He campaigned all the way home. Finally, Lamb said, "It's okay with me if he wants to invite somebody."

"All right," Abby said. "*All right!*" He'd finally broken her down. "You can call Gus when we get back."

Two days later Gus Kline arrived, shaggy-haired, open-faced, loud, and slovenly. He walked in like he owned the place, checking out the fridge, helping himself to the leftovers from last night's dinner. "Hey, *Baumer* . . ." he said, pronouncing it *bomber* and doing a one-two punch. "How's it going?"

"Since you got here," Daniel said, punching him back and smiling for the first time, "things are definitely looking up."

Abby

SHE'LL BE DAMNED if she's going to let the kids spoil this. Never mind the hatred in Caitlin's eyes. It was a mistake to walk into her life unannounced and unexpected. She should have known better. It might take some time but she'll win her over. She's always wanted a daughter and this one looks like she could use some mothering. Besides, in less than ten years the children will be grown. But why is she thinking this way? She and Lamb have known each other just four months.

Before they met she'd been thinking about having another child. She's just thirty-seven. There's still time. Yet now that it looks serious between her and Lamb—at least she hopes it's serious—she's less sure. Three surly teenagers seem like more than she'd bargained for. Of course, a baby would be something else. A baby could bind them together. But she knows from experience it can also drive a wedge between a couple. It was never the same between her and Marty after Daniel was born. She'd never expected him to be jealous of the baby, to compete with him for her affections, making demands she couldn't possibly meet, but there it was.

In the year since she's left him she's grown stronger, more confident. She's not afraid to put her foot down now and she's sure she can see the respect in Daniel's eyes.

Truth is, she hadn't planned on falling in love so soon. Too soon, her friends say. But is she supposed to walk away from the best man she's ever known because it's too soon? How ironic, to meet him now, when she's determined never to be dependent on a man again.

She tries not to think about the old hippie girlfriend on the boat, even when Caitlin drops hints. *Trisha bakes the best muffins, and she's got incredible breasts.* Imagine this twelve-year-old child talking to her about breasts! She'd had to bite her tongue.

They have sex together . . . fellatio and cunnilingus. Ask Lamb if it's not true.

She'd wanted to belt her that time. Instead, she'd said, *This is not an appropriate subject.*

Why not?

Because it isn't. She'd walked away but could feel Caitlin's pleasure.

She'd gone to Lamb in a jealous rage. *This thing between you and Trisha . . .*

There hasn't been a thing between Trisha and me for a long time.

Why does Caitlin think there is?

Caitlin's twelve, Ab. What does she know?

But she told me . . .

She's just trying to ruffle your feathers.

She talked about fellatio and cunnilingus.

What?

My feelings exactly.

He started laughing. *I told you it wouldn't be easy with her.*

I should have believed you.

6

VIX SUPPOSED a person who vowed never to be ordinary, never to be boring, would welcome changes, but when it came to the Vineyard Caitlin wanted things exactly as they'd always been and was furious that the house had been renovated without her knowledge, not to mention her permission.

"What the fuck?" Caitlin said, a look of total disbelief on her face when she took her first look at the new and improved Psycho House.

"We wanted to surprise you," Abby said.

"Surprise me?" Caitlin asked. "*Surprise me!*"

Abby and Lamb had been married over Easter. Caitlin had flown to Boston for the wedding. Vix pressed for details but Caitlin didn't want to talk about it. It was too depressing. "At least Phoebe doesn't *marry* her boyfriends."

Caitlin pushed past Abby and marched through the house without a word, her hands clenched, her mouth tight. Vix dutifully followed. When Caitlin stopped dead in the middle of the living room, Vix did, too. Personally, she thought the house looked fantastic. Skylights had been cut into the ceiling flooding it with light. Big windows and French doors had been added. The huge pine trees that blocked out the sun and cast weird shadows at night had been relocated to the woodsy side of the house, opening the view to the pond and to the Sound, beyond. You could see the ferries coming and going and the sailboats flying their spinnakers. The old furniture was dressed in crisp blue and white slipcovers. There were vases filled with zinnias and sisal rugs that felt prickly underfoot.

Abby waited, a hopeful look in her eyes, but Caitlin raced up the stairs and flung open the door to her room. Nothing in there had been touched. It was exactly as they'd left it. Vix was disappointed but Caitlin said, "Thank God!"

Abby had followed and was standing in the doorway. "I thought you'd like to do your room yourself," she told Caitlin. "You know, choose your own colors and accessories."

Vix was thinking what a great time they'd have painting the drab wooden walls, organizing the collections, shopping in town. But Caitlin said, "I like it exactly the way it is, thank you!" and she slammed the bedroom door in Abby's face.

If Abby thought she was going to win points with Caitlin by making changes, she was mistaken. Vix wished there was a way for her to let Abby know that trying to please was *not* the way to win Caitlin's affection. People who tried too hard disgusted her.

A minute later Caitlin kicked off her shoes and smashed them against the wall. She beat her mildewed pillows against the books on her shelves until one of them opened, its feathers flying in all directions. She attacked her rock collection, sweeping it onto the floor. She hurled tennis racquets and swim fins across the room, then grabbed her desk chair and crashed it against the door of her closet. She cursed and cried as she destroyed everything in her path.

Vix was in shock. She'd never seen anyone behave that way. Once, in fourth grade, she'd come home from school crying hysterically because a boy in class had called her a *whore*. She'd had no idea what the word meant. Neither did he but she didn't know that at the time. *Whore, whore, whore* . . . the other boys in the class chanted, taunting her for a week.

Tawny had shown no sympathy. "Save your tears for something important, Victoria. There's no need to display your emotions in public. Do you want those boys to have power over you?"

"No."

"Then remember what I'm telling you. Keep your feelings to yourself. Don't ever show anyone your disappointment."

That was the last time she'd let Tawny see her tears.

As she crouched between the twin beds, protecting her head with her hands, she thought about Tawny's advice and felt proud for knowing how to keep her feelings to herself. Obviously no one had taught Caitlin to save *her* tears for something important.

Finally, Caitlin threw herself on her bed.

There was nothing Vix could say to comfort her. Instead, she handed Caitlin a box of tissues then sat beside her, rubbing her back.

Caitlin blew her nose. "You're the only one in this

house I don't hate. You're the only one who cares about me."

Caitlin didn't even hate her when Vix got her period, though Caitlin wanted desperately to be first. "I guarantee I'll be first with everything else!" she promised.

Maybe . . . maybe not, Vix thought. This was the first thing she'd had that Caitlin wanted and she liked the feeling.

They hiked the two miles to town without telling anyone, to buy pads for Vix, then Caitlin escorted her to the secret bathroom behind Patisserie Francaise on Main Street and helped her stick the pad inside her pants.

Outside, they ran into Trisha, who was delivering muffins to the gourmet food shop. "Lordy . . . look who's here!" Trisha set the tray on the hood of her truck and handed each of them a peach muffin. She was wearing short shorts and an orange T-shirt. Vix thought of those gigantic breasts and warned hers not to grow that big.

"So how's the bride and groom?" Trisha asked.

Caitlin made a retching sound.

Trisha nodded. "You think you know somebody really well and then they go and do something so outrageous . . . so totally off the wall . . ."

"He should have married you!" Caitlin said.

"Oh, honey . . . you're not the only one who's thinking that."

Only when Caitlin decided to hitch home did Vix balk. "I'm not allowed to hitch." Though the idea of walking back with the sun beating down on her when she was already feeling queasy, made her wish she could.

"This is the Vineyard, Vix. Everybody hitches."

"I can't. It's the one thing I've promised my parents I'll never do, along with drugs and sex before marriage."

"That's three things."

"You know what I mean."

But moments later an old blue Camaro screeched to a halt. There were two guys in the car, both wearing baseball caps and wraparound glasses. And the driver was *him*, the National Treasure.

"Heading up island?" Von asked.

Caitlin turned to Vix. "You can walk if you want but *I'm* riding." The other one, Bru, let his seat fall forward so Caitlin could squeeze into the back of the car.

"You getting in or not?" Bru asked Vix. "Because we're holding up traffic as you can see."

She followed Caitlin into the car, thinking there had to be exceptions to every promise. Besides, if they were going to be killed it would be better to be killed together, otherwise she'd have to explain to Lamb why Caitlin was murdered and she wasn't.

Caitlin yanked Von's ponytail.

He lowered his shades and looked at them through his rearview mirror. "I knew this was my lucky day," he said, turning on the charm. "Hey, Bru . . . get a look at what we caught."

"Uh-huh," Bru answered, about as excited as if they'd reeled in two sardines.

They were heading out of town, past the Italian Scallion vegetable stand, past mini golf, past the Tashmoo

Overlook, to Lambert's Cove Road where Caitlin told Von to take a right. "How far up?" he asked.

"I'll let you know." When she did, Von slammed on the brakes making them fall forward against the front seats, which he found funny.

"Thanks for the ride," Caitlin said. "See you at the Flying Horses."

"Not this year," Von told her. "I'm working at the fish market this year."

"Which one?" Caitlin asked.

"That's for me to know and you to find out," Von said.

"Yeah . . . well, save me a fish head," Caitlin said.

"I'll save you something better than that," Von told her. "See me in about three years to collect."

"Don't hold your breath," Caitlin sang, slamming the car door.

They could hear the boys laughing as they pulled back onto the road and floored it.

Caitlin took this as a sign that all was not lost. She threw an arm over Vix's shoulder as they walked the mile down the dirt road leading to their house. "Aren't you glad we hitched?"

"Maybe," Vix said. She wondered if the boys knew she had her period, if they'd noticed the bulge in her shorts when she'd stepped out of the car.

"Just maybe?" Caitlin asked.

"Probably. Is that better?"

"Yes, definitely better."

That night they sat facing each other in the old claw-footed tub which had somehow escaped renovation. Caitlin had convinced Vix no menstrual blood would come out in the tub, but if it did she wouldn't mind. "You're really growing," Caitlin said, focusing on Vix's chest.

Vix felt her face grow hot. "I know." They hadn't seen each other naked since last summer. Caitlin was still flat.

"What's it feel like?" Caitlin asked.

"What's *what* feel like?"

"To have tits?"

"I don't know. It doesn't feel like anything."

"Can I touch them?"

"I guess."

Caitlin leaned over and cupped her hands around them. Vix had touched them herself but this was the first time anyone else had. It made her feel funny, as if she couldn't breathe.

"Do you still have The Power?" Caitlin asked.

Vix nodded.

"Do you use it?"

"Sometimes. Do you?"

"Sometimes." Caitlin gave Vix a sly smile then slid underwater. Her hair fanned out and for a minute she looked dead.

Vix had worried that Caitlin would find another summer sister, someone to replace her. It wasn't until they'd boarded the plane at the end of last summer that Caitlin had broken the news. She was going to Mountain Day, a private school in Santa Fe. Vix had been completely crushed.

"Cheer up!" Caitlin had told her. "For all we know we'll die today. The plane might crash, anything could happen."

But the idea of losing Caitlin was even worse than having the plane crash. She wondered if Caitlin and her new school friends shared The Power. She never shared hers. Sometimes at home, after Lanie was asleep, she'd use The Power by herself. Mostly, it went to waste. There was too little time and too little privacy.

She hadn't expected Caitlin to invite her back to the Vineyard, and when she did, Vix worried that her mother wouldn't let her go. It had been a difficult year for her family. Nathan was sick on and off all through the winter and hospitalized with pneumonia in March. A few weeks later Lewis broke his arm. The roof started leaking with the heavy wet spring snow and Tawny let them know she was worried about the stack of bills piling up on the desk in the living room. There was talk about selling the RV but Ed decided against it for the moment. Instead, he took a second job, driving for UPS, but was laid off after a few weeks.

Tawny surprised her. She seemed relieved there'd be one less person around for the summer, one less person to worry about.

In mid-May Tawny reported that Phoebe had been a guest at the Countess's party the night before. "She was there with someone at least ten years younger," Tawny sniffed.

"So?" Vix said, trying to prove how sophisticated

she'd become. "Phoebe has a lot of friends. It doesn't necessarily mean they're lovers."

For a second she thought Tawny was going to slap her face and she jumped back. Instead, Tawny shouted, "I've had enough of your impudence, Victoria!"

The week before she'd called Vix *impatient . . . impatient* and *irritating.* Vix had no idea why her mother was so angry with her. She'd overheard Tawny on the phone, telling someone the Countess was drinking again and smoking two packs a day, and when the doctor issued a stern warning the Countess had told him to *fuck off!* "I don't have the strength to worry about her, too, but if she goes . . . my job goes," Tawny said.

Was the Countess going to die? Was that what Tawny meant? Vix didn't ask. She tried to stay out of her mother's way but as the end of the school year approached Tawny was always hostile, blaming everything on Vix. One night, when the chicken she was supposed to baste got overdone on the grill, Tawny yelled, "Look at this!" She jabbed a fork into a piece and waved it around for the other kids to see. "If Victoria weren't so self-centered we wouldn't have to eat burned chicken tonight!" Vix ran to her room and didn't come out.

Later, while she was finishing her math homework, Lanie said, "You know why she hates you?" Vix looked up from her notebook. "It's because you get to escape," Lanie said, trying to braid Malibu Barbie's hair. "We all hate you for that." Lanie spoke without emotion, and suddenly Vix understood everything. She got to escape and they didn't.

She felt sad about leaving Nathan, especially when he

shoved his raccoon puppet in her face. "I want him to go to Martha's, too. Then he can tell me all about it."

"But I told you all about it last summer," Vix said. The stories she'd told were generic island stories, about the ocean, the birds, the storms.

"How do I know you didn't make it all up?" Nathan asked.

Could he see through her so easily or was this his idea of a joke? "Okay, Rupert," she said to the puppet. "You're going to Martha's with me!"

"His name isn't Rupert anymore," Nathan said. "It's Orlando."

"Orlando?"

"As in Disney World," Nathan said.

Vix knelt in front of Nathan's chair. "Someday I'm going to take you to Disney World," she told him.

"When?"

"As soon as I earn enough money."

"How many years will that take?"

"I don't know. Not that many." She wrapped her arms around him. His body felt so small, so frail.

"I missed you last summer," he whispered. "Lewis and Lanie don't care about me the way you do."

She knew this was true and she felt guilty, but not guilty enough to stay home. It wasn't that Lanie and Lewis were cruel or unkind to Nathan, it was more that they were involved in their own lives and sometimes forgot about him. Especially Lewis. He'd always resented Nathan, for being born in the first place, and then, for being born the way he was. She could tell sometimes that Lewis was thinking, *Why did they have to have him? Why didn't they stop after the three of us?* She knew they'd all asked themselves the same questions, even her parents. Tawny used to tell them Nathan was a gift from God, to teach them to be strong, to teach them to count their blessings. But what about Nathan? What kind of gift had God given him?

7

THE SECOND WEEK in July, when the hydrangeas turned a deep blue and ran rampant around the porch, Lamb threw a party to celebrate Abby's MBA. "She just loves showing off her new husband and her renovated summer house," Caitlin snickered.

"What about her lovely stepchildren?" Vix asked.

"Oh, definitely."

They both looked across Abby's newly planted flower garden to Sharkey, who had turned into a stranger, growing seven inches without gaining a pound, which left him looking like Lurch, his arms hanging like fishing poles from his shoulders, his hands dangling at his sides as if he couldn't figure out what to do with them.

"Almost as perfect as her own son," Caitlin said.

Daniel and Gus had arrived the day before, for a three-week visit, which meant she and Caitlin had to share the bathroom not just with Sharkey but with *three* teenage boys. Three disgusting fifteen-year-old boys who left the toilet seat up, peed on the rim, farted wherever and whenever. And one of them regularly forgot to flush or else was so proud of what he'd made, he wanted to share it with the rest of them. There was always toothpaste stuck to the sides of the sink from where they'd spit, wet towels tossed on the floor, and the tub was strewn with hair from God knows what parts of their bodies.

They overheard a guest at the party telling Abby how attractive the children were, then asking if she'd found a job yet. Abby answered, "No, I really haven't starting looking. I'm giving myself some time off to just enjoy."

"Now that she has her meal ticket she'll probably never get a job," Caitlin whispered to Vix.

Meal ticket?

The day after the party the weather turned rainy and windy, and for a week it stayed that way. Vix and Caitlin bought a stack of paperbacks at Bunch of Grapes and, except for meals, spent the entire week in bed, reading. Abby tried luring them out with boxes of old jigsaw puzzles. Sharkey hovered over Vix after dinner, his breath on her neck, as she put them together.

"What's your secret?" he asked after she'd completed a particularly complicated sailing scene.

"Secret?" she said. "I don't have a secret." All she knew was she was good at putting the pieces together, at making the picture whole.

Gus referred to her as the *Cough Drop*. Maybe Tawny knew what she was talking about when she'd said, *If I'd wanted to name my daughter after a cold remedy I would have.* "Hey, *Cough Drop!*" Gus would call. "What's happening?" He was the most irritating person she'd ever known. Caitlin wasn't the only one who couldn't stand the Chicago Boys. They definitely didn't get it!

The girls escaped by closing themselves in their room at night where they became Disco Queens, dancing to the Bee Gees. They'd seen *Saturday Night Fever* six times. They were in love with John Travolta. Caitlin swore if you looked close at those tight white pants, you could see the outline of his Package.

On the night that Gus came to dinner wearing a mop on his head and tennis balls inside his shirt, singing *Ah, ha, ha, ha, stayin' alive, stayin' alive* . . . as if he were capable, as if he were worthy of imitating either them or John Travolta, Caitlin dubbed him *The Pustule.*

"That's good," Gus told her, not the least bit offended. "I like my women on the clever side."

"Your women?" Caitlin snorted. "Dream on!"

Even Caitlin didn't mind that the old cracked mirror above the bathroom sink had been replaced. No more scar faces. She began to brush her tongue with toothpaste, sticking her toothbrush halfway down her throat in the process, so when the time came she'd be ready for the fellatio thing. She encouraged Vix to do the same but every time Vix tried, she gagged. "You're going to be hopeless at oral sex," Caitlin told her, shaking her head.

"Maybe you don't have to stick it down so far," Vix suggested.

"You do."

"How do you know?"

Caitlin shrugged.

"You've seen pictures?" Vix asked.

"I've seen Phoebe."

Vix opened her mouth but no words came out.

Caitlin grabbed her by the shoulders. "Swear you'll never tell a soul!"

"I swear."

"Have you ever . . . you know . . . seen your parents?"

Vix shook her head.

"I didn't think so."

"But one time," she began, partly to make Caitlin feel better, "I saw my father flirting. It was a real shock."

"How old were you?"

"It was . . . recent. They were sitting in the window of the sandwich shop at La Fonda. I was outside, walking by."

Caitlin was quiet for a minute. "That's not exactly like having sex."

"I know." Vix couldn't find the words to explain how she'd felt that day, like an intruder in her father's life. Until tonight she'd put it out of her mind. "She had big hair . . ." Vix said. "Frosted. They were laughing. I saw her reach across the table to pat his arm."

Caitlin patted *her* arm. "It's probably nothing. Don't worry. Flirting doesn't count."

Caitlin was straightforward in her flirting. If she found someone attractive she'd let him know. She didn't waste time playing games. On Vix's thirteenth birthday Lamb dropped them at mini golf. When she and Caitlin stepped into the clubhouse and found Bru behind the register they were beside themselves. Bru, all business, asking them, *How many games?* She and Caitlin elbowed each other and tried not to laugh. Who said thirteen isn't a lucky number?

Even though he wasn't totally gorgeous like Von, and his lips weren't the kind you'd suck on all night if you were inclined to suck on lips at all, there was something about Bru that appealed to Vix even more. His eyes were a warm golden brown and his hair, the same color, fell below his ears. She wished she could touch it. He didn't smile all the time like Von, but when he did it was a slow smile, the kind that sneaked up and took you by surprise. She had no trouble imagining those sinewy arms wrapped around her.

"How many games?" he asked again.

"Two," Caitlin told him, digging her money out of the pocket of her dress.

He handed them two scorecards and a pencil, acting as if he'd never seen them before. "What color balls?"

That sent them into gales of laughter.

"Okay . . . okay . . ." he said. "Let's get this over with. Pink, orange, yellow, green, blue . . ."

That made it worse yet. Finally Caitlin pointed to pink and Vix pointed to yellow. They were still convulsed as they started walking away. Then Caitlin pulled herself together, turned back and said, "I can't believe you don't remember us."

That caught his interest. But after a long look all he came up with was "Can't say I do."

"*Double Trouble* . . ." Caitlin told him. "Does that ring a bell?"

When he still looked blank she added, "You and Von gave us a ride . . ."

He was waiting on someone else now, a young couple

with a little boy. But he stopped and gave them the once-over again. "*Double Trouble* . . . yeah, maybe . . . but you look different . . ."

Of course they looked different! They were wearing matching sundresses with strapless bras underneath, sandals that tied around their ankles, strawberry-flavored lip gloss, and dangling skunk earrings—the official scent of Martha's Vineyard, as the bumper stickers claimed—all purchased with Lamb's credit card, which Caitlin had borrowed to take Vix on a shopping spree for her birthday. And they smelled different, too, of Charlie, which they'd splashed all over themselves.

Caitlin tilted her head and threw him a smile. "See you around," she called.

"Not if I see you first," he answered.

The father with the little kid was drumming his fingers on the counter. "Could we get going here?"

"Sure," Bru told him. "What color balls?"

They exploded again, laughing even harder than the first time. While they were waiting to tee off Caitlin said, "Someday they're going to fall in love with me."

"Who?" Vix asked.

"Bru and Von."

"Why both?" Vix said. "Why not just one?"

"Because it's more interesting if it's both," Caitlin answered.

But that didn't strike Vix as fair so she pushed Caitlin to choose. "Let's say you could only have one. Which one would it be?"

"I don't know."

"Let's say your life depended on it. You have to choose or you'll die."

"Which one would *you* choose?" Caitlin said.

"I asked you first."

"Okay," Caitlin said. "I guess I'd take Von."

Good, Vix thought. Because she had already chosen Bru for herself.

A week later they buried Cassandra and Vixen. They built sand sculptures of themselves on the beach, complete with breasts. Vix made hers round, Caitlin made hers pointy, and they both gave themselves purple stone nipples. They used black stones for their eyes, chunks of seaweed for their hair, tiny white shells for their fingernails and toenails, and wispy strands of beach grass for pubic hair. They smoothed out the sand all around their bodies and wrote, *Here lie Vixen and Cassandra. They had a good life while it lasted.* Then they chanted and danced around their former selves.

Two women with a springer spaniel stopped for a minute, admiring their work. Caitlin and Vix continued to dance, ignoring them.

It wasn't that they didn't have The Power anymore, it was that they couldn't use it together. They didn't know why. Something about it just didn't feel right. They agreed that for now they could use The Power by themselves, but Vixen and Cassandra were dead. Dead and buried.

8

VIX WOULDN'T have thought twice about Lamb's boyhood if Caitlin hadn't said, "Lamb was raised by his grandmother. She's coming soon. I forget when. She's a real bitch. But you'll see that for yourself."

Her interest was piqued even more when Caitlin fished an old eight by ten photo out of her bottom dresser drawer. "Lamb's parents," Caitlin said, tapping the photo. "Amanda and Lambert. Killed in a car crash on the island when Lamb and his sister were just babies. You know how old they were when they died? Twenty-five. Is that pathetic or what?" She didn't wait for Vix to respond. "They were both drunk on the night of the accident. That's why Lamb never touches the stuff. *She* was driving. I look like her, don't you think?"

Vix covered the thirties hairstyle with her fingers. She did look like Caitlin.

"They wouldn't have been very good parents anyway," Caitlin said, slipping the photo back into a glassine envelope.

"They might have stopped drinking," Vix said.

"I doubt it."

"Some people do."

"Well, it doesn't matter, does it? Because they're dead!"

"Why are you getting angry at me?"

"Who's angry? Did I *say* I was angry?"

"No . . . but you're acting like you are."

"You take everything personally, don't you?"

"Just *some* things!" Vix told her. Now she *was* getting angry. And over what? She took a couple of deep breaths and said, "Lamb turned out okay."

"Lamb was perfect . . . until he married *her*!"

Vix wondered if Caitlin was ever going to get over Abby.

Grandmother Somers looked elegant in her white linen pants suit and wide-brimmed straw hat. Her face was still beautiful and hardly wrinkled, even though she had to be really old. Caitlin said Grandmother had plastic surgery the way other people had their teeth cleaned. "She's got staples in her scalp."

"Staples in her scalp?"

"And maybe behind her ears, I'm not sure."

While Vix was contemplating having staples behind her ears Caitlin introduced her to Dorset, Lamb's sister, who was tall and muscular, with long honey-colored hair held off her face with tortoiseshell combs. She'd been married three times and had been at Hazelden for rehab twice. At the moment she was living with Grandmother in the big house in Palm Beach. Caitlin said anyone who could live with Grandmother Somers deserved a medal. Dorset had a great tan.

"No matter what Grandmother says," Caitlin whispered, "don't talk back."

"Me, talk back to somebody's grandmother?" Vix had to laugh it was such an absurd idea. Besides, she was still in shock that the name, *Regina Mayhew Somers*, neatly printed in green ink inside all the hottest books in the house, belonged to somebody's grandmother. "A grandmother read those books?" she'd asked Caitlin.

"What are grandmothers supposed to read . . . the Bible?"

"I wouldn't know," Vix said. "I don't have any grandparents."

Grandmother Somers was so polite, so refined, that Vix couldn't believe it when she came inside and after a quick look around, said, "So this is what the Jew did to my house. Well, it's quite something, isn't it? Quite a statement."

Vix felt prickles down her spine but she remembered Caitlin's warning. *Don't talk back*. Lamb winced but didn't say anything either. Vix was grateful Abby was in the kitchen and hadn't heard Grandmother's remark.

Regina Mayhew Somers

SHE TRIES NOT to let her memories of this island intrude. The police at her door on the night of the accident. The hastily arranged double funeral. The realization that it would be up to her and Lamb Senior to raise those tiny orphans, to begin again just when they'd planned on celebrating his retirement with a round-the-world cruise. And his anger at *her* for devoting herself to the babies! She never could understand that. What was she supposed to do, walk away from her responsibilities? To get out of it he'd keeled over one Friday afternoon at the club, on the seventeenth hole, dumping it all in her lap. The children, the responsibilities, and, yes, the money. Not that the Mayhews didn't have their own. She'd trusted Charlie Wetheridge to advise her, until Charlie had gone and died on her, too, literally, in bed at the Ritz. She'd stayed close with Lucy, his widow, who'd never suspected Charlie was more to her than a financial counselor.

No, it wasn't easy, raising two children by yourself in those days. And having to listen to that awful music. Elvis, and then those English boys. And the most unbecoming clothes and hairdos. As far as she's concerned you can take those years and flush them down the toilet. *Revolution*, indeed! *Make love not war!* Where did that get them?

And now her house! He's let this new woman have her way with it. This *Jew*! It was all more than she could bear. Really.

Dorset

SHE PRAYS FOR Grandmother's death. Get it over with while they're all together so Lamb can take care of the details. She doesn't wish her pain or suffering. Just closure. So she can take control of her own life.

Why does she have to die for you to grow up and take control of your own life? her shrink wants to know.

You tell me, Dr. Freud.

So far he hasn't.

WHEN DORSET ASKED for a volunteer to help her run errands, Vix jumped. Last stop on the list was John's Fish Market, to pick up the poached salmon Abby had ordered for lunch. The second they walked into the fish market Vix stopped dead, because who should be working behind the counter wearing a long white apron but the National Treasure himself. Wouldn't Caitlin be sorry she hadn't come!

"Well, well . . ." he said when he finally noticed her. "Look what the cat dragged in."

Vix was flattered he remembered her, although her loyalties lay with Bru. Still, the heat from his smile drifted across the counter and made her fidget. She ran her hand over the lemons sitting in a basket while Dorset asked if Abby's order was ready. Von disappeared into the back and came out carrying the salmon arranged on a platter, decorated with flowers. He presented it with a flourish, singing, "Ta-da . . ."

"Flowers . . ." Dorset said. "How pretty."

"Yeah . . . and they're edible," he said, eyeing Dorset up and down even though she had to be old enough to be his mother. "I never knew you could eat . . . you know . . . flowers until I started working here."

Dorset cleared her throat and took her time signing the charge slip. Then she said, "Could you get the door please, Victoria?"

"What?" Vix asked, because by then *she* was locked into a staring contest with Von.

"The door," Dorset repeated.

"Oh, sure . . ."

"Wait . . ." Von called. "I've got something for your friend."

He disappeared into the back again.

Vix could see Dorset wondering what all of this was about. Von returned and handed her a small brown bag. "Give her this, with my regrets . . . I mean, *regards*."

Just when she thought it couldn't get any better she stepped outside and there, sitting in a parked truck with his feet propped up on the dashboard, was Bru. *Oh God, oh God, oh God* . . . she couldn't believe her luck!

"Hey . . ." he said when he saw her. He was doing something to his finger with a pocketknife, maybe digging out a splinter.

"Hey," she answered.

"What've you got?"

"Got?"

"In the bag . . . I'm starving."

"Oh. I doubt you'd want what's in the bag."

"Let's have a look."

"I don't think it's . . ."

"Vix!" Dorset called. "Let's get going."

"I have to go."

"Take it easy," he said.

"Yeah . . . you, too."

"He's a little old for you, isn't he?" Dorset asked, on the way home.

"Oh, it's not like that," Vix explained. Was she talking about Von or Bru? "We're just sort of . . . friends."

Dorset mulled that over. "Good. Because I don't like to see young girls getting in over their heads. It's just not wise."

Vix nodded, as if she knew exactly what Dorset was talking about.

The minute she got home she handed Caitlin the bag from the fish market. From the way Caitlin sucked in her breath when she opened it, Vix knew it must really be a fish head.

"Have either of you seen my Percocet?" Dorset asked, dumping everything out of her purse onto the kitchen counter. "Because I was sure I had it with me."

"Sorry," Caitlin said and she and Vix took off, running all the way to the beach, tripping over each other, laughing hysterically as they fed Von's gift to the cormorants.

9

UNTIL THE NIGHT BEFORE Vix hadn't realized Lamb's full name was Lambert Mayhew Somers the Third, or that Sharkey was named Lambert Mayhew Somers the Fourth, like some king, some king who pumped gas at the Texaco station on Beach Road. They'd planned on calling him Bert, Caitlin told her, to distinguish his name from Lamb's, but when he was little he became so fascinated by sharks they started calling him Sharkey and the name stuck.

"When they made *Jaws* Lamb took him down to the lagoon to meet Steven Spielberg," Caitlin said, "but all Sharkey cared about was that huge mechanical monster. Then Lamb made the mistake of taking him to see the movie and Sharkey totally freaked out. He hasn't gone swimming since. Did you see it?"

"The shark?"

"The movie."

Vix shook her head. "My parents wouldn't let me."

"If they show it again we'll go together. It doesn't scare me," Caitlin told her. "You know what a shark bite feels like?"

"No, what?"

Caitlin suddenly jumped onto Vix's bed and bit her on her rear end.

"Cut that out!" Vix yelled.

When Sharkey joined them at the house for lunch, Grandmother bopped him over the head with her purse. "Straighten up, Bertie. Walk tall. You're a Mayhew."

Sharkey slumped into a chair at the porch table, set for lunch with Abby's blue and white dishes. Vix could feel the tension building and wished she could escape to the beach with a peanut butter sandwich and a book. Maybe she'd run into Bru and Von again. Now that would be interesting!

Dorset sat across from her, a blank expression on her face. Her eyes were unfocused, as if she were already somewhere else, probably back at the fish market with Von. She fiddled with the combs in her hair, first taking out one and repositioning it, then the other.

The conversation at the table centered on Grandmother's health. "But you're looking so well, Mrs. Somers," Abby told her.

"Oh, pfoo," Grandmother said.

Vix had to remind herself that this woman was *Regina Mayhew Somers*, that she'd once read *Valley of the Dolls* and *Peyton Place*. She probably knew all about *coitus interruptus*.

"I'm not well at all," Grandmother continued. "And those Florida doctors can't find the problem. But you know who you get down there . . . doctors looking for sunshine, doctors who want to fish all day or sail boats

. . . and so many of them of the Jewish persuasion. Not that they don't make good doctors," she hastily added.

"Now, Grandmother . . ." Lamb said, putting down his fork.

"Oh, I knew you would take that wrong!" she cried, as if she were a naughty girl. "But Abby understands, don't you, dear?"

"Yes, I understand completely," Abby said.

"We all understand, Grandmother," Caitlin added.

"Well, that's good, isn't it?" Grandmother asked lightly.

Regina Mayhew Somers

OH, WHAT FUN, making them squirm in their seats! But if they're going to treat her like some kind of relic she'll act the part. Not that she's denying her years . . . far from it . . . she's proud to be an octogenarian. Of course, she doesn't look a day over sixty-five. She could easily be taken for Lamb's mother, not his grandmother. There's still plenty of spunk in the old girl.

Caitlin is quite a beauty, isn't she? She should marry well. What about Charlie Wetheridge's grandson? An investment banker, she hears. But Caitlin isn't ready yet, is she? No . . . she's just thirteen or fourteen.

Bertie's an odd one. And that noise he makes. Even with her hearing loss it's obvious. Isn't Lamb aware? Can't he do something about it?

This salmon is quite tasty, actually. Maybe she'll ask for a second helping. Good thing the Jew doesn't go in for those ethnic dishes. She's heard they have strange dietary habits.

Dorset

WHAT A NUMBER Grandmother is doing on Abby, calling her the Jew, testing her. And that story about doctors! What doctors? There's nothing wrong with her. She'll probably outlive all of them. Ha!

Where the fuck is her Percocet? She'd wrapped it in a tissue, hidden it in the pocket of her pants. If they hurry and finish lunch she'll still have time for a quick trip back to the fish market. Maybe *fishboy* can get away for an hour. Now there's a positive thought. What a body, and those lips . . . she can feel them on her already . . . on her mouth, her neck, her breasts, between her legs. Yes, think about that, Dorset . . . that'll get you through this meal. Where's her vibrator? In her overnight bag? Maybe she can excuse herself. If she can't have fishboy she can at least think of him while using her magic pole.

Sharkey

WHAT A JOKE his family is, sitting at the table with the Old Bird, every one of them wishing they were someplace else. And what's Dorset thinking about with that weird little smile on her face? She's not bad looking, his aunt. No trouble picturing her in underwear. The old-fashioned kind, white cotton panties, pointy bra. Like in the old Sears catalog he keeps hidden in his closet. Probably goes back to the Old Bird's day. So what?

Wonder what Vix is thinking, licking the crumbs off the corner of her mouth when she thinks no one's looking . . . like a cat.

He's got to get back to work. Zach's going to be real glad he hired *him*. He can do a whole lot more than pump gas. He's almost sure he can convince Lamb the Datsun truck makes sense. Twenty thousand miles. Almost new. Jet black. Like something James Bond might drive if he drove a truck. Perfect for next summer when he has his license. With a VIP plate spelling out SHRKY. Then Carly can write a song about him. *Nobody Does It Better* . . .

———————

ALL THROUGH LUNCH Vix watched as Caitlin seethed. She waited for the explosion, surprised when it didn't come. It wasn't until later, after Grandmother and Dorset left, that Caitlin stormed into the kitchen where Abby and Lamb were cleaning up. "I don't see how you can stand it," Caitlin said to Abby. "She's such a prejudiced old bitch!"

Abby looked stunned. So did Lamb. "I won't have you bad-mouthing Grandmother!" Lamb said in a tone Vix had never heard him use.

"I wouldn't have to if you'd tell her off yourself."

"If it weren't for Grandmother—" Lamb began.

Caitlin cut him off. "What? You'd have been sent on the orphan train?"

"Watch your step, Caitlin."

"It's disgusting, the way you just let her say anything . . . without thinking how it comes across to the rest of us!"

"That's it!" Lamb said. "Go to your room."

"Oh, please . . . isn't it a little late in the game for sending me to my room?"

Abby reached out and touched Caitlin's hand. "Thank you, Caitlin. It means a lot to me that you care."

Caitlin pulled away. "Don't take it personally," she said. "I was talking about prejudice in general. And now, if you'll excuse me, I believe I'm being punished!"

Upstairs, in their room, Vix wondered herself why Lamb let Grandmother Somers get away with those rude remarks. She didn't have to ask. Caitlin volunteered the information. "You know what it's all about? *Money!* You don't tell off the one who controls the big stuff."

Oh, the Big Stuff. She couldn't believe how naive she'd been, assuming Lamb was struggling to support his family, because who did she think paid for the fancy house, the new Sunfish, the camera Lamb and Abby gave her for her birthday—a gift so extravagant, she'd never show her parents? She'd heard Tawny refer to some of the Countess's friends as trust-fund babies—always with disdain—but until now she'd never known any personally.

"The one with the big stuff has a lot of power," Caitlin said.

"I wouldn't know," Vix said.

"You're lucky."

"No," she argued. "You are."

"You have no idea what you're talking about."

She was right, of course. But Vix knew her parents would do anything to have plenty of money. Well, not anything, maybe, but close to it. And they wouldn't need a lot. Not as much as Grandmother Somers, however much that was. Not even as much as Lamb. Just enough so they'd never have to worry. Just enough to buy a nice house, maybe one of those new places off the Old Taos Highway, and a couple of vacations a year, maybe to Hawaii, and plenty of help for Nathan. She could hear Tawny reminding her, *The rich are different, Victoria.*

Yeah . . . right, she thought. They have more money.

Abby

SO, CAITLIN HAS a social conscience. Well, good for her! She's a spunky girl. Challenging but spunky. Just last week when she'd joined the girls on a bike ride, Caitlin had stopped off at the cemetery on Spring Street to show Vix Lamb's parents' grave.

If they'd lived they'd be my grandparents, Caitlin said.

If they'd lived they'd be my in-laws, she told Caitlin, placing a small stone on top of the double gravestone. Then she'd ambled through the cemetery checking out the Somers and the Mayhews, all of them Lamb's ancestors. Caitlin and Vix followed. When she came to a wrought-iron arch with the words *Martha's Vineyard Hebrew Cemetery*, she stopped. *I could be buried here*, she told the girls.

What are you talking about? Caitlin asked.

I'm Jewish. You know that.

But if there's only one god, what difference does it make which part of the cemetery you're buried in?

She looked at Caitlin for a minute. *That's a profound question.*

I'm a profound person, Caitlin told her, *in case you haven't noticed.*

I've noticed, she said, trying to keep a straight face.

10

VIX ALTERNATELY dreamed of striking it rich and becoming Mother Teresa. If she were rich she'd be able to take Nathan to Disney World. She'd take him to the best doctors, hire the best physical therapists, send him to the finest schools. She'd build a hot tub in the backyard so her parents could relax when they came home from work. She might even buy Lewis the ten-speed bike he'd been begging for, and Lanie . . . she wasn't sure about Lanie because Lanie was a handful that year, willful and wild and not even thirteen.

On the other hand, if she opted for Mother Teresa she wouldn't have to worry about having money. She'd have God. She'd spend all her time praying and ministering to the sick and needy. And she wouldn't have to worry about her breasts growing too big because her habit would hide them. Not that she had the time to worry about the size of her breasts, though sometimes she wondered if she might have caught some rare disease from Trisha.

With summer, the problems of the world; her world anyway, magically lifted from her shoulders. It was the hottest July on record, with humid tropical air blowing in on southerly winds. The flowers in Abby's garden wilted, the crackers and cereals in the pantry went slack, a disgusting green mold grew on anything that wasn't thoroughly dried. Everyone was talking about a Chilmark family who had fallen ill with a rare, infectious type of pneumonia. Was it Legionnaires' disease? Abby lectured them about scrubbing their hands before meals, keeping their nails cut short and scrupulously clean. She bleached their bedding and towels, their clothes.

Sweetie spent the long muggy days dozing under the trees. She had no more energy or appetite than the rest of them. How lucky they were not to be in the city where people were dropping like flies from the heat, Abby reminded them, while they could stand in water up to their chins all day if they felt like it. Even Sharkey, who never got wet, turned the garden hose on himself.

At night the foghorn lulled them to sleep.

It was the first time Vix had come away without feeling guilty, thanks to Nathan's doctor, who'd arranged for him to spend two weeks at a camp for disabled kids in the Colorado Rockies. "No parents," Nathan had told her proudly. "Nobody to tell me what to do."

"Promise you'll be careful?" she said.

"What do you mean?"

"You know . . . watch out for yourself."

"I'm not a little kid anymore. I'm nine. So you don't have to worry about me."

"I'm not worried."

"Good. Because I'm going to have fun. It's going to be like school but better. No Tawny."

She'd laughed with him over that. "You're going to have a great time," she agreed, hugging him.

"And if you're lucky I'll tell you about it."

For two months she wouldn't have to plan her life, baby-sitting every afternoon and as many nights a week as Tawny would allow, determined to do something about her future and the future of her family. For two months she could just lie back and let Abby take care of her.

She didn't mind the cloying dampness or the heat and humidity. She had come to the Vineyard that summer with a delicious secret, a secret she'd been savoring for months. She'd seen an announcement on the bulletin board at the public library in Santa Fe. *Reluctant Swimmers. It's Never Too Late to Learn.* She'd signed up at the town pool without a word to her parents, shoving the bottom half of the permission slip in front of Tawny one night, telling her it was for a class trip that didn't cost anything. Tawny scribbled her signature without even reading it. Vix paid for the course out of her baby-sitting money and had enough left over to buy a neon yellow maillot, the latest in swimsuits according to *Seventeen.*

And what good timing! True, her stroke was crude, clearly that of a beginner. And she wasn't going to win any races. But the first time she marched out to the end of the dock, jumped into the water, and swam out to Lamb's boat, the expression on Caitlin's face made it all worthwhile. "I thought you didn't know how to swim."

"You shouldn't jump to conclusions," Vix told her.

"I was hardly jumping. This is your third summer

here and until now I've never seen you in water above your knees."

"I wasn't hot enough to swim until now."

Caitlin laughed. "I just love the way your mind works."

They prepared for the arrival of the Chicago Boys by installing a hook-and-eye lock on their bedroom door. But nothing could have prepared Vix for the day Gus took her by surprise in the pond, grabbing hold of her foot while she was swimming out to Lamb's boat. She panicked, going under, coming up gagging and choking, flailing her arms. The second her feet touched bottom she ran for shore.

Gus was right behind her. "Hey, *Cough Drop*," he called, tossing her a towel. "You've got snot coming out of your nose."

Daniel stood by slapping his thigh as if she were performing a comedy routine for his pleasure. To get back at them she and Caitlin raided their room. Caitlin found a jock strap dangling from a hook on the back of their door. She sniffed it and proclaimed the owner this summer's winner of the Dingleberry Award.

They found a Victoria's Secret catalog under a pile of dirty clothes, which only enraged Vix more. Imagine a sexy underwear catalog with *her* name on it! And one or both of the Chicago Boys had annotated the pages: *best tits, best ass, best all-round-lay.*

"These guys don't think about anything else!" Vix said. Not that she and Caitlin weren't thinking about it, too. Their Power had turned into an itch that never went away. But at least it was hidden, not dangling between their legs for all the world to see.

Caitlin taped a photo of Georgia O'Keeffe to the Chicago Boys' bunk bed.

> *Dear Baumer and Pustule,*
> *Try jerking off to a real woman for a change!*

After that Vix tried to ignore them, until the night they all wound up on the ticket line at the Strand to see *Alien*. While they were waiting a group from Camp Jabberwocky passed, on their way to the Flying Horses. "Retards," Daniel said to Gus, and the two of them did a number, pretending to be spastic.

She exploded. "You stupid assholes! Not everyone with physical disabilities is retarded. You're retarded if that's what you think!" Although some of the Jabberwocky campers were retarded they had no right to make a joke of them. God, they were beyond stupid . . . beyond hope!

The two boys were amazed. They couldn't believe that she, who never showed anything, had raved and ranted in public. "What?" Gus said. "What'd we do?"

"Her brother has muscular dystrophy," Caitlin told them. "He's in a wheelchair. But he's a million times smarter than either one of you pathetic slobs will ever be."

That shut up the Chicago Boys. Even Gus couldn't come up with a smart remark. Vix was fuming. Inside the theater they went in separate directions and the second the movie ended she marched up the street to Murdick's Fudge and sent Nathan a one-pound box of assorted flavors. She knew it was stupid, that the camp wouldn't let him have more than one small piece at a time, if that, but she figured he could share the rest with his friends and they'd all know she'd been thinking of them.

After that, she refused to speak to Daniel or Gus. She looked the other way when and if she passed either of them in the house. Two days later they approached her as she came out of the bathroom on her way to bed. Gus did the talking. "We didn't mean anything. We were just fooling around. We didn't know you had a brother like that."

"He's not *like* anything. He's a *person* who just happens to have been born with something he can't control. It could have happened to you. It could have happened to any of us. So the next time you see someone in a chair, someone spastic, just imagine if that were you! The same *you* who's standing here now, but your mind's been trapped inside a body you can't control!" She'd surprised herself, sounding so clear and strong and angry. Her heart was beating so fast she could feel the blood pumping to her face.

"I never thought of it like that," Gus said. He elbowed Daniel, signaling that it was his turn to speak. But Daniel just turned and walked away.

"He's having his own problems," Gus said.

"Who isn't?" She knew Daniel's father was about to remarry, someone Gus referred to as the *Babe*. *A real dish, not even thirty*, he'd told them, making sure they got his point.

"Are your parents divorced, too?" he asked.

"No. Not all parents are divorced. And not all problems are about parents."

"You don't have to be so hostile. I *said* we were sorry."

"Actually, you didn't."

"Well, we are."

"Okay." She realized then she was standing outside the bathroom in an oversize T-shirt and underpants, with a toothbrush in her hand, talking to some sixteen-year-old boy she didn't even like.

And then Gus did the strangest thing. He leaned over and kissed her on the cheek. "I really am sorry, Cough Drop," he said. "We acted like *shits*. Good night."

Which left her completely speechless.

Gus and Daniel gave Vix a belated birthday present, a jigsaw puzzle, "Seeing Red," five hundred pieces all in one solid color. They bet Sharkey twenty bucks she wouldn't be able to finish it in a week.

"What's in it for her?" Caitlin asked. "Why should she bust her ass for any of you?"

"What are you, her agent?" Daniel said.

"That's right," Caitlin told him, "I'm her agent."

"Okay . . ." Daniel said. "She gets twenty if she makes it, which means we're laying out forty. Are you and Sharkey going to match us if she doesn't?"

Caitlin nodded at Sharkey, who looked at Vix for confirmation. She gave him a thumbs-up. "You're on," Sharkey told the Chicago Boys.

For two nights the four of them pulled chairs up to the card table and watched Vix, as if she were Bobby

Fischer. But with everyone staring she couldn't concentrate. She made almost no progress. Daniel and Gus eyed each other smugly. Vix was determined to prove them wrong. She rose at sunrise the next day and for two days after that. The others would find her there when they came down to breakfast, studying the pieces, locking together the edges, constructing separate sections, until the end of the sixth day, when she knew she had it.

She let them watch that night, enjoying every step toward victory, and when she placed the final pieces Sharkey pumped his fist in the air and cried, *"Yes!"* He lifted her out of her chair and before she could stop him, swung her around. She was totally amazed. But when she smiled down at him he released her without a word, collected his share of the winnings, and disappeared. Gus and Daniel hung around to help the girls celebrate.

"How about a consolation prize?" Gus said.

"What did you have in mind?" Caitlin asked.

He smiled and looked her over. "Whatever you're willing to give."

"You wish!" She threw the empty puzzle box at him. He and Daniel laughed and went off together.

11

VIX WONDERED if Abby ever guessed how she fantasized about being her daughter, how she dreamed of being beautiful and rich and living in the big house in Cambridge, not that she'd ever seen it, but she'd seen pictures. Just weeks earlier, on the night of Vix's fourteenth birthday, when she and Caitlin had dressed up for dinner at The Black Dog, Abby had said, "You both look so pretty. You remind me of how much I've always wanted a daughter."

"Don't get any ideas," Caitlin had told her. "We already have mothers."

Vix could see the hurt in Abby's eyes, hear it in her voice. "I only meant . . ." Abby started to say, but then she looked away and never finished.

Vix asked Caitlin once if she didn't miss Sharkey and Lamb during the school year, if she didn't want to live in Cambridge, too.

"I miss them," Caitlin answered. "But Phoebe needs me, to prove she's not a failure as a mother."

Vix thought of Phoebe's postcards. Last summer there had been just one, from Tuscany.

Dear Ones,
Hope your having a grand summer, as always.
I'm about to leave for a few days in Venice.
See you soon!
All my love,
Phoebe

The card was addressed to Caitlin and Sharkey Somers. One card for two kids. One card every summer. Sharkey dismissed it as fast as he'd read it, telling Caitlin she could add it to her collection. Caitlin stuck it in her bottom dresser drawer with all the others. Phoebe had misspelled *you're*.

Vix didn't understand why Lamb and Phoebe had divvied up the kids when they'd divorced. "I was only two when they split up," Caitlin told her. "I didn't have a lot to say about it then."

What about now? Vix wondered, almost certain she knew the answer. You weren't always born to the right parents. And parents didn't necessarily get the kids they were meant to raise.

When Vix found out Tawny was coming to the island she grew sick with fear, sure Tawny had somehow found out about her fantasies and was on her way to fight for her rights as a mother. She imagined a raging court battle like the one over Gloria Vanderbilt in the book she was reading, *Little Gloria, Happy at Last*.

"I knew Lamb and the Countess were old friends," Abby said to Vix as they worked side by side in the

garden, "but I had no idea your mother was her amanuensis." Whenever Caitlin went sailing, Vix spent her
time with Abby. In the garden Abby wore a coolie hat, a
long-sleeved white shirt, drawstring pants, gloves, and
red vinyl clogs she'd ordered from some gardening catalog.

If Lamb and the Countess were old friends how come
no one had ever told her? And what was an *amanuensis*?
It sounded sexual.

Abby pulled up a lady's-mantle, mistaking it for a
weed. "I can't believe I did that," she said, holding it
tenderly, as if it were a pet. In her garden, unlike in real
life, Abby's enemies could be identified and destroyed.
Japanese beetles were collected in bags hanging from
trees, slugs were lured into saucers of beer, and mites
were sprayed with a solution of soapy water. A picket
fence, lined with chicken wire, helped to keep out rab-
bits. "I know they're adorable," Abby would tell her
guests, "but just one little bunny can destroy your garden overnight."

The deer were another story. To keep them away,
Abby tied bars of Irish Spring soap to the fence posts.
When that didn't work she scattered dried blood. Last
summer Vix had seen a deer tear through the woods,
leap into the pond, and swim all the way across. When
he got there, he looked around as if he'd made a mistake, then turned and swam back, disappearing into the
woods. Vix wondered if he had a family, if he was running away but changed his mind at the last minute.

"When your mother gets here maybe we can sit
down together and talk about school," Abby said. She'd

given up on the lady's-mantle and was deadheading the fairy roses.

What did she mean, *school*?

"Lamb and I have been wondering if you'd like to go to Mountain Day with Caitlin?"

"Mountain Day is a private school."

"Suppose you had a scholarship?"

"A scholarship?"

"Of course high school is just the beginning," Abby told her. "Have you thought about college yet?"

No one in her family had ever gone to college. She was hoping for UNM, though Tawny wanted her to become a medical technician. *Healthcare, Victoria. That's where the jobs are going to be. Listen to me. I know what I'm talking about.*

"I know it seems far off," Abby continued, "but actually it's right around the corner. You've got to start planning now. Maybe we can talk about the big picture when your mother gets here."

Vix kept weeding the same patch even after all the weeds were pulled. Was Abby having fantasies, too? She began to feel sweat trickle down inside her bra, a new kind of wetness that could spring from her pores in an instant, without warning, releasing a pungent odor, even if she'd just showered. She hated the unpredictability of her body. She hated being fourteen. It felt like a punishment. She just didn't know for what.

"I'm not making you uncomfortable, am I?" Abby asked.

"No," Vix said, too quickly, swiping her face with her arm, trying to get a whiff of her underarms. "It's just that . . ."

"I understand completely," Abby said.

"You do?"

"Of course."

As much as she dreaded the idea of Tawny invading her space, Vix was relieved to find that the visit had nothing to do with Abby. She'd come because the Countess could no longer travel on her own and the Countess had too many friends in too many places to sit at home brooding over her emphysema and failing eyesight.

Fortunately, the Countess kept Tawny busy. Everyone on the island wanted a piece of her. How did all these rich people know one another? Was there some sort of club? Vix decided the Countess's popularity had to do with the fantastic stories she told—stories about running away to join the circus at sixteen, winding up in Paris at eighteen, finding herself stranded with the Count in a stalled elevator at some hotel called *George Sank*, marrying him a week later. Even though the marriage didn't last more than six months she came out with gobs of money, or maybe she had money all the time.

Vix, trying to picture the Countess atop an elephant under the big top, once asked her mother if the Countess's stories were true. "All I know is what I'm told," Tawny had replied, which was no answer at all. When Vix had balked she'd added, "I don't ask questions, Victoria. That's *why* I'm still employed."

With her pixie haircut, outlandish outfits, and infectious laugh, the Countess was still in center ring. She was never boring. She was definitely not ordinary. On the last full day of her whirlwind visit, the Countess gave Tawny the afternoon off to spend with Vix, who couldn't remember an hour, let alone an afternoon, she'd been alone with her mother, and the idea frightened her.

They drove up island in the red convertible rental car, all the way to the scenic overlook at Gay Head, and when Tawny peered through the telescope—a dime for each minute—and saw the colors in the cliffs below, she said, "But this is just like New Mexico!"

"Except there are no crashing waves in New Mexico," Vix reminded her mother. "There's hardly any water at all."

"Yes, but we have mountains," Tawny said. She didn't sound angry, the way she usually did if Vix disagreed with her. She didn't call her impossible or irritating or even immature.

They ate lunch outside, overlooking the ocean, with the wind blowing their hair and the sun in Vix's eyes. Tawny ordered fried clams and drank a beer she'd brought with her. "I can see why you like it here, Victoria," she said. "It has a magic quality . . . something I haven't felt since I first got to Santa Fe." She let out a deep sigh. "But that was so long ago . . ."

Vix could not believe how different Tawny seemed away from home.

"Things change . . . things happen . . . things you can't even imagine when you're young and full of hope." Tawny gazed out over the ocean. "I always thought I'd travel, see the world, but this . . ." she said, looking back at Vix and rapping her knuckles on the table, "is as far away as I've ever been."

Was this stranger swigging beer out of a bottle, this stranger who suggested they kick off their shoes and walk along at the ocean's edge so she could say she'd not only seen the Atlantic, she'd dipped her toes in it, really her mother?

Tawny

ALL RIGHT, she admits it, just for a minute this afternoon, she'd envied Victoria her freedom, even her youth. She's glad the Countess convinced her to come here. She hasn't felt so relaxed since . . . she can't remember when. The anger she carries around with her most days, that extra weight on her shoulders, has lifted since she's been on this island. Yes, she feels more like herself. Her old self. Too bad Ed can't see her laughing and talking as if she doesn't have a care in the world.

She just wishes Victoria wouldn't look at her that way. The same way *she'd* looked at her mother, sizing up the situation, trying to figure out Darlene's mood. That Abby is a lucky woman! Lamb is an attractive man, and well-to-do. How long since she's allowed herself to feel attracted to a man other than Ed? She can't remember that either. She's going to fix herself up for dinner at their house tonight. She'll wear her new white shirt, cinch her belt a little tighter, use the lipstick that came free with her sunblock. She's still a woman. She still has feelings and desires.

12

THE COUNTESS addressed Lamb as *Dear Boy*. "Dear Boy, it's been far too long!" she said, kissing him on the lips. He called her *Charlotte*. Vix had never thought of the Countess as having a regular name.

Drinks were set up on the porch. The Countess belted down two vodka and tonics. When she lit up, Abby didn't say a word, even though no one was allowed to smoke in the house. When she began to cough, Lamb and Abby looked concerned. But it wasn't until the coughing racked her body, leaving her gasping, that Vix was convinced she was going to keel over and die. Abby probably thought the same thing because she jumped up and grabbed the phone, ready to dial 911. But Tawny remained calm, waving them away, administering medication to the Countess.

After, the Countess laughed, which almost sent her into a second attack. "When my time comes, scatter my ashes in the mountains, have a drink, tell yourselves '*She lived well . . . she had a few laughs.*' No religious mumbo jumbo for me, Dear Boy. Remember that. Tawny has my instructions."

A few minutes later the Countess decided she'd like

to take a walk. But when Tawny started to get up she said, "Lamb will escort me. You stay here with Abby." Then she beckoned to Vix. "Victoria, come with us."

You didn't argue with the Countess. Vix did as she was told.

Lamb

A VISION POPS into his head. He's four or five and he barges into the bathroom to get his tugboat because his nurse is going to give him a bath in the kitchen sink. He's startled to find someone soaking in his tub, the tub where he and Dorset are usually bathed. He remembers too late he's supposed to knock when the bathroom door is closed. Grandmother will scold him for forgetting. But the lady in the tub doesn't mind. She's smiling. He knows her name—Charlotte, like his favorite treat from the bakery. She takes a puff on her cigarette. *Precious child* . . . she says, and her voice is as warm and soft as his blanky. *Would you like to come in with me?* He takes off his underpants because you're supposed to get naked before you get in the tub. She holds his hand as he steps over the edge and sits opposite her. He offers her his tugboat. *Thank you*, she says and she makes it swoosh through the water. *This is what it would be like to have a real mother*, he thinks, someone who likes to play in the tub. Someone with a laugh that bubbles up like the ginger ale Nurse brings him when he has a tummy ache.

She takes a sip from the glass that's resting on the floor. *Want some?* she asks. *It tastes like grape juice*. He knows it's not grape juice. It's something grownups drink. *No thank you*, he tells her.

Her breasts bob up and down in the water. He reaches out to touch them, looking into her eyes for approval, wondering if she'll slap his hands like Nurse. But no, she laughs. *I have a good pair, don't I?*

He chokes up for a minute, thinking about her. She must have been in her twenties then. A young woman with long chestnut hair pinned on top of her head. His mother's best friend. She gave him a photo album filled with pictures of the two of them. *Charlotte and Amanda*. Summer friends like Caitlin and Vix. It's a shock to think his mother would be *her* age now.

OUTSIDE, the Countess lit up again, took a few puffs, then flicked the butt into the woods, where it sparked. Lamb raced after it and stomped it out before it could catch fire. "That's a dangerous thing to do, Charlotte, especially this time of year, with everything so dry."

"I've always lived dangerously, Dear Boy."

"Now, Charlotte . . . as much as I like you, I can't let you burn down the island. There are laws . . ."

"Oh, fuck the laws . . . fuck the island!" She took Vix's hand, raised it to her lips, and kissed it twice. "Remember this, Precious Child . . . nothing matters but the moment. There might be no tomorrow and even if there is, nobody gives a damn."

Vix didn't have a clue what she was talking about. Or if she was waiting for her hand to be kissed. Vix hoped not. She was relieved when the Countess laughed and headed back to the house, where she asked for another vodka and tonic.

This time Tawny put a hand on her arm. "Tawny is my savior," the Countess said. "I don't know where I'd be without her. If only she didn't have that family. Such a burden. Such an albatross. Why anyone has children when they could have dogs is beyond me." Sweetie raised her head and yawned as if she understood perfectly.

Vix was miffed. Two minutes ago she'd been *Precious Child*, now she was a burden, an albatross around her mother's neck.

"You get everything from a dog you'd get from a child," the Countess continued, "plus total acceptance, absolute gratitude. I've never met a grateful child, have you?"

Abby grabbed Lamb's hand and they smiled at each other knowingly, probably wishing they had three dogs instead of three teenagers. Where were Caitlin and Sharkey? They'd promised to be back in time for dinner.

When Abby brought up the subject of the scholarship Vix held her breath. This is it, she thought, the Big Picture. She still wasn't sure what the Big Picture was but Tawny had been in such a good mood all day maybe it would be okay. As she glanced up from her position on the floor she saw Tawny fiddling with a cocktail napkin, one that said, *Fly First Class. Your Children Will.* She folded it into quarters, then eighths, until it grew small enough to swallow. "Having her as your guest for the summer is one thing," Tawny told Abby. "A scholarship to private school is another."

"Yes, but we want . . ." Abby began.

"Victoria doesn't need to go to private school," Tawny said, cutting her off. "She can get a fine education at the high school."

Lamb tried to explain the Somers Foundation and how one of its programs provided scholarships to worthy students. But Tawny wasn't listening. "Do you want to go to the Mountain Day School, Victoria?" she asked. "Is that what this is all about?"

"It was our idea, Tawny," Lamb said, "mine and Abby's."

Abby gave Lamb a grateful look but Tawny wasn't having any of it. "Victoria?" she said and she wasn't a stranger anymore. She was the mother Vix knew from Santa Fe.

"I would like to go," Vix said.

"Why?" Tawny asked.

Damn! She could have come up with a million reasons if only she'd thought about it. She could have told them about Raymond Kurtis, who made ugly, sucking sounds when he passed her in the halls at school and who had bets going with his disgusting friends that one or the other of them could grab a feel or get his hand up her skirt. She could have said, *To get a better education* or *To be best friends with the most popular girl at school.*

"We're waiting, Victoria," Tawny said.

The Countess boomed, "Oh, for gawd's sake, Tawny! Why are you making such a thing of it? Four thousand kids at one school is too damn many kids in one place if you ask me."

"I'll have to discuss it with my husband," Tawny said.

The Countess rolled her eyes skyward and muttered, "Thank gawd *I* don't have a husband."

13

SOMETIMES CAITLIN acted like the one who didn't get it. When Vix broached the subject of finding jobs Caitlin was incredulous. "A job . . . but why . . . are you bored?"

"No, I'm not bored."

"Then, what?"

"I need the money."

"Oh, the money."

Caitlin had trouble remembering not everyone had an unlimited amount to spend. Not that she was a big spender. Like Lamb, she played down the money thing. She had no idea the scholarship had caused an uproar at Vix's house.

"The world has changed since we were young," Ed had told Tawny. "This will give Vix an—" He'd dropped the last word.

"A what?" Tawny asked.

"An *edge*," her father repeated, this time so Tawny could hear the word.

"An edge to topple over," Tawny scoffed.

"She deserves the chance," Ed argued. "After that,

it's . . ." He'd mumbled the rest but Vix, listening intently, was sure he'd said, *After that, it's up to her.*

Yes, she thought, it would be up to her!

She was beginning to see her father as her champion within the family. She just wished he'd be more demonstrative, more open in his love, if love was what it was about.

Another thing Caitlin didn't get was that friendship carried certain obligations. Otherwise she'd never have said, "Even though we're summer sisters and always will be, I have another life at Mountain Day, a life apart from the two of us."

Vix felt like she'd slammed into a concrete wall. Her head throbbed with the titles of every insipid self-help article she'd ever read. "When Your Best Friend Betrays You!" "Are You a Victim of Your Circumstances?" "How to Handle Your Hurt."

"I'm doing you a real favor," Caitlin said. "You understand, don't you?"

Understand? She'd willed herself not to cry, not to allow Caitlin to see her pain or disappointment. If Caitlin was afraid she'd cling to her at school, she didn't have to worry. "I have another life, too," she said, sounding as if she couldn't have cared less.

"I know you do," Caitlin said. "And I'm not offended . . . really."

After that Vix had to remind herself that Caitlin could have asked any of her Mountain Day friends to spend the summer, but she didn't, did she? Sometimes, at school, Caitlin's behavior annoyed Vix. She'd act as if she were some other person, some person Vix didn't even know. Then Caitlin would look at her as if to say,

You and I understand this is just a game but the others think it's for real so don't give me away . . . okay?

After a month at Mountain Day Vix got sick. A kidney infection. It burned when she peed. She had a high fever and a pain in her back. She needed antibiotics. She felt terrible, as bad as she'd felt in her entire life. Her mother blamed it on the new school. *Just because it's an expensive school doesn't mean you don't need paper on the toilet seat to protect yourself.*

She assured her mother she'd been careful. And the doctor swore this wasn't something she'd caught from a toilet seat. But Tawny didn't believe him. "Thank God your father's job comes with health insurance," Tawny said. "Do you know what these antibiotics cost?"

She didn't want to know.

The Countess sent flowers with a card that read, *Darling Child, Get well!* It was signed with the names of her five dogs.

Nathan offered Orlando. Orlando had magical powers. He would make her better. But if he didn't and she died, he'd be really pissed. "You know what *pissed* means?" he asked her.

"Yes," she said, "I know."

His first taste of freedom had changed Nathan. "No more Mr. Nice Guy," he'd announced. "Just because I'm in a chair doesn't mean you can *push* me around!" His wheelchair jokes drove Tawny up the wall.

"We never should have let you go to camp," she told him.

"Too late. I've already been." He pressed for more freedom, for privacy, respect. He'd even shouted at Vix one night when she'd come into the bathroom without knocking. "Out . . . right now! Only guys allowed."

"Okay, sorry . . ." She was glad he was struggling for independence but that didn't make living with him any easier.

In her feverish dreams Bru came to her every day, kissing her so passionately he set her body on fire. In her dreams he didn't speak at all, which was just as well since the one time she'd seen him all summer, as she was coming out of the Porta Potti at the Ag Fair and he was waiting his turn to go in, he'd looked right at her and said, *When you gotta go, you gotta go*. She'd been mortified at the idea of him knowing she'd just used the toilet and hadn't been able to respond.

Later, he'd come up behind her while she was lined up for the Tilt-A-Whirl. He'd tapped her shoulder and when she turned he shoved a giant panda bear at her. "Keep him warm for me . . . okay?"

Then he was gone.

Caitlin couldn't believe it. "You are the luckiest person in the entire world!"

She slept with her arms around the bear every night, one fuzzy leg between hers, igniting her Power.

Since she'd fallen ill, Caitlin came to see her every day. She stood a kachina doll on the shelf above Vix's bed. "If your medicine doesn't ward off evil spirits, this will." Then she sat at Vix's bedside holding her hand. "You

know what I told you before school started . . . about
having another life at school?"

Vix nodded.

"Well, I never would . . . that is, I didn't mean . . .
to hurt you or anything. I would never hurt you. Never.
Compared to you my school friends mean nothing to
me. Less than nothing."

"You're not the reason I got sick, if that's what you're
thinking."

"Who said that's what I'm thinking?"

"You're acting guilty, like it's your fault."

"I am not!"

"Okay . . . fine." Vix rolled over in bed.

"You really make it hard," Caitlin said, "you know
that?"

"Make what hard?"

"Never mind. Just forget it. I'll come back tomorrow.
Or maybe not."

If Vix hadn't gotten sick, if Caitlin hadn't felt guilty,
would they be sitting together on the old glider swing
now, arguing about summer jobs? Would their friendship have survived? Tawny said, *You can fill a lifetime with
if-onlys . . . or you can get on with it. In our family, we get
on with it.*

"So . . . what kind of job did you have in mind?"
Caitlin asked.

"There's only one thing we can do until we're older."

"Please . . . tell me it's not what I'm thinking!"

Vix shrugged.

"I don't even like little children," Caitlin cried. "They're so . . . demanding."

"Do me a favor. Keep that to yourself if you decide to go with me."

Caitlin decided to go with her. They were hired on the spot by the first person to interview them, a woman named Kitty Sagus, whose grandchild was coming for a month. As soon as she heard Caitlin was Lamb Somers' daughter she was sold.

On their first day on the job they discovered Kitty's daughter and son-in-law were Famous TV Stars. They recognized him right away—Tim Castellano. And even though she was pregnant and hiding behind huge sunglasses it was obvious she was Loren D'Aubergine.

Vix knew she was supposed to act cool, as if she didn't notice they looked familiar, because, after all, this was the Vineyard and plenty of celebrities came here to get away from it all.

Right away The Stars announced that Max wasn't toilet trained. "You mean he's still in diapers . . . at three?" Caitlin asked, in her I-cannot-believe-this tone.

Max looked up at her with huge baby eyes. "I like diapers."

You could tell Tim and Loren were embarrassed. Loren blushed and said, "If you can get him to use the potty, there's a bonus in it for you."

"A bonus?" Vix asked.

"Yes, a handsome cash bonus," Tim explained.

"So long as you don't threaten him or make him feel guilty," Loren said. "We don't want his toilet training to be traumatic in any way. It's very important that it be his decision."

"I get M&M's if I go potty," Max said, crashing his dump truck into his excavator. "Three for a pee, five for a poop. Yellows and reds are my favorites."

One morning during their second week of work, Tim accompanied them to the beach. At first Vix thought he was checking up on them, not that she minded. The idea of being seen with Tim Castellano was pretty exciting, even though he wore a baseball hat and dark glasses to keep people from recognizing him. And maybe he did look like just another guy with his family at the beach because no one stared or paid extra attention.

Vix was trying to get up the guts to ask for his autograph for Tawny, who never missed his show. But when she saw the way he was watching Caitlin slather herself with suntan lotion, she changed her mind. "Want me to do your back, Spitfire?" he asked. That was his special name for Caitlin. He didn't call Vix anything.

"Oh, thanks . . ." Caitlin said, lowering the straps of her red bikini. She was shooting up at an alarming rate, already taller than Vix who had reached her full height of five feet five a year ago—and even though she ate twice what Vix did she wasn't gaining an ounce. Her breasts were still tiny. But Vix didn't like the way Tim looked at her. Something was going on, something that made her uncomfortable. And she didn't like it when he asked how old they were either.

"Fifteen," Vix told him, loud and clear, though he hadn't directed his question to her. "How old are you?"

"Thirty-five," he said, laughing. "Old enough to be your father."

But he wasn't acting like a father. Especially when,

just before they were ready to pack up and head home for lunch, he suggested that he and Caitlin take a dip.

Caitlin said, "Sure."

"You'll watch Max, won't you?" Tim asked Vix.

"That's my job," she told him.

"Be right back." Caitlin tossed her hair out of her face, raised her eyebrows at Vix, then raced for the water. She dove under and began swimming out, with strong, confident strokes. Tim had thrown off his baseball hat and glasses and was hustling out of the shorts he'd worn over his bathing suit.

"Where's Daddy going?" Max asked.

"For a swim," Vix told him. "Let's go watch."

"Carry me."

She held him in her arms, breathing in the sweet smell of his hair, while she tried to keep an eye on Tim and Caitlin. By the time they came out Caitlin's lips were blue. Tim wrapped her in a towel and rubbed her down, the way they did with Max when he was wet and cold. But something about it didn't feel right. When Tim took away the towel she could see Caitlin's erect nipples through her wet suit.

She was scared Caitlin might do something foolish like that time last summer in the dinghy, when she'd taken off the top of the same bikini, just to see if anyone would notice. An older couple passing in a canoe waved at them, as if nothing were unusual. Caitlin had waved back while Vix picked up the oars and began to row as fast as she could in the opposite direction. "Maybe they thought I was a boy," Caitlin said, disgusted. "Bet they'd have noticed if I was stark naked."

"Why would you want them to notice in the first place?"

"So I don't feel invisible."

How could Caitlin possibly feel invisible?

This time Vix threw Caitlin her sweatshirt and was relieved when she pulled it over her head without taking off her suit.

"Your friend is a good swimmer," Tim told Vix.

"Yeah . . . she's a regular mermaid."

He bent over to pick up his hat and sunglasses and as he did Vix let her eyes wander down his body to the curly hairs on the insides of his upper thighs, to his skimpy wet bathing suit, then to the bulky area in front. As he straightened up, he caught her in the act and smiled, though she'd already looked away.

Tim was the one who suggested a different route back to the house. He'd noticed a house under construction just down the road from the beach and knew Max would love it. He pushed Max in his stroller while she and Caitlin lagged behind. A hot, ugly feeling was building up inside her but she couldn't express it. She hated the way Tim made her feel, as if she barely existed. *Buy one, get the second one free.*

When they reached the construction site Tim lifted Max out of the stroller, and hiked him onto his shoulders, moving in for a closer look. Max announced for the zillionth time, "I'm into construction!"

Vix and Caitlin followed though they hadn't exchanged a word since the beach. As they approached the house Caitlin suddenly grabbed her by the arm.

"What?"

Caitlin pointed and Vix saw that Bru and Von were

part of the crew. Bru and Von looking unbelievably sexy in low-slung jeans, with strong, lean, suntanned backs and muscled arms. She was hit by a sudden wave of heat, making her face flush and her knees go weak. *Eat your heart out, Tim Castellano, because next to them you're nothing!*

A minute later both guys were coming toward them. Von recognized Tim. "Hey . . . you're that cop on TV. No, wait . . . don't tell me . . . *Sukovsky* . . . something like that, right?"

Actually, it was *Wolkowsky*, but Tim didn't correct him.

Von said, "How're you doing?" and put out his hand for Tim to shake. "That's a damn good show."

"Thanks, man," Tim said, all of a sudden one of the guys. "And this is my kid, Max. He likes construction."

"Hey, Max . . ." Von said.

"I have a hard hat," Max told him. "It's yellow."

"Yeah . . . you want a job? We could use another helper."

"I have to go to Kitty's house," Max said. "I'm having peanut butter for lunch. I always have peanut butter for lunch. With grape jelly."

"Sounds good to me," Von said. Then he focused on Caitlin.

"These are our baby-sitters," Tim said. "Caitlin and . . . Vicky."

"Vix," she said under her breath, annoyed at Tim for getting it wrong.

"Oh yeah . . ." Von said. "We know them."

Bru just stood there gulping Coke from a can. After

an uncomfortable silence, Von asked, "So . . . where've you two been hiding?"

"You're the ones who've been hiding," Caitlin said.

"How would you know unless you've been looking?" Von asked.

Caitlin punched him in the arm, like in the old days. But this time he grabbed her and threw her over his shoulder like a sack of dirty laundry. She was laughing as she whacked his naked back. "Put me down, you idiot!"

Max clapped his hands and started singing "Upside Down," a three-year-old Diana Ross impersonator.

Vix could feel Bru watching her as she watched them.

"Okay, that's enough," Tim said, the expression on his face changing. "It's time for Max's lunch."

Von returned Caitlin to the ground. She was glowing. "See you around," she said to him.

"Not if I see you first," he answered.

"Yeah . . . see you around," Bru said to Vix.

"Not if I see *you* first," she answered, playing their game. Oh, she was glad she'd given her sweatshirt to Caitlin. Glad she was wearing just shorts over her yellow suit. Glad she was tan and her long dark hair swung from side to side, that her skin was clear that day, and most of all, that she filled out the top of her suit, that she filled it out *really* well.

They went to see *My Brilliant Career*, about a young Australian woman who's determined to have a career as a writer, and the man who loves her. Afterward they had a heated discussion. "She made the right decision,"

Caitlin said. "He was an asshole. She'd have been miserable the rest of her life with him."

"Not necessarily," Vix said. "She could have had him *and* her career."

"Please!"

"Well, maybe not back then. But now . . ."

"Now? You think things are different now?"

"Look at Tim and Loren. They both have brilliant careers."

"Oh, sure . . . but which one is pregnant?"

"So . . . she'll have the baby and then she'll go back to work."

"I suppose you want a dozen screaming brats. I suppose your *brilliant* career is going to be *mother*."

"I really hate it when you tell me what *I* want! Just because I like kids doesn't mean I'm going to have them. For your information I haven't made that decision yet."

Tim asked if they could baby-sit one night during his last week of vacation so he and Loren could take Kitty out to dinner. Max was already in his pajamas when they got there, ready for bed. Loren looked pretty in a loose white dress, funky earrings, her hair French braided. Tim made a big thing out of admiring her. "Do I have the most beautiful wife in the western world . . . or what?" he asked, kissing Loren in front of them while Max danced in a circle, hugging their legs.

They got back just before eleven. Loren was yawning. "I'm exhausted," she said. "I'll be glad when this baby is born."

"That makes two of us," Tim said, kissing her good

night. Then he offered to drive them home since Kitty had trouble with her night vision. Caitlin sat up front next to Tim and Vix climbed into the back, grateful that it was just a ten-minute drive. Tim tuned the radio to WMVY. From time to time he'd glance over at Caitlin but she stared straight ahead, speaking only to tell him when to turn off the main road, then directing him down the dirt road leading to their house. But instead of swinging right, into their driveway, he kept going, as if he knew he would wind up at the beach. When he did, he turned off the ignition. You could see the lights from Woods Hole across the water.

It was very quiet. Vix was aware of the sound of Tim's breathing, of Caitlin's, her own. Finally, Tim spoke. "I don't want you hanging out at that construction site. I don't want Max's baby-sitters messing around with guys like that. You hear what I'm saying?"

"Excuse me?" Vix said. "It was *your* idea to go by the construction site, not ours. I mean *we* didn't even know they were working there, did we, Caitlin?" She had to poke Caitlin to get a response and even then all Caitlin did was shake her head.

"I want you to be very, very careful." He spoke slowly and softly, turning in his seat to face Caitlin, and Vix could see he was talking only to her. She had the feeling he wished *she* weren't there. And to tell the truth, she was wishing the same thing herself. This was getting too weird.

"You come on strong, Spitfire. You give a guy the wrong idea."

It wasn't his business to talk to them about guys, especially at night in a dark car parked at the beach.

"Some guys," he continued, in that seductive voice, "once they get turned on, can't help themselves. They can't think rationally. Some guys follow their pointers through life. Do you get what I'm saying?"

Caitlin made an odd sound, almost a laugh, but not quite.

"I think you should take us home now!" Vix said, leaning forward, her hand on Caitlin's shoulder. She could not believe he was talking to them this way . . . and about *pointers!*

"Relax," he told her. "I'm just trying to talk some sense into your friend. It's for her own good."

Vix didn't like the husky quality of his voice. Maybe he enjoyed talking to them about sexy stuff. Maybe it turned him on. She wondered how her mother would feel if she read about this in *People* magazine? Her favorite TV personality and his *thing* for fifteen-year-olds. Then she started to get scared. Suppose he was dangerous? Suppose he . . . you know . . . pulled his pointer out of his pants? The palms of her hands were clammy and she felt dampness under her arms. "Open your door," she told Caitlin, leaning way over to make Tim aware of her presence. But Caitlin just sat there, mesmerized. So she reached across and tried to open the door herself but it was locked. He had them automatically locked from his control panel.

That did it! She threw herself over the seat, tumbling into Tim's lap, taking him by surprise as she grabbed the car keys out of the ignition. He tried to hold her still, tried to wrestle the keys away from her but she was no fool. There was no way she was going to give them up.

"Vix . . . Vix . . ." Caitlin said over and over. "What are you doing?"

What was she doing? Saving *her*! She was prepared to scratch out Tim's eyes if she had to. She'd read about situations like this. Stick the key all the way into his ear . . . or up his nose, to cause maximum pain. But somehow she couldn't get herself to stick a key up Tim Castellano's perfect nose.

He twisted her arm until it hurt and wrenched away the keys. "Jesus," he said, "what's with you?" He started the car, backing up so suddenly Vix tumbled into Caitlin. He came to a screeching halt at their driveway and released the automatic door lock. Vix shoved open the door on Caitlin's side and practically dragged her out. "Run . . ." she said. But Caitlin shook her off and chased Tim's car down the dark road, calling, "Tim . . . wait . . ." He must have seen her following him because the car stopped. If Caitlin couldn't protect herself, then Vix would have to do it for her. She headed toward them. But after a minute, Tim's car pulled out and Caitlin called, "Vix . . . where are you?"

"Here . . ."

Caitlin followed the sound of her voice. "Isn't he incredible!" she asked, grabbing Vix. "I think he's attracted to me. I could feel it."

"I could feel it, too," Vix said. "When I fell over onto his lap. Inside his pants, if you get what I'm saying."

"He was hard?"

"I refuse to answer that question."

"That's so exciting."

"Are you crazy? He's lewd. He's sick."

"He just wanted to give us some advice. It's not like he touched us or suggested anything."

"Is that what you were waiting for?"

She shrugged.

"I can't believe this!" Vix said. "What would have happened if I hadn't been here?"

"He wouldn't have done anything. I mean, maybe he was thinking about it . . . but . . ."

"He shouldn't be thinking about it," Vix told her. "We're fifteen and he's thirty-five, remember?"

"Actually, I think he'd be a good one for my first time, don't you?"

"He's married. His wife is pregnant. They have a three-year-old. So no, I don't think he'd be a good one at all!" Where was her judgment?

Caitlin held up two bills. "He almost forgot to pay us. He gave us each a twenty."

"I don't want his money!" She knocked the bills out of Caitlin's hand.

Caitlin bent down, picked them up, and stuck one in the pocket of Vix's jeans. "I'm not going back to that house," Vix said. "I'm never going back!"

"We only have three more days."

"Fine. You can tell them I've got the flu . . . or poison ivy or something highly contagious. And if you get raped don't say I didn't warn you!"

"He's not even going to be there. He and Loren are going to Nantucket tomorrow morning. It'll just be Kitty and Max."

"Who told you that?"

"Tim. Just now. That's why I kissed him goodbye. We're not going to see him again."

"You kissed him?"

She nodded. "I stuck my tongue in his mouth."

"Are you completely crazy?"

Caitlin started laughing. "I don't know. Maybe."

Vix couldn't let Caitlin go to Kitty's house alone. Who knew what trouble she might get into without her protection. But when they got there the next morning, Tim and Loren *were* gone.

"A little honeymoon," Kitty told them. "A romantic getaway." She sighed. "You have to work to keep romance alive in a marriage. Remember that when your time comes."

14

EVERYTHING SHE KNEW about a loving relationship came from watching Abby and Lamb. They knew how to keep romance alive in their marriage. That's what she would remember when and if her time came. Until the last Saturday of the summer when it all seemed to fall apart. She was in the kitchen with Caitlin arguing with the Chicago Boys over whether or not to mix the tomato sauce with the spaghetti before it was served. She and Caitlin wanted the sauce on the side, with basil and parsley from the garden, but Daniel said, "No green stuff in our pasta! Put it on yours after it's on your plate."

"I don't want mine drowning in your Ragu," Caitlin told him. Sharkey, who was buried in a crossword puzzle, asked, "What's a four-letter word for undulate?"

"Flow?" Vix said. "Or maybe gush?"

"Gush . . . that's it!" Sharkey said. "Thanks."

Outside it was raining, a slow, soft rain.

Abby and Lamb had been cool and remote all day but now their voices, coming from the living room, heated up and as they did, the kitchen crew grew more quiet.

"I keep telling you, it's no big deal," they heard Lamb say. "Everybody hitches on the island."

"You're oblivious!" Abby told him. "You live in some other world."

"If you'd learn to cut them some slack, Ab, you wouldn't have such a hard time. You bring it on yourself . . . that's all I'm saying."

It was *her* fault they were arguing, Vix thought, hers and Caitlin's. If Abby hadn't bumped into some guy she knew in the dairy aisle at Cronig's she might never have found out they'd been hitching. Not that they'd told him their names. But he'd recognized Caitlin. "I'll bet you're Lamb Somers' girl," he'd said, oh so proud of himself. "I've got a good eye for faces and you and Lamb are dead ringers." Caitlin neither confirmed nor denied.

Vix felt a tightening in her chest that grew worse as Abby shouted at Lamb. "You think it's enough to love them, but I don't. They're fifteen years old. They need guidance. It's up to us to encourage them to act responsibly."

"Save the lecture for the kids, Ab."

"Dammit, Lamb! When is the last time you took a good look at your daughter? She's not a little girl anymore. And neither is Vix . . . in case you haven't noticed."

Ohmygod! This was so embarrassing. Vix felt her face grow hot and she looked at the floor.

"Caitlin's right," Abby said. "I don't fit in. I'm never going to fit in. I don't even know if I *want* to fit in."

"Don't make this into something you're going to regret," Lamb told her.

"I'm going to regret? You'd have plenty to regret if that man had driven into the woods with the girls. I don't even want to think about what might have happened."

Vix prayed she'd never find out about their adventure with Tim Castellano.

"You worry too much about things that are *never* going to happen!"

"I'm glad you have some special god watching over you while the rest of us . . ."

"Are you getting your period, Ab? Is that it?"

She must have thrown something at him then, a book or her purse, because they heard a thud, then Lamb calling, "*Jesus!*"

"I'm not sure how much more I can take of this family," Abby shouted, before she burst into tears.

Daniel severed a head of lettuce with a chopping knife. Gus glanced over at Vix. She looked away, ashamed of having had any part in this. By then she'd grown so used to hitching it hadn't seemed like a big thing. How else to get to all the beaches, to town to browse, to the construction site where they'd hang out, waiting for Von and Bru to take a break?

"Come on, honey," Lamb said, "let's talk about it in the car. We're already half an hour late."

"Don't patronize me!" Abby said in a hoarse voice. "I hate it when you patronize me."

"I only meant . . ." Lamb began.

"I know exactly what you meant."

They heard Abby blowing her nose, then nothing. A few minutes later the two of them came through the kitchen. Abby avoided their eyes, grabbed a poncho off a peg, and pulled the hood up over her head. Vix wanted to rush to her side and hug her, tell her she was a wonderful mother, the best, that *she* appreciated her even if no one else did, that she was right to worry about them, that *she* was sorry she'd caused this trouble and she'd never do it again.

"We'll be home by ten-thirty," Lamb told them, "eleven at the latest. We'll talk about this tomorrow, okay?"

Tomorrow her world would come apart. Goodbye scholarship. Goodbye magic summers. Tomorrow it would all be over.

As soon as they were gone Gus let out a long, low whistle. "Trouble in River City."

Daniel said, "Six months. I give them another six months and she'll be out of here."

"Sounds good to me," Caitlin said.

"Listen you little bitch . . ." Daniel grabbed her and spun her around. "You're the reason she's miserable!"

"Like hell I am!"

"Get your slimy paws off my sister," Sharkey snapped, coming up behind Daniel.

Daniel reeled. "Stay out of this, *Sharkolater*!" Gus stood close, ready to spring into action if necessary. For a moment he and Vix looked into one another's eyes.

Daniel

HE HATES WHAT this family is doing to his mother. If they think he's going to stand by while they destroy her, they're wrong! Tomorrow he'll go to her, pledge his loyalty, tell her whatever she decides to do, he'll stick by her. She doesn't have to worry. They'll be okay. They don't need Lamb or his money or his repulsive kids.

Sharkey

GOTTA GET THEM out of here before all hell breaks loose. Before Daniel really loses it and chops up something besides lettuce. *Come on . . . come on*, he tells the girls, ushering them out of the house and into his truck. He drives into Oak Bluffs. For the first time he can remember the yakkers keep their mouths shut. Nobody wants to think what this could mean. Not even his sister. He gets lucky, finds a place to park on Circuit Ave. and leads them up to the pizza place. He hopes he has enough cash on him. He'll tell them they can each order a slice. That's it. A slice and a soda.

BEFORE THEY EVEN PUT in their order they heard raised voices and turned to see Bru sitting at a small table up front, arguing with a redheaded girl. She pushed her chair away from the table. "That's it . . ." she shouted through her tears. "*Fini, finis, finito.* Get it? It's over in any language!"

"Calm down, would you?" Bru said. "The whole fucking place is listening." Which was true.

The redhead grabbed her mug of beer, lifted it, and tossed it in Bru's face. "Grow up!" she cried before storming out of the restaurant.

For the rest of her life, every lovers' quarrel would remind Vix of this night, this night when anger crackled in the air. She vowed then and there no guy would ever make her feel that bad.

PART TWO

Rapture
1982–1983

15

ALL HER LIFE she'd dreamed of being seventeen, like the Dancing Queen. And now she was, or would be very soon. On July Fourth she and Caitlin were singing along with Debbie Harry as they cruised up island in Caitlin's rusted red pickup. By the time they hit Menemsha it was after five. They figured they'd do sunset there, then head for home. But as soon as they stepped onto the beach they spotted Bru and Von tossing around a Frisbee.

Caitlin pushed her canvas tote at Vix, kicked off her Tevas, and flashed her a wicked smile as she raced down the beach, leaping into the air to snatch their Frisbee in mid-flight. Vix hung back, watching, as if she were in sixth grade again, studying Caitlin for the secret to success.

Caitlin was dazzling at seventeen. Her hair cascaded down her back, her skin was moist and flawless, and the expression on her face dared anyone to mess with her. She'd reached her full height that year, leaving Vix three inches behind. She was all legs, like Barbie, but without the ridiculous chest. Caitlin saw this as a defect, some trick nature had played on her.

The girls at school encouraged her to send a photo to *Elle* or *Cosmo* or even *Seventeen*. The boys drooled over her. Even the teachers found her irresistible, but irritating. She was so bright. Why didn't she apply herself? She could be anything, do anything, with just a little effort. But half the time she didn't turn her papers in when they were due, and she refused to study for tests. "School has nothing to do with life," she'd say.

She'd gone skiing with Phoebe over spring break, to the Italian Alps, and returned with big news for Vix. "Congratulations are in order," she'd announced. "I'm no longer a virgin."

So, Caitlin had been first, just as she'd guaranteed. Well, Vix wasn't surprised. She wasn't even disappointed. "Who?" she asked. "Where?"

"A ski instructor," Caitlin said. "Italian. Very physical. You know the type."

Vix didn't.

"We met on the tram. He was all over me by the time we got to the top of the mountain. We could hardly ski down fast enough."

Vix felt her heart beating faster. "And?" she asked, not certain how much she wanted to know.

"It just happened."

"It can't *just* happen."

"Well, first we had to get out of our ski clothes if that's what you mean."

That wasn't what she meant. "Did it hurt? Did you feel the Power? Was it exciting?"

Caitlin laughed. "Exciting? Yeah, I guess so . . . for about two minutes. That's how long it took till he finished."

Vix laughed, too. "Did he use something?" she asked.

"Of course. I'm not totally crazy!"

"Do you love him?"

"Love him? I hardly know him. I'll probably never see him again. It was mostly . . . curiosity. But at least I got it out of the way."

Vix had no intention of doing it just to get it out of the way. Caitlin called her impossibly romantic, swearing that sex and love not only *can* be separated but *should* be. "What gets women into trouble is the way they confuse the two," she said. "Men have always understood the difference. That's one thing I've learned from Phoebe."

And so, as Vix watched Caitlin whooping it up with the guys on the beach, she assumed there would be no holding back this summer. When Caitlin called "Vix . . . catch!" and the Frisbee sailed overhead, Vix reached up and grabbed it, then zigzagged along the beach, trying to avoid Bru who was heading straight for her. She managed to get rid of the Frisbee just before she hit the ground. She heard Caitlin shriek, then she was flat on her belly, wrists pinned, with Bru straddling her.

"Promise to be good and I'll let you up," he said.

"I'm not making any promises," she told him, spitting out sand.

"Then you can't get up."

"Okay." She wished she'd left her T-shirt on over her bikini because eventually she was going to have to get up and when she did he was going to get an eyeful.

She never should have bought this stupid suit with strings instead of straps.

The second he let go she raced for her beach bag, rummaged through it, but couldn't find her shirt. She pulled out a towel instead, quickly draping it over her shoulders, and just in time, too, because he was back, dropping to his knees beside her in the warm sand, offering a beer.

She still hadn't learned to like the taste of beer. She couldn't understand why the Chicago Boys went on and on about it, debating the merits of ale versus lager, draft versus bottled, but she was thirsty, so she took it, held the can to her mouth and tried swigging. It made her cough and when she did, she dribbled beer down her chin and onto her chest—reminding her of that night two summers ago when the redhead had thrown beer in Bru's face.

"So, what's behind that mask, Double?" Bru asked, pulling the towel from her shoulders. They were no longer *Double Trouble*, the team. As of today they'd become individuals. She was *Double* and Caitlin was *Trouble*.

"Mask?" Vix asked.

"Yeah, that mask you're always wearing."

"You're the one with the mask," she told him, whipping off his mirrored sunglasses. Right away she regretted it because now he looked directly into her eyes, making her squirm. She broke the spell by looking away first.

"Now *Trouble* . . ." he said, leaning back on his elbows, watching Caitlin and Von frolicking like puppies, "she wears it like a badge. But you don't need to advertise, do you?"

The side of her brain that could still think, still function, was impressed by his observations. He reached up and caught a strand of her hair as it blew across her face, then tucked it behind her ear, letting his fingers drift to her neck, across her shoulder, down her arm, making her breasts ache and her Power tingle. When he got to her hand, he turned it over. If he kissed it the way the Countess once had she'd faint. Faint dead away. She'd tell him it was the sun, that she always passed out from too much sun. But no problem, he traced a line across her palm instead. She could hardly breathe. *So this is what it's like, this is how it feels.*

He let go of her abruptly, cleared his throat, chugalugged some beer. "How old are you now?" he asked.

"Seventeen." Her voice came out a whisper. "Seventeen this month."

"Seventeen," he repeated.

"And my name is Victoria." She couldn't believe she'd said that. Never once had she called herself Victoria.

"Victoria," he said.

"How old are you?" she asked.

He found this funny. "How old do you think?"

"I don't know . . . maybe twenty . . ."

"Twenty-one in September."

"You *were* or you'll *be*?"

He looked at her and shook his head. "You worried about me being legal?"

No, that wasn't what was worrying her. She reached

into her bag again, determined to find her T-shirt. This time she came up with it.

"Cold?" he asked, as she began to pull it over her head.

"No."

"Then don't . . ."

So she didn't.

His hand was on her shoulder again. She tried to swallow, as if by swallowing she could make her thoughts go away. Her skin was burning. All she could hear was her heartbeat and Pat Benatar warning her— *Heartbreaker . . . love taker . . .*

Finally he said, "You're not scared of me, are you, Victoria?"

"Scared?" she said, too loud, as if she were some parrot who could only mimic words. She shrugged, wishing she could say, *No, I'm not scared of you. I'm scared of these feelings.*

"Don't be scared." And he gave her that slow smile, the one she'd first seen at mini golf the night she'd celebrated her thirteenth birthday.

Later, during the famous Menemsha sunset, Bru leaned back against a rock with his legs outstretched. She fit into the space between and relaxed into him, her back against his chest, his arms around her, although by then she was wearing a sweatshirt and wasn't really cold.

There were no official fireworks up island but someone with a yacht delivered an impressive show, lighting up the sky for fifteen minutes. When the display ended Bru walked her back to Caitlin's truck, stroked the side of her face with the back of his hand, then kissed her good night, a warm kiss, but quick, as if he didn't want to get started. She felt dizzy, weak, the crotch of her bathing suit was damp. She didn't want it to end yet. "You're not scared of *me*, are you?" she teased in a husky voice, a voice she didn't recognize as her own.

"Yeah, I am . . ." And from the way he said it she was almost sure it was true.

16

ABBY BROUGHT HOME a pair of Jack Russell terriers and named them for her grandparents, Irene and Jake. Caitlin was indignant. "She thinks those little *rodents* can take Sweetie's place? And naming them after her *grandparents*! Can you imagine naming your dogs after your grandparents? I mean, what is wrong with that woman?"

Sweetie had grown old and tired last summer. She'd hardly been able to walk. Still, when she'd collapsed and with one final shudder died at Lamb's feet, Caitlin was devastated. They all were. They'd had a service for her on the beach. "Lord, we give you our Sweetie," Lamb said. "She asked for nothing, she gave everything." Caitlin, tears streaming down her face, ran up and down the jetty, scattering Sweetie's ashes. Later, Vix helped her build a memorial to Sweetie out of sand and shells, but when the first storm washed it away Caitlin begged Lamb for a proper stone. They planted it near the house, between the big pines.

Sweetie
Faithful Companion
1970–1981

After that, Caitlin was consumed by death. Did Vix believe in past lives? Because Phoebe did. Phoebe had her own channeler, the same channeler who was helping Shirley MacLaine find her previous selves.

But Vix was more interested in this life than any other.

Caitlin asked how many times a week Vix thought about death, because she thought about it every day, sometimes more than once a day, like Woody Allen. He was obsessed by it. Most creative geniuses were.

"Are you planning on being a creative genius?" Vix asked.

"Absolutely," Caitlin said. "What else is there?" Then she laughed and gave Vix a jab in the ribs. "You take everything so seriously."

"Sometimes it's hard to tell with you."

"I'm going to be a woman of mystery, don't you think?"

"Either that or a schizo."

Caitlin's face froze. Now it was Vix's turn to laugh. "Who takes everything seriously?" But just to prove that she, too, could speak of the unspeakable, Vix said, "I saw a dead person once."

"Really . . . who?"

"Darlene."

"Who's Darlene?"

"My mother's . . ." She hesitated before spilling the beans, before admitting Darlene was her grandmother, knowing Tawny wouldn't like it. Instead, she said, "She was an old family friend."

"How'd she look?"

"I was really young. I don't remember that much."

She was sorry she'd brought up the subject in the first place.

"Was she in a coffin?"

"No, she was at the hospital."

"Were you there when she actually . . . died?"

"I wasn't in her room if that's what you mean." She'd been in the hallway with Lewis and Lanie, trying to engage them in a game of Go Fish because Tawny had told her to keep them out of the way and quiet. But she couldn't get Lewis to stop crying, not even by letting him go first. When she went to tell her mother, she found the curtains drawn around the bed and doctors and nurses all over Darlene. Her mother had grabbed her arm and led her back outside.

The following week Caitlin woke her in the middle of the night. "Vix . . . are you afraid to die?"

"I don't like to think about dying."

"But we're all going to, aren't we? I mean, nobody lives forever. In order to get to our next life, or whatever's on the other side, we have to actually . . . die."

"I suppose . . ."

"I wish I were a dog."

"They die, too."

"But they don't lie awake at night thinking about it."

"Maybe it's like *Our Town*," Vix said, trying to calm her. "Maybe we get to stand around after . . . and watch."

"But then we'd be invisible."

Vix liked the idea of being invisible, of watching and listening without anyone knowing. But she didn't say so.

"Could we finish this conversation some other time because I'm really, really tired."

Caitlin didn't say anything else and Vix fell back asleep. She'd no idea how much time had passed when she felt Caitlin's hand on her arm. "Vix . . ." Caitlin was kneeling beside her bed. "I've made a decision. I'm not going to hang around waiting for it to happen. I'm cutting out before it all falls apart . . . before I'm old and ugly and nobody wants me."

Vix feigned sleep, uneasy with the direction of Caitlin's thoughts. Woody Allen was one thing, this was another.

"Promise you'll go with me," Caitlin said. "I'd be too scared to go by myself."

When she didn't respond Caitlin shook her. "Vix . . . promise you'll go with me?"

When she *still* didn't say anything Caitlin said, "Vix . . . I'm scared. Can I get in with you?"

She moved over and Caitlin slid in beside her. Only then, with Vix's arms around her, could Caitlin get back to sleep.

Caitlin's fear unnerved Vix. She was almost relieved when last summer's focus on death turned into this summer's obsession with sex. Caitlin was drunk with her Power. It wasn't enough to have Von lusting after her, she flaunted it at home, too, coming on to Gus and even Daniel. The house was abuzz with sexual vibes. Caitlin was alive and well and anxious to prove it.

Sharkey hardly ever crossed paths with them, except for the night he came out of the bathroom and found Caitlin and Vix waiting their turn in the hall. Caitlin was in a short robe, loosely belted, with nothing underneath.

"Cover yourself up, will you!" Sharkey growled, shoving his towel at her.

"Shark . . ." Caitlin said, "we used to take baths together. What's the big deal?"

"You're not *four* anymore, that's the big deal." And with his head down he pushed past them.

A minute after she and Caitlin stepped inside, closing the bathroom door behind them, Gus knocked. "Bathroom in use?"

Vix opened the door a crack. "What does it look like?" she asked, her toothbrush sticking out of the side of her mouth. He was in shorts but no shirt. His chest had a patch of dark curly hair. Bru's chest was hairless and smooth. She wondered for half a second how it would feel to press her naked breasts against Gus, then looked away, totally embarrassed by such a revolting thought.

Gus

JESUS! When she opened the bathroom door and he caught a glimpse of her in that flimsy T-shirt, and under it the swell of her breasts, he was right back where he'd been two years ago, that night Abby and Lamb had almost blown it. Something happened to him that night, something he didn't want to think about because his father always said, *You don't shit where you eat.* But that night, just for a minute, he'd wanted to take her in his arms, feel her body against his.

He'd warned himself. *Cool it, she's just fifteen.*

Yeah . . . so? he argued. He knew girls her age who put out. Hell, he knew a fourteen-year-old who gave great hand jobs.

He's kept his distance since then, afraid to give in to his feelings. But now she's seventeen and it's a whole different ball game, isn't it?

17

CAITLIN CALLED IT the Summer of Their Brilliant Careers. They were working as a team for Dynamo, a cleaning service, earning good money, and Caitlin never complained about the long days or the foul condition of some of the houses. She was proud of herself for learning to clean out a toilet bowl, for scrubbing a tub until there was no scum left, things she'd never learned from Phoebe. They awarded the most disgusting bathrooms the New and Improved Dingleberry Award.

They never met or even saw most of their clients but they were privy to the most intimate details of their lives. They knew who was constipated by the boxes of Fleet enemas hidden in bathroom drawers or the prune juice and raw bran stocked in the fridge. They knew their clients' medications and why they were taking them. They knew what their clients were reading, what music they listened to, and who watched porno tapes on the VCR.

They knew who was having regular sex by the pubic hairs and bunched up tissues under the blankets, the lubricants on the bedside tables, the condom wrappers in the trash. Unlike some of the girls working for the service, they were discreet. They never tried on their clients' clothes or experimented with their makeup. They had their standards.

Their favorite clients were a gay couple out on Squibnocket Pond who left them beautifully printed lists of chores and always some little goody along with it, an unusual shell or a perfect rose or a sample box of Chilmark Chocolates.

They made up for the assholes on Middle Road who smashed every dish in the house and left the pieces all over the floor. When the slimeball and his girlfriend came home in a huff that afternoon and found Caitlin and Vix *still* cleaning up, listening to Stevie Nicks on the tape deck, he exploded. Vix wanted to take off before it got serious, but Caitlin looked right at him and said, "I believe you're responsible for the cost of replacing the dishes."

He reached into his pocket and began to throw hundred-dollar bills at them while his girlfriend tugged on his arm crying, "Honey, stop . . . honey, please . . ."

Hundred-dollar bills, five of them, two of which they pocketed, as he yelled, "Replace the goddamn dishes and get the fuck out of this house!"

Abby

SHE CAN'T SLEEP. The strain of having all five of them in the house is taking its toll. She's worried sick, especially about Caitlin and Vix. She has the feeling, from the way they get themselves up at night, there are boys in the picture this summer. But who are they? What are they doing together?

And just because Daniel has finished a year at Princeton, and Gus, at Northwestern, they think they're grownup, beyond rules. Gus has turned into a man overnight. Last summer he'd still been a teenager, her son's best friend. Now, when he looks at her she sometimes feels herself blush. How can she possibly tell him what to do? She supposes she'll have to learn to let go, as Lamb says, learn how to live with grown children. But where's the manual on that?

She's grateful they all have jobs. Not that she's thrilled Daniel and Gus are working nights, bussing tables at the Harborview, never getting home before midnight, never getting out of bed before noon. The girls are another story. Out of the house at seven every morning, home after work to shower and snack but never sitting down to a proper meal. The only one she doesn't fret over is Sharkey. At least she knows where he is— working at the garage all day, locked up in his room at night with the new computer. Sharkey, who went off to Reed a year ago and has never said a word about it, not to her anyway. He doesn't give her any trouble. Maybe she should be worried about that!

ABBY INVITED VIX to try her new yellow kayak. Lamb had surprised her with it at the start of the summer. They'd christened it with a bottle of champagne. Now Abby could paddle off her anxieties in the pond.

On their way down to the dock Abby said, "You know, Vix . . . I'd like to think if I had a daughter she'd be a lot like you." She took off her sunglasses and wiped the lenses with her T-shirt. "That's a compliment. I hope you take it as one."

Vix stammered. "I do . . . absolutely."

"I consider you a person of real values and ethics." She paused, then added, "That's a compliment, too."

Real values and ethics? She wondered what Abby would say if she knew how Vix used to dream about changing places with Caitlin, of just walking out on her family to live with *them* in Cambridge. God, had she ever been so young, so naive?

Now Abby tried to talk to her about drinking, drugs, sex, about herpes. Vix listened politely, then assured Abby she didn't like the taste of beer, let alone the hard stuff, that she'd promised her parents she'd stay away from drugs, which were more plentiful in Santa Fe than the Vineyard, and as for sex, she was still a virgin and intended to remain one. She just didn't say for how long.

Abby handed her a stack of college catalogs left over from the Chicago Boys and urged her to study them. "You know there's a scholarship waiting."

She felt as if she were fourteen again, with Abby encouraging her to plan for her future. But this time the only future she was interested in was that night and the next night and the night after that, with Bru.

18

Paradise was a shack that served as the on-site office of Bru's family's construction business. Three of Bru's uncles had seen the eighties building boom coming and had bought up a group of rundown cottages on Menemsha Pond. Bru and Von were part of the crew renovating the first place, turning it into a five-bedroom house. The shack had no water or electricity, just a table made from a sheet of plywood sitting on sawhorses and a couple of beat-up chairs. But who cared?

They lit candles, slipped their tapes into the boom box—*Don't you want me, baby? Don't you want me, oh*—and danced until they'd heated up the place and themselves. Then Bru led Vix out to his truck, leaving the shack to Caitlin and Von. The truck had a cap on the back and orange shag carpet on the floor. The first time Vix lay down on it without her shirt she got carpet burns on her back. After that Bru spread out an old cotton comforter to protect her skin.

This time it was Caitlin who wanted details. "Does he nibble on your earlobes? Does he suck your nipples? Does he press it up against you as if you're doing it but without actually doing it?"

The answer to all of the above was yes. *Yes . . . yes . . . and yes.* But Vix couldn't talk about it. She couldn't tell Caitlin how he'd ease down her jeans and reach inside her panties, touching her gently, slipping a finger into the moist delicate tissue where only her fingers had been before. And how she loved it! Loved the fire inside her, the explosion at the end. He knew she was a virgin and he never tried to rush her, though he said it had been a long time since he'd been with a woman that way. *A woman!* He taught her how to make him come, dipping her fingers into the jar of Abolene he conveniently kept in the glove compartment, wrapping her hand around him, sliding it up and down until his Package throbbed and sputtered while Van Halen played on the tape deck.

Not that he didn't want more, not that *she* didn't. But it was his decision to wait. She thought he really was nervous about making it with some seventeen-year-old summer girl from a prominent family, because by then he and Von knew Lamb Somers was Caitlin's father, that *she* was Caitlin's summer sister. And neither of them was looking for trouble.

He asked about her boyfriends in Santa Fe. She told him there weren't any, which was true. Until then her sexual experience with guys had been limited to Mark Shulman, a tall, awkward classmate at Mountain Day, whose tongue darted in and out of her mouth when they kissed, like a frog's catching flies. *Please . . . please . . .* he'd whimper, grabbing her buttocks through her jeans.

Please, what? She wanted him to spell it out, but he never did. He was kind to her the night she got drunk on margaritas and puked out the window of his Bronco.

But she wasn't seriously attracted to him and when they decided it wasn't going to work he started sniffing around Lanie.

Vix asked about the redhead. *Fini . . . finis . . . finito . . .*

"She was older," he said. "She wanted me to make promises I wasn't ready to keep."

Bru

JEEZ . . . SHE'S SWEET. So sweet. Hard to resist. And she doesn't seem that young when they're together. Not too young for him. He has to keep reminding himself to go slow, not to rush her. There's something about being her first, about teaching her everything his way. Like training a puppy but better. That silky hair, those soft, round tits, nipples that stiffen before he even touches them. Says she's never had a real boyfriend. Hard to believe. But why would she lie? He's never known a girl who's so wet, who comes so fast. Not like the redhead. He could go down on her all night and still nothing. Victoria wants to know what happened between them. What can he say? She's five years older. Ready to tie the knot. Wants kids. No thanks. Not yet. Anyway, she's got a new guy now. Maybe he can make her come. Maybe he doesn't care if she doesn't.

That expression on Victoria's face the first time he led her hand to his cock. *I can't believe I'm touching a penis*, she'd said. Then she'd giggled like a little kid. He'd tilted her chin up, kissed her.

Von's always telling him *Trouble* is hot. He can believe it. He's had a couple of dreams where both of them come on to him at once. The *Double Trouble* thing.

———————

"I DID THE FELLATIO THING," Caitlin said as she and Vix were driving home one night, the rumble of thunder in the distance. "He loved it. It made him crazy."

"But what about . . . you know?"

"It wasn't *that* bad, if you don't mind warm gooey laundry detergent. But to tell the truth, by then he couldn't have cared less. I could have spit it onto the floor and he wouldn't have noticed. That's how out of it he was. You should try it . . . that is, if you haven't already."

Vix knew Caitlin was fishing but she wasn't taking her bait.

"Oh, now I've embarrassed you!" Caitlin said.

"I'm not embarrassed."

"You are . . . I can tell."

"Okay, fine. I'm embarrassed."

Caitlin laughed, squeezed Vix's thigh, and sang all the way home.

Sharkey

SOMETHING'S GOING ON and he doesn't like it. He follows them one night way the hell out to Menemsha Pond. Sees Vix climb into the back of a truck with some guy. What's she doing with him? She could get herself in real trouble. And who knows what Caitlin's up to with the other one? Should he say something to Lamb? If he does and they find out they'll accuse him of being weird, of never having sex except by himself. The Portnoy of his generation. He can't fall asleep without jerking off, imagining how it would be if they got into the back of *his* truck, his sister and her best friend. He can't even look at them anymore without being scared he'll get a hard-on. Lamb would kill him if he knew. But he's never going to know. No one is.

Daniel

CAITLIN. THAT BITCH! A couple of years ago he'd wanted to blow her away. Now he wouldn't mind her blowing him. He can't get her out of his mind. The way she taunts him when she's in the outdoor shower, using her hands, not a washcloth. Her hands on her perfect little tits. Her hands on her soapy pussy. She closes her eyes, tilts her head way back, and sings "Eye of the Tiger." A command performance. She knows he's watching. Lamb would kill him if he knew. But hell, it's not like he's her blood relative.

It's a damn good thing he's got Bailey to take his mind off the bitch. Bailey, who's working as an au pair in Edgartown, going into her sophomore year at Smith. *You'll come to Northhampton, right, Daniel? You promise?* Sure he'll come . . . any second now. So what if he has to tell her he loves her during the act? At that moment he does.

—————————

ABBY WAS growing suspicious. "Where do you two go every night?" she asked Caitlin and Vix.

"We hang out with friends," Caitlin told her, which wasn't exactly a lie, except the friends Abby thought they were talking about were the other girls from the cleaning service. "Sometimes we take in a movie," Caitlin added. "We can't get into any of the clubs. They card everyone."

"I wish you'd invite your friends to our house," Abby said.

Vix felt so deceitful. If it had been up to her she'd have gladly brought Bru to the house. But Caitlin said *never*. Abby was never going to know about Von or Bru.

Okay, okay . . . Vix had to swear never to mention them although she didn't see why. She wanted to show off Bru to everyone. She wanted to write home about him. She wanted to tell the world she was in love with Joseph Brudegher and he was in love with her.

She made the mistake of admitting that to Caitlin.

"Oh, please . . . they all say they love you during sex. It doesn't mean a thing."

"Bru doesn't say things he doesn't mean," Vix told her.

"Vix . . . don't make this into something more than it is. I mean, what do you think happens when we leave here on Labor Day? You think they sit around waiting for us to come back? It's a summer romance. End of story."

It was still July. Why did she have to think about Labor Day?

"I just don't want you to get hurt," Caitlin told her.

Vix remembered the redhead crying her eyes out at the pizza place. *No guy will ever make me feel that bad!* And she hated Caitlin for reminding her. So what if it was just a summer romance? Did that mean she shouldn't enjoy it?

Caitlin wrapped her arms around Vix. "I'm glad you're happy. Really. I'm glad you're in love. Just remember, no matter how many guys come and go *we'll* always be together. Friends last longer than lovers."

19

ABBY ENCOURAGED THEM to throw a party for Vix's seventeenth birthday. "You can invite the girls from work . . . and Daniel and Gus will bring their friends from the Harborview." She said this as if it were a brilliant idea. "We could do a barbecue or even a clambake." Poor Abby. She wanted so much for things to work out between all of them, to play *mother* to her brood.

But Caitlin had her own plans and they didn't include Abby or the Chicago Boys. She chose a remote beach on Chappaquiddick as the site for Vix's party. And the only people she invited were Bru and Von.

Vix had never been to Chappy but she'd heard plenty about the scandal involving the senator and the young political assistant, and how she'd been trapped inside his car when it rolled off the Dike Bridge and into the dark waters.

"Talk about following your pointer!" Caitlin said. "And God knows what *she* was following."

"Maybe she thought she was in love."

"That was her first mistake," Caitlin said.

"And her last." Vix hadn't intended to make a joke of it but Caitlin laughed anyway.

In Edgartown she and Vix waited for the tiny car ferry to shuttle them across to Chappy, then Caitlin drove for miles, as if she knew exactly where she was going, as if she'd been there a million times before, though Vix couldn't imagine when. Finally the ocean came into view, as calm and blue as Vix had ever seen it, rimmed by a long white sandy beach, almost deserted. Bru and Von were already there, waiting.

Caitlin was wearing her black bikini that day, the one with the bottom cut up to her waist. She coated herself with suntan lotion, slowly, asking Von to do her back. He lifted her hair to get her neck and her shoulders, and as he did she stood with her face upturned to the sun, her eyes closed. Something about it was so sensual Vix felt uncomfortable and turned away, meeting Bru's gaze.

The midsummer heat wave was making headlines and the temperature of the ocean made it feel like a pond. Vix always kept both feet on the ground in the ocean, fearful not just of the waves washing over her, suffocating her, but of the undertow and, even worse, a riptide. If you were caught in a riptide and weren't able to swim parallel to shore it could carry you out so far you'd never be able to get back. Her worst nightmare was to be trapped underwater like Mary Jo, the senator's friend. But today, with no surf and hardly any undertow, she floated on her back as the water gently lifted then released her, like a seesaw. With Bru watching there was no reason to be afraid.

Late in the day, she and Bru walked hand in hand along the water's edge, stopping once to lie in the wet sand, their bodies pressed together, his hand pushing up the top of her bikini as they kissed hot, salty kisses. When he promised a surprise for her birthday, she smiled. After all, wasn't *he* what she wanted more than anything? But not here, not now. It would happen later, after dark, with the stars overhead and Stevie Nicks singing.

By the time they got back Caitlin and Von had the picnic supper spread out on Abby's best blue and white cloth. "I know you'll be disappointed," Von told them, "but Caitlin forgot the tofu."

This had become a running joke between them since Caitlin had convinced Von to give up his Marlboros. She'd told him how she hated the smell and the taste of tobacco and just like that, he'd gone cold turkey. *Hey . . . what guy in his right mind wouldn't trade his Marlboros for Caitlin?* he wanted to know. But give up his barbecued chicken, greasy burgers, and fries? *Give a guy a break.* There was a limit to his adoration.

He came up behind Caitlin, his arms around her waist, his mouth against her neck. "I guess I'm gonna have to eat *her* instead," he said, nibbling his way down to her shoulder, while she closed her eyes.

It was a rare, sultry Vineyard night and Vix threw Bru's old shirt over her bikini but she didn't button it. After they'd polished off the chips and salsa, the couscous and veggies, the bread and fruit, after the guys had each put away a couple of beers, Caitlin carried out the birthday cake with one sparkler blazing in the center. They sang to her, making her laugh with their off-key rendition of "Happy Birthday," then Caitlin dropped to her knees, taking Vix's face between her hands like a lover, kissing her directly on the lips, embarrassing the guys and Vix. "Did you make a wish?" she asked.

"Yes."

"What'd you wish for?"

"I can't tell . . . if I do, it won't come true." But she looked at Bru and knew her wish was going to come true.

Caitlin laughed, then flopped down beside Von. "And now . . ." she said, pulling a fat joint out of a Baggie, "a little something to help us celebrate."

"What's this?" Von asked, totally disbelieving. "Since when does the Tofu Queen indulge?"

"Oh, come on . . ." Caitlin laughed. "It's not tobacco . . . it's homegrown stuff . . . direct from Santa Fe." She lit up, took a drag, and passed it to Von, who didn't argue, but closed his eyes and inhaled deeply, before passing it to Vix.

Somebody always had a joint at school parties. By then she'd been to her share and that was the least of what they had. Sure, she'd tried it a couple of times, not enough to get really stoned though. It made her more sleepy than silly. But that night she already felt so high —from the moonlight, from the music, from the promise of what was to come—that when Von passed her the joint she took a deep drag, then lay with her head in Bru's lap watching the stars overhead. If you concentrated on the sky on a night like this you could almost always find a shooting star. On the boom box James was singing "How Sweet It Is" . . . then Carly joined in on "Devoted to You," which made Vix sad because everyone knew they'd split up. She had no idea how much time had passed, how many drags she'd taken on the

joint, when Caitlin jumped up. "Wait . . ." she cried.
"I forgot to give Vix her present!" She grabbed a flashlight and raced back to the truck, returning with a big,
beautifully wrapped box. "For you, Vix . . ."

"For me?" Vix sat up.

"Yes . . . open it."

"Open it?"

"Yes."

Vix pulled off the paper and ribbon, slowly raised the
lid off the box, and lifted out something delicate and
white. She wasn't sure what. She started laughing. Was
it a nightgown or a prom dress? And where did Caitlin
think she would ever wear it?

"Try it on," Caitlin said.

"Try it on . . . now?"

"Yes . . ."

"But I've got citronella . . . and sunscreen . . ."

"It's washable," Caitlin said and now she was laughing, too. "I made sure before I bought it . . . that it
was . . . you know . . . washable."

"Washable . . ."

"Yes . . . washable."

This struck Vix as hysterically funny. She wondered
why Bru and Von didn't get it, didn't get that this dress,
or whatever it was, that was suitable for a princess to
wear to a garden party, was washable. The word itself—
washable—was enough to send her into gales of laughter.

Caitlin held out her hand. Vix took it and Caitlin
pulled her to her feet, then led her behind the dunes.
Vix tossed Bru's shirt up in the air, still laughing. She
untied her bikini top and flung that aside, too.

Caitlin dropped the dress over her head. It fell

around her, cool and smooth, a perfect fit. Well, maybe it was cut dangerously low in front, but so what? Who was going to see it besides Caitlin and Bru and maybe Von, but he had eyes only for Caitlin.

Caitlin adjusted the silky rose centered between Vix's breasts. "Here . . ." she said, "I think it goes more like this . . ." and she eased the dress off her shoulders. She stepped back to admire her work. "God, Vix . . . you look so beautiful!"

Then they were dancing on the beach, Caitlin and Vix, twirling to "Wild thing . . . you make my heart sing . . ." Vix had never felt more beautiful, more desirable. She couldn't wait to be with Bru! Couldn't wait to actually make love, to feel him inside her. Was she stoned? Maybe . . . probably . . . but so what? For once she wasn't self-conscious about her body. She was proud of her lush breasts, her shapely legs glistening with oil, her long dark hair swinging back and forth as she twirled, growing more and more dizzy. It was her birthday, she was seventeen, dancing on the beach in the moonlight as her lover watched, watched with desire written all over his face. Tonight she was the *wild thing*. The temptress.

Then they were all dancing together, all four of them, and she was thinking, *It can't get any better than this . . . ever!* They were hugging and kissing, so much in love. *This will be my best Vineyard memory. This will be the one I remember all my life.*

The kissing grew more serious, deeper, hungrier. Vix let her eyes close and she moaned softly, turned on by hot breath, soft lips, hands sliding the dress from her shoulders, hands on her naked breasts. She felt the hardness inside his shorts and reached down.

"Vix . . ." he whispered. "Oh baby . . ."

Oh baby . . . oh baby? Wait! Something was wrong with this picture. The hands on her body weren't Bru's, the lips on her lips weren't his. She tried to keep her eyes open but everything was so fuzzy.

Suddenly she felt sick. She broke away and raced down to the water. She bounded out in the low tide . . . farther and farther, until the water caught the skirt of her dress, making it billow out around her like a parachute. Then she leaped like the deer she'd once seen in the pond, until the water was deep enough to carry her. She lay down . . . lay down and let the rise and fall of the sea carry her away. She could hear Caitlin's voice screaming, "Oh my God . . . Vix . . ."

And Bru yelling, "Victoria . . . *Victoria!*" Then they were coming after her but she didn't care. She was swimming now, swimming straight out like a mermaid, all the way to China, or whatever was on the other side.

20

SHE WAS DREAMING of her own funeral. Tawny peered into the casket and yelled at her. *Drugs, Victoria! After you promised . . .*

One joint! Vix argued, sitting straight up in the casket. *One joint between four people.*

Tawny wouldn't accept her feeble excuse. *You see . . . you see now why we made you promise! But you broke your promise, didn't you? Drugs and sex and . . . I don't even want to think about what else. I should have sent you to parochial school.*

But I'm dead, Mother. What's the point in being angry?

Then act dead! Tawny shoved her back down and lowered the lid on the casket.

The scene switched. Vix was in the ocean and it was dark. So dark. She kept slipping under. There was no point in struggling. She might as well give in to it. Suddenly she was grabbed from behind. She thrashed, kicked, screamed. Then she was being carried, no dragged, across the beach. Someone else was there, too. She could hear them whispering as they dumped her body into the back of a pickup truck. But it wasn't really a truck, it was a hearse. They thought she was dead. She cried out and banged on the glass partition separating her from them. But it was no use. They couldn't hear her.

She awakened and sat upright, gasping, drenched with sweat. A terrible feeling washed over her, a feeling of impending doom. By sunrise she was dressed and throwing her clothes into the blue canvas duffel she'd bought with her own money to replace Tawny's old suitcase. She had to escape. Now . . . before it was too late.

As daylight lit the room Caitlin stirred. Vix stood absolutely still, willing her to stay asleep. But Caitlin opened her eyes, saw that Vix's bed was neatly made, looked around, then focused on Vix and her duffel.

"Don't do this, Vix. Don't ruin everything."

Vix felt like shouting at her, *I'm not the one who ruined it!* Even though she couldn't remember everything about last night she remembered enough. It could have been another Vineyard disaster. She could have been the next Mary Jo.

"So we got a little stoned," Caitlin said. "Big deal. Nothing happened." She gathered her hair with one hand and pulled it away from her face.

When Vix didn't respond Caitlin sat up and pointed a finger at her. "Where do you come off acting so fucking self-righteous? It's not exactly like you were playing jacks with Von!"

Vix felt her legs begin to tremble.

"Look at you . . ." Caitlin said. "You're so scared of that side of yourself you have to run away."

Suddenly it all became clear to Vix. "You planned it, didn't you?"

"Don't be ridiculous. It was supposed to be the best damn birthday you've ever had. So maybe it got a little out of control. I'm sorry. Is that what you want me to say?"

"Was Bru in on it? Just tell me . . . was he part of your plan . . . or was it just you and Von?"

"You're paranoid if that's what you think," Caitlin said. "Nobody planned anything. It just happened." She lay down again with the blanket pulled up to her chin.

Vix's head was pounding. *If she didn't get away . . . if she didn't get out of here . . .* She zipped up her duffel, expecting Caitlin to jump out of bed and beg her to stay, reminding her that their friendship was more important than anything or anyone.

"You know something?" Caitlin said, her voice a disgusted whisper. "You're an emotional iceberg, terrified of your own feelings."

Keep your feelings to yourself, Victoria. Don't ever show anyone your disappointment.

She slung the duffel over her shoulder. "And you're a disaster waiting to happen!" she told Caitlin.

"Fine, go . . ." Caitlin dismissed her with a wave of one hand. "Have a mediocre life filled with mediocre people. Forget NBO . . . forget our pact. Because that's exactly what you're heading for . . . a boring and ordinary life."

"Which is better than what you're heading for!" Vix longed to slam the bedroom door. Instead, she pulled it closed behind her, tiptoed down the stairs, left a note for Abby and Lamb on the kitchen table, then let herself out the door. Only then did a single sob escape from deep inside. But she swallowed that, too.

She'd hiked halfway out to the main road when she heard a truck coming from behind. She shifted the duffel to her other shoulder. But she didn't turn, not even as the truck slowed down.

Gus

WHAT WERE THEY going on about at the crack of dawn? He'd tried holding the pillow over his head but he couldn't breathe that way. Fuck. He'd been out until after two A.M. Not that he was complaining. You don't complain when a good-looking woman hands you a slip of paper with her room number on it while you're clearing away her grilled swordfish, even if she is wearing a wedding band.

They'd have to use the bathroom, she whispered, when he'd knocked on the door, in case her girlfriend returned while they were at it.

Okay . . . sure . . . the bathroom. What did he care? She'd padded the tub with a blanket and towels. If by chance her friend came back early, she'd say she was taking a bath. A bath, right. Whatever she wanted. She was wearing a silky pajama top with nothing underneath. Nothing. He was hard just thinking about it.

He took off his jeans, climbed into the tub, lay on his back. She straddled him, talked herself through it. *That's it, oh yes . . . keep going . . . oh . . . you're so strong . . .* She bit his shoulder, pulled at his hair, clamped her hand over his mouth so he couldn't cry out when he came. *Thank you, very nice . . .* she'd said, shooing him out as soon as they'd finished.

Now he can hear the door across the hall open, then close. He listens. *Cough Drop.* He's sure of it. Recognizes her footsteps. He pulls on his jeans, sneaks downstairs, gets into the truck, trails her down the road. She's carrying her goddamn duffel over her shoulder like some kind of navy recruit. Where does she think she's going?

21

VIX NEVER FOUND OUT how Gus happened to be driving down the road early that morning. Or how he knew the Homeport was looking for mid-season replacements. She got in beside him and stared straight ahead. He didn't try to make small talk. He asked only one question and that not until they'd stopped to buy juice and doughnuts which they ate overlooking the cemetery in Chilmark.

"You want to talk about it?" he asked.

She shook her head.

"You sure you don't want to go home?" Gus said.

She thought he meant Santa Fe and shook her head again. No way could she deal with her parents now.

The Homeport hired her just like that, without even checking her references. It meant a big cut in salary unless she could make it up in tips. But as she explained over the phone to Joanne, the owner of the cleaning service, her circumstances had changed and she couldn't come back.

"What about Caitlin?" Joanne asked.

"I can't speak for her."

"Well, this is very disappointing," Joanne said. "You

and Caitlin were the perfect team. I depended on you to finish the season."

"I'm really sorry. It was a great job. But I have no choice."

Joanne didn't get it and tried wooing her back with more money.

"I'm sorry," she said again, feeling even more foolish. "I've already taken another job."

Joanne sucked in her breath. "With the competition?" Joanne never referred to the other cleaning services by name.

"No . . . at the Homeport."

"The Homeport? Why would you want to work there?"

"It's . . . personal."

"I see." She paused and Vix imagined her chewing on her pencil, the way she did when she was talking to a dissatisfied client. "Well, if you change your mind give me a call. I'll always have a job for you."

"Thanks."

Vix dragged her duffel halfway out the long dock, to Trisha's boat, and caught her just before she left for work. When she explained that she'd left Lamb's, that she had a job waiting tables at the Homeport and needed a cheap place to stay, Trisha said, "You're looking at it, honey."

Trisha tossed her a key to the hatch lock, told her to take either of the berths in the main cabin, then left for Vineyard Haven. "I should be back around seven, unless I meet Arthur, my new squeeze, for dinner."

The second Vix was alone, she crumpled. She wept, she wailed, she soaked her T-shirt with her tears, sobbing until she gagged. She was not an emotional ice-berg! Then she lay down in the tiny berth and fell into a deep sleep.

She'd have slept all day if she hadn't heard banging on the hatch and voices calling her name. She jumped up, disoriented, needing a minute to figure out where she was and why. When she finally opened the hatch and squinted in the bright sunlight, she saw Lamb and Abby.

"Vix," Abby began, "we were so worried!"

"Didn't you get my note?"

"Yes . . . but you didn't say where you were going, or why."

"I'm sorry. I wasn't sure where I was going when I wrote it." How had they found her? Had Trisha called them already?

"Look . . ." Lamb said, "whatever happened be-tween you and Caitlin I know she regrets it."

"All friends have disagreements from time to time . . ." Abby added. "It's only natural . . . it's like a marriage . . ." She looked at Lamb, then back at Vix. "Oh, Vix . . . no boy is worth this kind of grief."

How did she know there was a boy involved? How much exactly had Caitlin told them?

Abby came toward her, steadying herself as the boat rocked in the breeze. "Come home," she said, hugging Vix. "We're family. You belong with us."

"I can't . . . please . . ." There was no way for Vix to explain.

Finally Lamb said, more to Abby than to her, "If Vix needs some time and space . . . I trust her judgment."

"How much time?" Abby asked. "A day . . . two

days? We're responsible for you, Vix. We can't just let you live on your own. Your parents assume . . ."

Her parents! "Please don't tell my parents I've left. Not yet . . ." Then she added, "I'll understand if you want to give the scholarship to someone else, someone more . . . worthy." Her voice broke on that. They wouldn't be as lenient this time as when they'd found out she and Caitlin had been hitching. A few soft words, a promise they wouldn't hitch again, and that had been it. Not that it mattered because by the following summer Caitlin had her license. This time was different. This time there was more at stake.

Lamb and Abby looked at one another again. Then Abby said, "This has nothing to do with the scholarship. Nobody's going to take anything away from you."

Vix wanted to cry with relief. How easy it would have been to go back with Abby.

It wasn't until later that Vix remembered Abby saying, *I'd like to think if I had a daughter she'd be a lot like you.* Yes, but . . . if they had to take sides, no matter how much they cared for *her*, Caitlin would always come first. She would always be the daughter. And Vix would always be the daughter's friend.

When she came out of the Homeport, confused and exhausted after her first night on the job, Bru was waiting. "We have to talk," he told her. They walked out to the end of the dock, where they sat swatting mosquitoes. "Whatever happened last night, I can live with it," Bru said.

Was it just last night?

"I know it didn't mean anything," he continued.

She looked at him, puzzled. "What didn't mean anything?"

"You and Von."

"Me and Von? There is no me and Von. Is there a you and Caitlin?"

"Caitlin?" he said, as if he had no idea what she was talking about. He turned her hand over, studied it the way he had that first day on the beach, then covered it with both of his. "I think we should just forget about last night," he said. Then his voice went all soft. "You're my girl, Victoria. I knew it from day one. You'll always be my girl."

And just like that she melted. Just like that they were back together.

They saw each other every night, and Vix had no curfew, no one asking *Does he do this? Does he do that? When are you going to . . . ?*

This time she was the aggressor. She practically begged him. *Please*, she whispered. *Please . . . Bru.* What guy could resist? He rolled on a condom right there in the dunes where they'd spread out a blanket and left half their clothes.

Trisha

THIS WAS GETTING HEAVY, with Lamb calling two, sometimes three times a day, asking, *Can you handle it? Handle it?* What does he think she's doing?

Then Abby gets on the phone. *Please, Trisha . . . try to convince her to come back.*

Come on, guys! It's just been a week. Give the kid a break. Don't suffocate her. She tells them she'll do her best. But hey, if Vix and Caitlin have some kind of problem, Lamb should be trying to help the two of them work it out. He's the parent, after all. As for what happened between the girls, Vix doesn't want to talk about it. And *she* doesn't believe in butting in. *Mess around with the money folks, wind up getting burned.* Vix will learn the hard way, same as she did.

Anyway, Vix has a boyfriend. Nice guy. She knows the family. Spent a couple of nights with one of the uncles a few years back. What the hell . . . she's single.

22

THE HOMEPORT had a big, noisy dining room, where food was served family style. It was popular with tourists and locals alike, more for its location overlooking the harbor, the best place to view spectacular Menemsha sunsets, than for its food. It was impossible to get a reservation this time of year unless you called at least a week in advance.

The menu was simple and never changed. Swordfish and lobster were the two most popular dinners. They came with baked potatoes, corn on the cob, and cole slaw. For dessert it was pie and ice cream. The blueberries in the pie were canned, not fresh. If anyone asked, Vix was supposed to tell them the truth. But no one ever asked.

Because all the up island towns were dry, there was no bar. You could BYOB if you wanted beer or wine with your meal, but Vix wasn't permitted to open it because she was under age. Tips ran the gamut from generous to pathetic. She always tried to guess at the beginning of a meal how much her table would leave, but more than half the time she was wrong. One night she was sure she saw Barbra Streisand, another, Mary Steenburgen. But neither sat at Vix's tables. She did get to wait on a group from *Saturday Night Live*. They were loud and messy, dropping lobster shells on the floor, but they left her two twenties to make up for it.

The staff got to eat free. At first it seemed like a great deal but after the first week she couldn't look at another piece of swordfish, let alone eat it. She lived on corn, baked potatoes, cole slaw, and Trisha's muffins.

The manager considered her a hard worker but encouraged her to become more of a team player. She was always polite, always efficient, but she didn't hang out with the other servers and they resented her. When one of the girls finally asked where Vix headed every night after work, Vix told her about Bru. After that the others were more accepting. Everybody loves a lover.

Probably no one at the Homeport would believe she was still a virgin . . . technically, anyway. But it was true. The first time they tried it hadn't really worked. He'd never been with a virgin, Bru told her. Maybe it was always like this but he was afraid if he pushed too hard he'd hurt her. And he didn't want to hurt her.

Hurt her? She loved it that way, couldn't imagine it feeling any better, until the blustery morning when the weather prevented him from working and he came to the boat looking for her. She invited him aboard. There was no way the two of them could fit into her narrow berth so they moved forward, to Trisha's cabin. She hoped Trisha wouldn't mind. And there, on the v-berth, with the rigging creaking, the halyards slapping against the mast in the wind, the boat gently rocking, there, with a lubricated condom and taking it slowly, so slowly, Bru got all the way inside her and it didn't hurt that much, not that much after the initial quick, sharp pain, because she was so hot, so ready. And when she cried out the pain was mixed with pleasure. But she didn't come, not that day. After, she found a few spots of blood, but they washed right off the vinyl cushions.

The next day she was sore. But not so sore she wasn't ready to try it again. When she did she began to understand what all the fuss was about.

One morning Trisha asked her about Bru. When Vix told her they were lovers Trisha pressed her hand and said, "Oh, honey . . . are you being careful? You're using condoms or something?"

"Yes," she answered, secretly thrilled to be discussing this with a woman of experience.

"Because you have to think ahead. You don't want to get pregnant or catch some disease."

"We're careful."

"And is it . . . enjoyable for you?"

Vix felt herself blush.

"You don't have to answer. It's just that in the beginning . . . well, some guys have no idea what they're doing. No idea how to make it good for you."

Vix didn't tell her about Bru's slow moves, about how he loved to feel her quiver.

Lamb

HE KEEPS ASKING Trisha if she can handle it when he doesn't know how to handle it himself! Abby's pushing for him to take a stand, to insist Vix come back. She goes on and on about responsibility, making his head ache.

He can see for himself Caitlin is miserable without Vix. Quit her job. Just sails the Sunfish all day. If he asks her anything she answers, *What is this . . . the Spanish Inquisition?* What's he supposed to do?

Trisha tells him Vix is okay. She's keeping an eye on things. The boy is from a decent family. They're using birth control. *Birth control!* He doesn't want to think of some boy taking advantage of Vix . . . or Caitlin. And he remembers very well what boys of that age are after . . .

SOMETIMES VIX would get a pang, realizing it was already the middle of August, that summer would be over in a couple of weeks and she'd be thousands of miles away from Bru, a schoolgirl again. Maybe she should stay on island for senior year. She was sure Trisha would welcome the company, and if not, she and Bru could get a cabin. He'd been talking about moving out of his uncle's house. She'd find an after-school job and help pay their expenses. That way they wouldn't have to be apart.

But she never had to make that decision because three weeks after she'd packed up and left Caitlin, while she was setting up tables for dinner, the manager came over and whispered that someone was here to see her, outside.

Her first thought was Bru. But no . . . it was Caitlin and, a few steps behind her, Lamb and Abby. Vix saw it right away, in the expression on Caitlin's face, in her eyes. "What?" she asked.

Caitlin said, "It's Nathan."

"No," Vix said.

"Vix . . . I'm so sorry. He died this morning."

Vix screamed. "No . . . please God, not Nathan!"

Caitlin grabbed her, kept her from keeling over. Then Abby was pushing a glass of something in her face. Vix knocked it out of her hand. "They didn't even tell me he was sick!"

"It happened too fast," Abby said.

"I have to go home." Vix broke away. "I have to see him."

"We've already booked a flight, kiddo." Lamb had his arm around her shoulders and was holding her tight.

Caitlin slid into the back seat of the Volvo next to Vix. "I'm coming with you."

Vix shook her head.

"I know how much he meant to you," Caitlin said, reaching for her hand. "Please, Vix . . . let me be your friend."

She never had the chance to say goodbye to Nathan, never had the chance to keep her promise. Instead, she slipped the Disney World brochure into his coffin, along with Orlando and a letter telling him she loved him, apologizing for thinking only of herself that summer, for being too much in love.

When she asked her family why no one had called to tell her he was sick, Lanie answered, "He wasn't *that* sick. It was just a summer cold. Two days later he had pneumonia. We didn't know he was going to . . . die."

23

AFTER NATHAN DIED nothing was the same.

She felt more like an outsider in her family than she ever had. Tawny sat stony-faced in the living room. "His suffering has ended," she repeated over and over, like a mantra. "He's with the Lord now."

Her father lay on Nathan's bed, shutting her out, leaving her alone with her feelings, alone with her grief.

"Come back to the Vineyard with me," Caitlin said.

Vix shook her head.

"It's just for a week, just until Labor Day. It'd be good for you."

As much as Vix wanted to see Bru, have him hold her, comfort her, she felt guilty for making love while Nathan lay dying. And it crossed her mind that this could be her punishment for enjoying sex, for defying her mother. She tried to push those thoughts away. What kind of god would punish her by taking Nathan's life just because she was having sex with someone she loved?

"I can't leave my family," she told Caitlin. "Not now." Only weeks ago Vix had been convinced her friendship with Caitlin was over. How childish that seemed to her now. If a friend is someone you can depend on when life gets tough, then Caitlin was her friend, traveling home with her, holding her hand at the funeral, even staying behind at the house afterward to clean up the kitchen once those who had come to pay their respects had left.

She started a letter to Bru, but the words wouldn't come. So she asked Caitlin to give him her message. "Tell him about Nathan and explain . . ."

"Why you couldn't come back?"

"Yes . . . and also . . ."

"That you miss him?"

Vix nodded.

"What about love . . . should I tell him you love him?"

No, she thought, shaking her head. That would be too personal. That would have to wait until they were together again.

Vix helped her father dispose of Nathan's clothes, his toys, the contraption for his bath, his wheelchair. When she said she would like to keep Nathan's books for herself—*Green Eggs and Ham*, *Stuart Little*, *The Great Brain* —her father broke down and sobbed, the only time she'd ever seen him cry. She tried to console him but he bolted, unable to share his feelings.

If Lewis or Lanie were sad about Nathan's death they didn't say. They went on with their lives as if nothing had happened. Vix sometimes thought they were relieved. What kind of family were they? she wondered. What kind of family isn't able to comfort one another?

When Caitlin returned from the Vineyard she hand-delivered a sympathy card from Bru, stiff, formal, with some bullshit message that began *In your time of need . . .* It was signed, *I'm sorry. Bru.* She sent an equally formal card, thanking him for his expression of sympathy and signed it *Victoria.*

At Christmas he sent a card showing a snowy Vineyard scene. *Hoping to see you next summer. Bru.* She sent him a card showing a Santa Fe scene. *Hoping to see you, too. Victoria.*

The Countess asked Tawny to accompany her on a trip to Europe. Tawny went and stayed away almost three months. When she returned she had very little interest in anything or anyone. Lanie was running wild and Lewis was sullen at home, when he *was* home, which wasn't often.

Caitlin decided men were too much trouble. "I'm applying to Wellesley," she told Vix at school. "I think I'll do better without men around to distract me. Besides, I'm thinking of becoming a lesbian . . . to make a statement. Are you interested?"

"This is a joke, right?"

"It's whatever you want it to be."

Vix laughed uneasily.

"I take it that means no?"

"Come on, Caitlin . . ."

"Where's your sense of adventure . . . your curiosity?"

"Obviously *not* where yours is!"

Caitlin sighed.

"Besides," Vix said, "if you're really a lesbian you'll be more distracted at Wellesley than a coed school."

"Good point," Caitlin said. Still, she didn't send in any other applications and in spite of her study habits she was accepted.

Abby convinced Vix to apply to Harvard. "It's Lamb's alma mater. He'll write a letter of recommendation for you."

Harvard? She'd never thought about any school but UNM. But Harvard was in Cambridge, close enough to the Vineyard to commute, if not every day then at least once a week. And Abby and Lamb lived there. She'd have family. So maybe those weren't the best reasons for choosing a school but who cared? She didn't think she had a prayer of getting in but she filled out the application anyway.

When it came to listing her special talents all that came to mind was *Victoria is a good listener*. Her seventh-grade English teacher had written that on her final report card. Was there a way to translate *listening* into a talent? And if so, how would she describe it? *Caitlin Somers chose me as her summer sister because I was smart but quiet. She knew I wouldn't ask a million questions and get in the way.*

She thought about the day she and Caitlin had gone to see *The Turning Point*, about best friends, ballerinas, who chose different paths, one giving up performing to marry and have children, the other giving up everything else to perform. "I can't imagine wasting all that talent," Caitlin had said, identifying with the character played by Anne Bancroft.

"Suppose you're not that talented?" Vix asked.

"Are you saying I'm not?"

"I'm just saying not everyone has that kind of talent."

"But we do."

"Really?"

"Yes," Caitlin said. "I can juggle and you can . . . do jigsaw puzzles."

"That'll get us far!" They'd exploded with laughter and rolled around on the floor until their sides ached.

She skipped the talent question and put her effort into the required essay instead, choosing as her topic *The Most Influential Person in My Life*. Instead of writing about a parent, a teacher, or a superstar like the other seniors, Vix wrote about Caitlin. She compared their friendship to a finely woven tapestry. They'd been pulling threads for years, one here, one there. So far the tapestry could still be mended, and each time it was mended it became stronger. But suppose they pulled the wrong thread? Would the whole piece unravel? Would she and Caitlin have come back together this time if it hadn't been for Nathan?

She had a local interview with a Harvard alum, Matt Sonnenblick. They talked energy, karma, alternative lifestyles, goals. He dug out his yearbook and showed Vix his senior picture. "I graduated at twenty and made it big before I was forty. I had it all, maybe too soon. That's why I came out here . . . to think, to reflect."

But Vix wasn't listening this time, because right above *his* picture was *Lambert Mayhew Somers III*. He'd played soccer and belonged to the Hasty Pudding Club, which made Vix think of instant tapioca. What did his graduation picture tell, anyway? Nothing, except he was good looking. It didn't tell a thing about how his parents had died when he was a baby, how he'd been raised by his grandmother, how he'd once loved Trisha but had married Phoebe, and then Abby.

By the time her mother returned from Europe, Vix had mailed in her application. "I don't like the way they're taking over your life," Tawny told her. "First the Mountain Day School and now Harvard. They're turning you into their own personal charity."

"They're not taking over my life. They're interested in my future, which is more than I can say for you!"

Tawny hauled back and slapped her in the face.

Vix was stunned.

"Don't forget where you belong, Victoria . . . where you come from. You think you can be one of them by going to their fancy schools? Fine. Go. See if you fit in. See if they accept you. The rich are different. Believe me, I know what I'm talking about. People who've never had to worry about money—"

"Well, I'll never be like that," Vix said, before Tawny had finished. "I know how to worry about money." She walked away, her hand against the side of her face. One thing she knew, she wasn't going to wind up like her mother, disappointed and pissed off at the world.

Tawny

SHE WAS GETTING MORE like Darlene every day. Bitter and hard. Slapping Victoria that way! Was she coming unglued again? The Countess had recognized the signs. Had taken her away before she'd done something to herself or one of the children.

Ed had given his blessing. *Just get well over there*, he'd said. *Just get over . . . what happened. We always knew we wouldn't have him for long. Be thankful he didn't suffer at the end.*

Was Ed God? Hadn't he been right there in the hospital room? Was that what he called not suffering? *The other children need you, Tawny*, he'd told her.

No, they didn't need her. They never did need her. They had *him*. He was the one they depended on. They wouldn't even notice she was gone.

I need you, he'd said.

She doubted that, too.

Sometimes she felt her mother was trying to take over her mind. She had to fight her every day. *Leave me alone, Darlene!* she wanted to scream. But she wasn't one to scream.

She should apologize to Victoria. She hadn't meant to smack her. But if they let her make this move . . . oh, what was the point? Victoria had turned into the same restless girl she herself had been, counting the hours until she could escape. They might as well write her off now and be done with it.

THE NEXT DAY Tawny approached Vix. "While you're at it, you might as well marry into it. Then you can take care of your father and me in our old age."

Vix was trying to come up with some smart remark, some remark that might or might not get her face slapped again, when Tawny asked, "What about the brother?"

"The brother?"

"You know who I mean."

"Sharkey . . . you mean, *Sharkey*?" Vix started to laugh.

"Why is that funny? He's not *that* way, is he?"

"What way is that?" she asked, but Tawny wouldn't say.

Sometimes she thought her mother wanted her to fail so she could say, *I told you so. I told you you don't belong in their world.*

Her father argued with Tawny on her behalf. "A good education opens doors."

"If she wants an education so badly she can go to UNM," Tawny said. "She doesn't need Harvard."

"This is a pointless argument!" Vix cried. "Who knows if I'm even going to get in?"

But she did get in. And while she was celebrating on her own, keeping her pride and excitement to herself, Lanie celebrated by announcing her pregnancy.

Abby

IT'S HER FIRST TRIP to Santa Fe and she's anxious about meeting Phoebe at graduation. She wears her taupe Armani, a string of pearls, little heels. She's going for an elegant, understated look. But she sees right away she's got it all wrong. The other women gathered in the quad at the Mountain Day School are dressed like cowgirls. "At best, Linda Evans in *The Big Valley*—at worst, Dale Evans as herself." She wishes Lamb hadn't dropped her off while he went to park.

The Countess rushes to her side. *Precious Girl*, she cries, taking her arm, leading her to a striking woman in fringed leather, silver and turquoise jewelry, her hair braided. *Darlings* . . . the Countess coos, *you two really must get to know one another. After all, you've had the same husband, you share the same children.*

Her instinct is to run, but her feet won't move. She can't swallow. Phoebe breaks the ice first. *What a wicked girl you are!* she tells the Countess, who laughs heartily, then excuses herself to greet someone else, as if she's the hostess at a garden party, leaving *her* alone with Phoebe, who leans close and says, *They don't call her the* Cuntess *for nothing!*

She imagines them in bed together, Phoebe and Lamb, then shuts her eyes tight, trying to erase the picture. She hadn't expected her to be so exotically beautiful, the long hair, the green eyes. Every male standing in the quad, every straight male, anyway, has his eye on her. And Phoebe knows it.

Phoebe

WELL, WELL, WELL . . . isn't she something! So chic, so East Coast elegant. In Armani, for God's sake. And all this time she'd been so sure it would be Trisha. She tries to contain her laughter.

She hears Caity warning her—*Be nice at graduation, Phoeb, okay?* How sweet of Caity to feel protective of Lamb's new wife, though she's not sure she likes the idea. Shouldn't Caity be protecting *her*?

She tries to imagine Lamb and his bride in bed together, but she's bothered by the image of him holding this woman the way he once held her. Does she have regrets? Let's just say she has fond memories. Maybe if he'd been willing to do the Aspen thing, the Santa Fe thing, but Boston . . . God help her! She wasn't about to wind up a proper Yankee wife. How ordinary, how boring!

Tawny

SHE HOLDS ON to Ed's arm, feeling out of place. Not that she doesn't recognize the faces gathered here. Most have been guests at dinner parties she's arranged for the Countess. And isn't *she* acting her part today, bringing the dogs to graduation! At least she's brought along a dog walker. Handsome young man. She doesn't recognize him. The Countess is full of surprises. *Oh, Lord* . . . she's introducing Phoebe to Abby! Well, that should be interesting. She doesn't trust Abby. Ed thinks *she's* crazy. *You're too suspicious*, he tells her. *The woman doesn't have any ulterior motive*. She'd like to know how he can be so sure. And now here comes Abby, waving at her as if they're long-lost friends. At least Phoebe understands the rules.

Lamb

HOW PROUD HE IS of his daughter. He tears up as she
marches in to "Pomp and Circumstance." And that
smile, as she accepts her diploma. *Caitlin Mayhew
Somers*. He's sure the audience is as awed by her charm
and beauty as he is. He holds Abby's hand tightly.
Sharkey sits on his other side and next to *him*, Phoebe.
Sharkey hadn't sent her an invitation to his graduation
from Choate. *Two parents at graduation is enough*, he'd
said. And as far as he knows, Phoebe never noticed the
snub.

Now Phoebe leans across Sharkey and whispers
something to him. He gets a whiff of her perfume, the
same one that used to drive him crazy. He moves closer
to Abby and smiles, letting her know it's okay, he's there
for her.

Then the headmaster calls, *Victoria Leonard*. Vix accepts her diploma plus a five-hundred-dollar award for
academic excellence. The audience claps politely. *Thank
you very much*, she says. *I couldn't have done this without
my family's support*. She finds him and Abby in the audience, smiles, then looks over at her parents. Abby
squeezes his hand, sniffles, and reaches for a tissue.
Their summer daughter. How lucky they are.

24

EVERY TIME SHE TURNED around Abby and Lamb dangled another opportunity in front of her. "Come on, kiddo . . ." Lamb said. "Go with Caitlin. See the world. Think of it as a graduation present."

She and Caitlin were standing in the shade of a cottonwood tree, both of them in white summer dresses, both of them clutching their newly earned diplomas. Vix hadn't known until then that Caitlin wasn't going back to the Vineyard. That she'd opted for a trip to Europe instead.

"What do you say?" Lamb asked.

"I can't," Vix told him.

"What she means is she can't leave her boyfriend," Caitlin said. "Isn't that right, Vix?"

"No . . ." She didn't even know if she still *had* a boyfriend. She had her eye on her parents across the quad, standing alone and looking uncomfortable, while Lewis and Lanie sat on the steps, bored out of their minds. You couldn't tell Lanie was pregnant. Vix hoped she wouldn't have a sudden bout of nausea and vomit on campus. She hadn't told anyone about the pregnancy, not even Caitlin, afraid Tawny would accuse her of washing their linen in public.

She caught a glimpse of Sharkey, checking out the new arts building, a gift from some Hollywood hotshot who had recently moved to town and enrolled his children at Mountain Day.

"It'll be an unforgettable experience," Lamb told her.

Every experience with Caitlin was unforgettable. That wasn't the point. "I can't," she told them. "Not that I don't appreciate . . ."

"It's her boyfriend," Caitlin said again. "Never mind the great time we could have. She cares more about him than seeing the world with me."

"That's not it," Vix said, the pressure building.

Abby said, "Vix has to listen to her heart."

Caitlin said, "I don't think her heart is what's making this decision."

"Will you quit answering for me!" Vix said.

"Sorry," Caitlin told her. "It's just that I know you're going to regret this decision."

"But it's her decision to make," Abby said.

Caitlin rolled her eyes.

Didn't they understand? The scholarship was one thing. That came from the foundation and she'd earned it, by graduating second in her class of thirty-two, with Board scores close to fourteen hundred. The scholarship wasn't exactly charity. But a trip to Europe . . . She wasn't their daughter. Besides, she'd already signed on full time with the cleaning service on the Vineyard and had a second job lined up, hostessing two nights a week at the Homeport, determined to earn her own spending money for college.

Tawny and Ed were heading in her direction. They were taking Vix to lunch at the restaurant in Tesuque where her father had a new job, as manager. The restaurant was described in *The New Mexican* as serving "traditional southwestern fare in a charming setting." Her father wanted to make it a party, inviting Caitlin and her family, but Tawny had vetoed the idea. "We don't have to pretend we can play in their league."

25

SHE WAS THE ONE to suggest Bru meet her at the Flying Horses. After all, that's where it all began. She got there early and, on a whim, bought a ticket and rode an outside horse. She'd worried for weeks about how it would be when she and Bru saw each other again. Would the feelings still be there or would they take one look, turn, and run in opposite directions? She wasn't the same person she'd been last summer. She'd never be the same person. She was amazed, when she thought about it, that she could still eat, fall asleep at night, get up, brush her teeth, even laugh with friends, when all the time there was a hollow numbness someplace inside her.

The boy who collected the rings was a thin teenager with unwashed hair and bad skin, nothing like the National Treasure of her first island summer, with his sun-streaked ponytail and muscled arms. A small girl in denim overalls rode the horse next to hers and as the carousel began to spin she grasped the pole tightly with both hands and shrieked.

When they were in full whirl she caught a glimpse of Bru, moving through the crowd. She resisted the urge to call out to him and watched, instead, as he scouted the area, his thumbs hooked in the pockets of his jeans. She didn't recognize his shirt. She was wearing something new, too, a white cotton pullover with a deep V neck. She'd let her hair hang loose, the way he liked it, and she'd dabbed Love's Baby Soft on all his favorite places.

When he spotted her he jumped onto the moving carousel. She held her breath as he worked his way toward her, that slow smile lighting up his face. Then he was alongside her. She licked her lips because suddenly her mouth went dry. He touched her bare shoulder, making her knees go weak, her stomach tumble.

"How're you doing?"

"I'm okay. How about you?"

"Pretty good." He looked deep into her eyes and she could feel the heat between her legs. So, that part of her hadn't died.

"How's Caitlin?"

She didn't want to think about Caitlin. "She's in Europe."

"Yeah, Von's disappointed. How come she took off like that without telling him?"

"I guess he wasn't that important to her."

"Not like you and me."

"No. Not like you and me."

Bru

WHAT TO SAY? Damn! He never can find the right words when he needs them. But she's waiting for him to say something. He feels it. Something about her brother's death. Something about how sorry he is. How he understands.

And he does. Really. He's been through it himself. Not the same thing, exactly. But close enough. His mother . . .

Tell her about his mother? No way . . . forget it. He never talks about his mother, about those two years she was sick. There are no words for what happened. Oh yeah . . . there's the C word. The Big Unmentionable. There's that. But that doesn't say shit. Doesn't say how she screamed and cried from the pain. Doesn't say how the fucking chemo made her so sick she begged them to put a plastic bag over her head. Or how, when it was over, he'd tried to end it, too. Swallowed a bottle of aspirin. Had to pump out his stomach. What the fuck? He was just a kid. Fifteen. How can he tell her that?

Instead, he kisses her, hoping his kiss says it all . . . how he's thought about her all winter, wants to be with her, wants to make love to her. It doesn't have to be tonight. He can wait until she's ready. He hopes it's soon though. Real soon.

FROM THAT NIGHT ON nothing else mattered. She counted the minutes until she could be with him, said his name a hundred times a day, smiled to herself just thinking about him. Every love song spoke directly to her. After feeling listless for so many months she had energy to burn. She could work all day and still stay up half the night making love. When she was with him, time stood still. Every cliché she'd ever heard about love made complete sense.

"I don't mean to pry, Vix," Abby said, "but how serious is it with you and Bru?"

How serious? Did she mean were they making plans? They never talked about the future. Wasn't it enough to be in love? Totally, completely, hopelessly in love?

"I just want you to give yourself every opportunity," Abby told her. "Don't mistake physical attraction for love. I did, when I was your age, and it cost me . . . and ultimately, Daniel, too. I was engaged to Daniel's father when I was just nineteen. *Nineteen*, Vix. What did I know at nineteen? And nobody tried to stop me. My mother was pleased because he was a law student, someone who'd be able to provide for me. She never thought I should learn to provide for myself."

"Don't worry . . ." Vix said. "I'm going to provide for myself. I have goals." Isn't that the motto she'd chosen for her senior page in the Mountain Day yearbook?

A life without goals isn't worth living.

"What the fuck is that supposed to mean?" Caitlin had asked when she'd seen Vix's yearbook.

"*Goals*. Haven't you ever heard of goals?"

"What goals are we talking about? I'd say a life without adventure isn't worth living, a life without learning, a life without sex, even . . ."

"It's just a quote," Vix said. "It doesn't have any hidden meaning." She couldn't admit that her goals included escaping from her family, finding out what else was out there, trying out life on her own, though she knew Caitlin would have applauded her. Instead she asked Caitlin, "What does *your* quote mean?"

"Mean?"

"Yes . . . since you're making such a *thing* out of mine. What exactly does 'Tiger, tiger, burning bright' mean to you?"

"It's who I am," Caitlin said. "It's how I define myself."

"Really," Vix said.

"Yes, really," Caitlin answered. Then she looked hard at Vix. "Why are we having this conversation? Why are we acting as if we're angry. Are we angry?"

"I'm not angry," Vix said.

"Good . . . because neither am I."

"Maybe we're scared," Vix said.

"Scared?"

"Of being apart. Of losing each other."

"We're *never* going to lose each other," Caitlin said, holding Vix in her arms.

It was strange staying at the house without Caitlin. Their bedroom, with all its memories of past summers, felt empty. Vix played a tape they'd made singing "Dancing Queen" . . . and laughed at how young they sounded. She lay awake on her bed running through the details of every summer, but she could feel the panic of her last morning in this room, too, the morning she'd packed and left at sunrise a year ago, never to return.

"Would you rather stay in the boys' room?" Abby asked when she'd arrived, anticipating her feelings. Neither Sharkey nor the Chicago Boys were coming back that summer. They were off doing their own things. She would finally have her chance to be an only child, the focus of Abby's and Lamb's attention, not that she wanted it now that she had Bru. She was grateful when Abby began to fill the house with guests—her college roommate, who lived in San Francisco; her parents, whom Vix had never met; old friends from Chicago; new friends from Cambridge. They'd eat dinner late and Vix was invited to join them anytime she wished, but after work she'd head for Bru's cabin in Gay Head.

He'd moved in mid-July—one room, woodstove, no plumbing or electricity, but cozy, with a real bed and curtains made by his aunt. Sometimes, as she slept in his arms after making love, she'd dream of Nathan. One night Nathan, his body straight and tall, was pushing her through the woods in a baby carriage. When they reached their destination, a beautiful vista at the top of a mountain, he tilted the stroller so she could see. But she wasn't strapped in and she slid out, then down, tumbling through space, her arms and legs splayed, a look of terror on her face. She cried out in her sleep, waking herself and Bru.

"What?" he asked.

"Bad dream," she said, burrowing into his chest.

"It's okay," he said, wrapping his arms around her. "I'm here . . . I won't let anything bad happen to you."

She never allowed herself to spend the night in his cabin. She forced herself to climb out of bed, night after night, throw on her clothes, and drive home along Old County Road, the road where Lamb's parents were killed.

The phone rang late one night at the house, rousing all of them. Lamb or Abby must have picked up and Vix fell back asleep until Lamb knocked on her door and called, "Vix . . . if you're awake, it's Caitlin. She wants to talk to you."

She picked up the bedside phone, the one they'd installed for Caitlin the summer before. "Hello?"

"Vix . . . I'm in Arles . . . you know, the place where Van Gogh cut off his ear? And it's so fantastic . . . the colors of the sky, the fields, the village. You've got to come . . . just for a week. And don't tell me you can't. If you want to, you can. That's all there is to it!"

"It's the middle of the night," Vix said, still half asleep.

"I know. That's what made me think of you. I don't want you to miss this. Joanne will give you a week off.

You know she will." She paused, then added, "And so will Bru . . . if he really loves you."

She wished Caitlin would stop tempting her, would just quit telling her everything she was missing. She'd get there someday. On her own.

"I just hoped . . ." Caitlin said, barely audible, "because I'm not coming back in September . . ."

"What do you mean, you're not coming back?"

"I'm taking a year off before Wellesley, to travel and study abroad."

"When did you decide?"

"Just now," she said. "But it's always been a possibility."

Caitlin began to send postcards, a series of them, each one from a different place, a few cryptic words printed on the back.

> *I am the most . . .*
> *You are my . . .*
> *In the whole world . . .*
> *We could be . . .*
> *If only . . .*

They reminded Vix of the messages printed on little candy hearts, the kind her father brought home for Valentine's Day. At the end of the week she laid them out, trying to find the hidden message, but there were too many possibilities.

———

Abby convinced her to bring Bru home for dinner. "Really, Vix . . . this is getting ridiculous. You can't keep him to yourself forever . . ." She knew Abby was right but she was nervous, afraid they would . . . what? Judge him and find him lacking? She didn't have to worry. He arrived on time with a bunch of cosmos for Abby. He was polite, almost shy, endearing.

Abby served a simple summer meal of grilled swordfish, island-grown corn, salad, blueberry pie. "We think of Vix as our daughter," Lamb said, during dessert. "We're her Vineyard family."

"Yes, sir. I know that."

"And we're very proud that she's going to Harvard in September," Abby added.

"I know that, too." He squeezed Vix's thigh under the table, letting her know he got the message, a gesture neither Abby nor Lamb missed.

"What are *your* plans?" Abby asked Bru. "Do you think you'll stay here, on the Vineyard?"

"I'm an islander. I've got a good job with my uncles' construction firm. So long as the market for second homes holds we've got nothing to worry about."

"He seems like a very decent chap," Lamb said that night, after Bru left. "With a bright future."

"But Vix is so young . . ." Abby argued, "with her own bright future."

"Vix isn't going to do anything foolish, are you?" Lamb asked, to ease Abby's fears.

Before Vix could answer Abby said, "But she's in love . . . anyone with eyes can see that."

By mid-August Vix was exhausted. The boundless energy of early summer had dissipated. She felt as if she could sleep for weeks. "I don't like the idea of you starting college in such a rundown condition," Abby said. "Why not stop working now and take some time off to just relax?"

"I'll be okay," Vix told her. But she wasn't so sure. She felt so down, so depressed.

Bru said, "Maybe you need vitamins."

"Maybe I just need more sleep."

"So what's the point of driving all the way down island every night?" he asked. "What's the point of sleeping in Caitlin's father's house when you could be sleeping here with me?"

She couldn't answer his question. She didn't really understand it herself. She only knew she needed Abby and Lamb. She needed to feel connected. She felt safe with them. But every time she tried to explain that to Bru he'd get defensive.

"You feel safe with them but not with me?"

"It's not a competition. It's not you against them."

"Sometimes I feel like it is. And there's no way I can win."

"You've got it backwards," she told him.

On her last night on the island they made love until dawn. "Think that'll hold you till we see each other again?" Bru asked.

"Don't worry," she said. "How about you?"

"I'll just think about tonight. And if that doesn't do it, there's always the phone." But when the time came, when she tried to get out of bed, he reached for her and whispered, "Stay with me, Victoria. I need you here, in my arms . . . please don't go."

And at that moment she felt that nothing . . . nothing would ever matter but this.

PART THREE

We Are the World
1983–1987

26

AT HARVARD she called herself Victoria.

Maia, her freshman roommate, an elfin princess from New Jersey, with colorless braces on her teeth—*Don't even ask! It's my second round of orthodontia. My parents are thinking of suing*—took one look at Bru's picture and said, "God . . . what a great-looking guy. I love those rugged, outdoorsy types. Where's he go to school?"

"He's out of school."

"Really. What's he do?"

"He's in construction."

"Construction?"

"He works for his uncles. They build houses . . . on the Vineyard."

"Oh, wow . . . the Vineyard. I hear that's a great place. So where'd he go to school?"

"On the island."

"Really? There's, like, a college on the island?"

She hated Maia already and they'd just met.

The freshman class was filled with high school valedictorians, people who'd scored in the high fifteen hundreds on their Boards. They were talented, brilliant, intense, and competitive, used to being number one in everything they tried. Graduating second in her class from Mountain Day meant nothing at Harvard. It was a joke. She couldn't imagine why they'd admitted her. She was out of her league, to use Tawny's expression.

Even her roommate had bagged straight A's. At least that's what she claimed. She drove Vix up the wall with her running commentary and questions. Not that she answered any of them with more than a *yes*, *no*, or *maybe*, not since that first day. And the way Maia bit her fingernails as she studied, like a hungry gerbil. Vix had fantasies of tying her hands behind her back, or painting her nails with some vile-tasting substance that would send Maia racing across the hall to the bathroom. She couldn't wait until Maia crashed at night so *she* could have some peace and quiet in their room.

Maia

SHE CAN'T BELIEVE she's stuck with this creature for a whole year! Disappointed doesn't begin to describe her feelings. They have absolutely nothing in common. She assumes the *creature* is at least smart. Otherwise, she wouldn't be here. But try to have a conversation and all you get is *yes, no, maybe,* like when she asks about the photos, not just the hunky boyfriend but the kid in a wheelchair. *My brother.* That's it, that's all she says. There must be a story there but the *creature's* lips are sealed. And then there's the beautiful girl looking right into the camera. There's something about that face that keeps drawing her back. And the tantalizing signature— *NBO, Your Summer Sister.* When she asks what it means, the *creature* says, *Nothing, really.*

When she complains about the *creature* to her mother *she* tells her to keep trying. *She could be shy, Maia.* No, that's not it, Mom. It's something else. Snobby, maybe. Aloof. Paisley, their suitemate, thinks Victoria is deep, even mysterious, that she's had experiences she isn't able to share. *Look into her eyes,* Paisley says, *and you'll see what I mean.* But when she looks all she sees is disapproval.

———————

THERE WAS A TIME when Vix thought she'd choose a career in social work or physical therapy, maybe teaching, something, anything, to give back to Nathan. At UNM she might have gone that route. But now that she was at Harvard, now that she saw all her options . . . She thought at first she'd choose English for her concentration, because students at Harvard didn't have *majors* the way they did at other schools. They had *concentrations.* But should it be just plain Literature or English in American Literature, or History in Literature? Or maybe she should go with Sociology or Social Anthropology or Visual and Environmental Studies, whatever that was. She was Charlie in the Chocolate Factory with too many choices, feeling she had to gobble up as much as she could as fast as she could, before someone wised up and kicked her out.

At night in their rooms at Weld South ideas were batted around like badminton birdies. Vix listened and absorbed but rarely spoke as the others discussed the equality of the sexes, genes versus environment, and the biggie—The Meaning of Life. Never mind that the Countess had told her there was no meaning. She was in Robert Coles's Gen Ed 105, The Literature of Social Reflection. He understood life. She wanted to.

On the first Tuesday in October, Vix's father called at dawn to tell her Lanie had given birth. Vix was an aunt to a baby girl named Amber.

Maia rolled over in her bed. "What?" she asked, half-asleep, as Vix hung up the phone, dazed.

"My sister had a baby. I'm an aunt."

"I didn't know you had an older sister."

"I don't. Lanie's just turning seventeen."

Maia sat up. "You mean she's like a . . . teenaged mother? A statistic?"

"Exactly. She's a statistic."

No teenage sister of Maia's would ever get pregnant and if she did, she'd have an abortion. Vix knew that Maia thought of New Mexico as a third-world country and Vix's family as something right out of *Tobacco Road*. But to Vix, Maia represented the worst of privileged suburbia. She found her naive and judgmental.

Vix's father sent a picture, one of those newborn shots taken at the hospital. The baby was a preemie, just four pounds but otherwise okay. Tawny would have no part of Lanie's life. *She made her bed, now let her lie in it.* Vix sent Lanie a copy of *Dr. Spock*, plus a snuggly for Amber.

The next time the phone rang at an ungodly hour it was Caitlin. "Where are you?" Vix asked.

"Rome. It's fantastic. I'm studying Italian . . . and art . . . and history where it really happened."

"When are you coming back?"

"I don't know."

"For the holidays?"

"They don't celebrate Thanksgiving here."

"Christmas?"

"Phoebe's coming for Christmas."

"Then when?"

"Maybe never."

"Don't say that."

Caitlin's voice turned low, seductive. "Do you miss me?"

"You know I do."

"I miss you, too. Is Harvard all it's supposed to be?"

"It's tough, if that's what you mean. I'm just trying to keep up."

"What about Bru?"

"What about him?"

"Do you get to see each other?"

"We talk on the phone."

"Is that enough?"

"What do you think?"

Every time she heard Caitlin's voice she felt an ache, a longing for something, she didn't know what. Even though it was almost a relief to be on her own with no one looking over her shoulder, no one questioning her every move, she missed her. To Vix she was still *Caitlin Somers, the Most Influential Person in My Life.*

"Does she *have* to call in the middle of the night?" Maia asked. "I need my sleep. I can't function with less than seven hours. Could you please tell her she's not just waking you, she's waking me, too."

But the next time Caitlin called and Vix asked if she could call before eleven P.M. Caitlin said, "Overnight rates are less expensive. I'm on a budget, you know. I'm learning to manage my money."

"You're serious?" Vix asked.

"Of course I'm serious."

"Okay . . . I'll try to explain that to my roommate."

"What's she like?" Caitlin asked.

"Nothing like you!"

"Good."

It was Maia who explained to Vix that Caitlin wasn't getting lower rates by waking *her* in the middle of the night. It was daytime in Rome when she placed those calls.

Forget commuting to the Vineyard. Forget once a week, forget once a month. Her course load was so much more than she'd bargained for she had to give up her second job working weekends at Filene's, and just stick with three nights a week at the Coop.

Bru came up for Columbus Day weekend. He took a room in a Motel 6 outside of town. She had a sore throat and a fever. All she wanted was to climb into bed and sleep.

He scolded her for getting sick. "You don't know how to take care of yourself."

"Now you sound like Abby."

"Maybe Abby knows what she's talking about."

Abby had called before the weekend urging Vix to set up an appointment with her doctor.

"I'm not that sick," Vix had told her. "It's just a little cough."

"Little coughs can turn into pneumonia if you don't take care of them."

"I'm taking care . . . really."

She could hear Abby sigh.

And now Bru was lecturing. "I keep telling you, you need vitamins. There's a new health food store in Vineyard Haven. The owner really knows her stuff. I'm going to talk to her about you. See what she says. There must be a reason you're always so run down."

Although he was concerned about her health he was turned on by her fever. Her body felt so hot, he said, inside and out. He couldn't get enough of her. No, he wasn't scared of catching her germs. And if he did it would be worth it. They had to make up for all that time apart. All those nights they'd fallen asleep dreaming of one another.

"You know what I've discovered about myself?" she asked him late Sunday afternoon, when her fever finally broke and she was soaking in the Motel 6 bathtub.

"That you're crazy in love with me?" he said, sitting on the edge of the tub, soaping her back.

"I've always known that."

"Then what?" He kissed her neck. "What have you discovered?"

"That basically I'm uneducated. I never knew until I came here how much there is to learn. How many ideas there are."

He backed away from her.

"I didn't mean . . ." Damn! He'd taken it personally. "Bru . . . this has nothing to do with you. It's just that sometimes, when I start thinking about all there is that I don't know . . . I get scared. That's all I meant."

"Why don't you start thinking of all you *do* know. I'll bet you know more about life than any of your new friends."

"That's probably true."

"Don't you ever wonder what you're doing here?"

"All the time."

She stepped out of the tub and he watched as she rubbed herself down with a towel. "You still love me?" he asked.

"Of course I still love you," she told him. "Did you think I wouldn't?"

"I wasn't sure, to tell the truth."

"Here, let me prove it . . ." she said, sinking to her knees.

A week later a package came from Vineyard Health. Six different kinds of vitamins and minerals with a personal note from the owner, someone named *Star*.

27

THOUGH PHILOSOPHY was a favorite topic, they were not above discussing Men and Sex. Maia was still a virgin. That might explain her fascination with Bru. Maybe she was more curious than meddlesome.

When Maia decided it was time to take action, Paisley and her roommate, Debra, encouraged her. "Winter is long and hard up here," Paisley said in her southern drawl. She was a big, rawboned girl from Charleston, with the kind of looks Abby would describe as handsome. "You might as well find a warm body to make the dreary nights more exciting."

Debra was Korean, educated at international schools, already a published poet. "If you consider *YM* being published. But I'm not Sylvia Plath. I don't want to be Sylvia Plath. I mean, really, look how she wound up."

"Because of some guy," Maia said.

"Most people say it was her mother," Debra said.

"She didn't stick her head in the oven over her mother," Maia argued.

"She might have," Debra said. "She might have had some innate imbalance."

"They're developing drugs for that," Paisley said.

"Soon none of us will be imbalanced. Unless we want to be."

"And creativity will go right down the tubes," Debra said, which got them talking about the neurotic personality and creativity for the next hour.

The warm body Maia found belonged to Wally, a guy she met in Justice, another coveted freshman elective. He was a virgin, too. They saw a lot of one another, spending hours analyzing their situation. Vix suggested maybe they were overanalyzing, maybe it would be better if they just went with their feelings. Maia accused Vix of being the least analytical person she'd ever met. Vix thought that was probably true, given the people Maia knew.

Before the blessed event Debra and Paisley presented Maia with an explicit how-to video. Maia sat stiffly, her hands ready to cover her eyes just in case, but instead of being grossed out by what she saw, Maia was turned on. So was Vix. She'd never guessed there were so many ways of making love.

Just after Valentine's Day Maia returned to their suite looking smug. "Well," she said, "we got through that!" Debra and Paisley crowded into their room. "We laughed a lot," Maia said. "That's a good sign, don't you think?" She searched their faces for agreement. "Well, maybe not during," she admitted. "During it's all moaning and groaning and sweat and glunk but after . . . when you start talking about it, it's like, *wildly* funny."

They looked at Maia, then at each other, and finally Paisley said, "How about it, Victoria? You're our resident expert."

She was the only one of them to have a serious relationship. Sometimes she wished she and Bru hadn't promised not to see anyone else. Sometimes she wished she could walk into a coffee shop or a bookstore and flirt. She wondered if Abby was right, if she was denying herself the pleasures of being young. Did Bru ever have similar thoughts? And how would she feel if he did?

"Well, Victoria?" Paisley said.

"Yeah . . . some of it is funny, I guess," she answered. She tried to remember if she and Bru ever sat around laughing after sex. She didn't think so. Usually they fell asleep in one another's arms. Just thinking about it made her miss him.

Caitlin called at four A.M. from Paris. "I had an affair with a woman. She reminded me of you."

"What do you mean?" Vix spit hair out of her mouth.

"Dark hair, full breasts, beautiful skin . . ."

"I don't think I want to hear this."

"Why . . . does it shock you?" Caitlin asked.

"Are you trying to shock me?"

Caitlin laughed. "I'm always trying to shock you." A long pause, then, "I've met a lot of LUGs here."

"Slugs . . . did you say *slugs*?" She held the phone to her other ear.

"LUGS. L-U-G-S. That's what they call themselves. Lesbians Until Graduation."

"Oh . . . LUGs."

"But she was possessive," Caitlin continued. "She accused me of being a political lesbian, not a biological one, and when I refused to give up men she got so pissed she cut my panties into little pieces and tossed them out

the window . . . right onto the Boul St. Germain. I
was lucky to get out of there alive!" Laughter. "Are you
still there . . . did I lose you?"

"I'm still here."

"Did you know this is the warmest February on record in Paris?"

"No."

"Flowers are blooming in the parks."

Bru had sent her an amaryllis for Valentine's Day. It
sat on her windowsill, its petals falling to the floor.

·

Paisley

WHAT SHE LIKES BEST about Victoria is that she listens and evaluates. She doesn't just run on endlessly for the sake of hearing her own voice, the way Maia does when she's feeling insecure. When Victoria invites her to dinner at Lamb and Abby Somers' house she's impressed. It's a gorgeous old place on Appleton, very smartly done, very Cambridge. She doesn't quite get the relationship between Victoria and the Somers. Victoria calls them her surrogate family. Surrogate as in *Baby M*? She'd love to know but she doesn't ask.

At dinner she's seated next to the Democratic State Chair. She takes this opportunity to expound on the state of politics in the U.S. of A. She lets him know exactly what she thinks of Nancy Reagan and her *Just Say No* campaign. As if simplistic slogans can solve the problems of the world! She's worried about the state of this country. Really. Someone has to take action before it's too late!

He's dazzled by her sharp thinking, she can tell, and encourages her to join the Young Democrats. *A bright young woman like you can go far. Have you thought of running for office one day?* Run for office? Is he out of his mind? She's got other plans. And was that his hand on her thigh or was it just her imagination?

———

The Young Dems love having a southern girl like her aboard. Of course, they don't know shit about the South. Half of them don't know what state Charleston's in. And this is Harvard! Which proves geography's another thing going down the tubes in the U.S. of A.

28

VIX AND PAISLEY worked their tails off trying to get out the vote for the Mondale–Ferraro ticket and were devastated by the landslide presidential election.

"Welcome to the eighties," Maia, the only Republican among them, sang.

"The eighties are half-over," Paisley reminded her.

"Too bad," Maia said.

Paisley groaned. "Four more years of Adolfo suits and tight smiles. Do you think she goes down on him?"

"Please!" Maia said. "She's the First *Lady*."

They were living in Leverett House. Vix had thought, when she'd signed up with Paisley last spring, she'd be getting away from Maia. But now they had two classes together and Vix was surprised by Maia's intelligence. Not only that, but they both enjoyed Mexican food, the hotter, the better, foreign movies, even bad ones, and Joan Armatrading. Besides, they weren't sharing a room, which made it easier. And Maia swore she was going to conquer her nail-biting habit.

———

Caitlin called from London on election night. "Politics are such a bore," she said when Vix griped about the results. "Look at it this way . . . anyone who's willing to run, I'm not willing to vote for."

"But you had an absentee ballot, didn't you? You voted."

"No, I didn't vote. I just told you."

"That's why we lost! Because people like you just don't care enough."

"People like me? Should I be offended by that remark?"

"No . . . well, maybe . . . sorry. I'm just disappointed. And tired. What are you doing in London anyway? I thought you were at the Sorbonne."

"I'm here to see a play. The producer invited me. I'll be back at school on Thursday."

"Are you coming home for the holidays?"

"I'm going to Gstaad with Phoebe. Our annual mother-daughter ski trek. Want to come?"

"I have other plans."

"I knew you'd say that."

Abby invited Vix for Thanksgiving dinner but she opted for the Vineyard instead. When she got there she was miffed Bru wasn't as affected by the outcome of the election as she was.

He didn't get her anger. He'd voted the straight Democratic ticket. What more did she want? It wasn't worth getting all steamed up over. Besides, Reagan was good for business. And business was what mattered.

They began to argue about everything. *What did you*

mean by that? she'd ask. *Nothing, just forget it,* he'd answer. For the first time it occurred to her that he had no books in the cabin, that she'd never *seen* him with a book. He probably never read more than the *Gazette,* if that. He was still listening to Van Halen. He hadn't even heard of Joan Armatrading.

When she complained about the Porta Potti, he asked what was wrong with it? What was wrong with her? Was she taking her vitamins?

"You think everything can be magically cured with vitamins?"

"Everything but us," he said.

She was tempted by Abby's invitation to join them in Barbados over Christmas, but angry at herself for behaving badly over Thanksgiving, finding fault with everything. It was probably hormonal, she decided, since she'd been premenstrual. So she went back to the Vineyard, to Bru.

And it went well over Christmas. The two of them bundled up and walked on the beach, shopped for gifts in Vineyard Haven, made love in the late afternoon in front of the woodstove. They shared Christmas goose with Bru's extended family—the three uncles and aunts, the twelve cousins, their significant others, their babies. All of them welcomed her into their homes, into their family. She should have felt at home. They were blue-collar, hardworking, a rowdy, beer-drinking crowd. They knew how to have a good time. They weren't all in therapy, they weren't all trying to find the meaning of life. They didn't sit around comparing their dysfunctional families, blaming their parents for all their problems like her friends at Harvard. True, a few of them were already in twelve-step programs, but that meant they were trying to help themselves. Let Caitlin call their lives ordinary, even boring. This was where she belonged, wasn't it? If she belonged anywhere.

Phoebe

SHE HASN'T SEEN Caity in ages, not since she caught up with her last July in Perugia. She's glad Caity's finally settled in Paris and that she's going to school. She doesn't usually admit this but she's always wished she were better educated. One year at Stephens College didn't do much for her.

She's been looking forward to their ski week together so she's slightly miffed when, on their first night, Caity picks up a handsome young man in the bar at their inn and stays out till all hours. She doesn't expect Caity to be a virgin but she's taken aback by the ease with which her daughter attracts men.

Next day, as they're riding up in the chairlift, she decides to bring up the subject. She explains that when she was Caity's age she'd traveled abroad, too. She knows the score. *I'm not going to tell you what to do or not to do, but you need to be discriminating. Just because men . . .* She pauses. What is it she's trying to say? *It's true variety is the spice of life but that doesn't mean . . .* Mean what? she asks herself. That Caity should follow in *her* footsteps? She's still thinking about it as they reach the top.

Thanks, Phoeb, Caity says, adjusting her goggles. *I'm glad we had this talk.* Then she turns and skis off.

Well, fine . . . if Caity's going to be out every night *she* might as well find some action herself. There's a charming Dane in her ski group . . .

Abby

SHE'S LESS WORRIED about Vix and Bru. Whatever understanding they have, it doesn't seem to be affecting Vix's chance for an education, and really, that's the most important thing, isn't it?

She's relieved Caitlin has agreed to study at the Sorbonne, though she wishes she hadn't entirely given up on Wellesley. They're all disappointed she's not coming home. Vix, especially, seems at a loss to understand. She's embarrassed to admit that last June she'd overheard a phone conversation between the two girls. She should have replaced the receiver but what mother isn't guilty of occasional lapses in respecting her children's privacy?

Why? Vix had asked when Caitlin gave her the news.

Because I belong here. Except for you and Shark and Lamb there's really no reason to come back.

It's time to get over her, Caitlin, Vix said.

Who?

Abby. Isn't that what this is all about?

She'd clapped her hand to her mouth so they wouldn't hear her sharp intake of breath.

This has nothing to do with Abby, Caitlin said.

Then what?

It's complicated.

What a relief! To know Caitlin's decision has nothing to do with her. Not that Lamb has ever hinted . . . but the thought has crossed *her* mind.

She has a plan to get Caitlin back, temporarily anyway. A surprise fiftieth birthday party for Lamb. Even though he claims he doesn't want to celebrate, she's sure he'll love it.

29

CAITLIN, in a tiny black Lycra dress and thigh-high boots, her hair cut stylishly short, looking like she'd stepped out of the pages of *Elle*, greeted Vix outside Lamb's house, shivering in the damp, cold, late April night air. She hugged Vix tightly, then held her away. "You look . . . older. Do you feel older?"

"Yeah," Vix said, "almost two years older."

"Almost two years. Has it been that long? Is that possible? Come inside. I'm freezing. I forgot how late spring can come here. In Paris . . ."

Vix cut her off. "Everything's in bloom."

Caitlin laughed. "It's so good to see you! I miss you every single day of my life."

Vix had been a wreck, charged with nervous anticipation all day, like a child expecting the return of a long-lost parent. If Caitlin felt Vix's cold shoulder, punishment for having abandoned her in the first place, she didn't show it. "I have so much to tell you," she said, "but it will have to wait until after the party. You'll spend the night, won't you?"

"I didn't bring . . ."

"Never mind. I'll give you a toothbrush. Do you still gag?"

"Only if I stick it down my throat."

"I wasn't talking about toothbrushes."

"I was."

Caitlin grabbed Vix's arm and led her through the crowd already gathered inside the house. "Fifty guests for fifty years. Is that cute or what? Sharkey's here and Daniel but I don't think Gus made it. What do you think of my hair? I hate it. I'm letting it grow. Lamb doesn't look fifty, does he?"

Vix began to melt.

All through the buffet supper Caitlin clung to her. "I need you tonight. Don't desert me. This is so hard."

"What is?"

"Being here. I feel like everyone's judging me."

Vix couldn't imagine who might be judging her or why Caitlin would suddenly care.

Sharkey

HE'S JET-LAGGED. Feels like shit. Took the red-eye from L.A. where the big guys at Cal Tech tried to convince him to do his graduate work. But M.I.T.'s after him, too. He's going to meet with them on Monday. Until then he's not going to make his decision.

Abby's asked him to make a toast to Lamb. Something short, she said. Something humorous. He's promised to try. He's been rehearsing it in his mind. He hates the idea of standing up in front of all those people.

When the time comes he raises his glass of champagne. *To Lamb . . .* he says, *a father who knows when to leave well enough alone.* The crowd grows quiet, like he's said something disrespectful when he meant to convey how lucky he feels that Lamb never pushed, that Lamb accepted him as he was, as he is. He was just trying to thank him, that's all. So how come they're all looking at him like that? Before he has the chance to figure it out Lamb is at his side, his arm around his shoulders. *Thanks, Shark,* he says. *No father could ask for a better son!*

Then it's Caitlin's turn and every guy in the room is drooling. And she's smiling at all of them, letting them think it's a possibility. *To Lamb . . .* she says, *the best man I've ever known. And I've known more than my share.*

Daniel

AT LEAST *he* stands up and makes a proper toast, which is more than he can say for the *bitch*. Christ, you could hear the guests hold their breath when she finished, until Lamb laughed. Laughed and kissed Caitlin, telling her no father could ask for a more loving and spirited daughter. Leave it to Lamb to get out of an uncomfortable situation. He's got to hand it to him. The guy is never at a loss. He should be running for office.

Gus

HE WOULD HAVE gone but he's got a paper due Monday and on top of that his grandmother's sick. It doesn't look good. They're keeping a bedside vigil. He can't stand the idea of her suffering even though they keep telling him she's not in pain. He and his grandmother have a special bond. He doesn't want to lose his Baboo. And he knows how badly she wants to make it to his graduation.

He calls during the party to wish Lamb a happy fiftieth. Just before they hang up he asks to speak to Vix.

Hello, she says.

Hey, Cough Drop . . . how's it going?

What? she says. *There's a lot of noise. I can't hear you.*

Gus Kline, he shouts. *Just wanted to say hello.*

Is this really Gus?

He laughs.

Because if it is . . . I can't hear a thing.

Never mind, he says. He'd like to see her again. He's curious.

AFTER THE CHAMPAGNE and cake, the poems and songs and silly gifts, Vix went upstairs with Caitlin, to the room that had always been reserved for her visits. Like Caitlin's room on the Vineyard, Abby hadn't touched this one either. Caitlin sat on the edge of the bed and hugged a pillow to her chest. "I suppose you can tell I had an abortion."

Vix was stunned. "God, Caitlin, I had no idea! Why didn't you tell me?"

"Do you tell me everything?"

Caitlin had her there. "When?" Vix asked.

"Six weeks ago. It was a mistake. I'm still not sure how it happened. The condom broke, I think."

"Are you still seeing him?"

"No. He's married."

"The producer?"

"What producer?"

"The one who took you to the play in London?"

"What play in London?"

"You told me . . . when you called."

"I don't remember."

"It wasn't that long ago."

"Well . . . I've been busy. A lot of things happen. I don't necessarily remember all of them."

How come Vix remembered if Caitlin didn't? "Did you love him?" She didn't know why she bothered to ask when she already knew the answer.

"No, I didn't love him. But I enjoyed his company, in and out of bed."

Could she say the same about Bru? They hadn't spent that much time together out of bed, but in it . . .

"I left the Sorbonne. I felt claustrophobic there. Everyone was so . . . French. It really got to me after a while. I'm better off in London, don't you think?"

Vix had no idea.

Suddenly, Caitlin's face lit up. "I've just had the most brilliant idea. Take junior year abroad. Wherever you decide to go, I'll go with you." She was dancing across the room now, singing out the names of cities. "Paris, London, Rome, there's even a program in Grenoble." She flopped back on the bed then rolled over to face Vix.

Paris, London, Rome . . . Maia had considered spending junior year abroad but her parents urged her to wait. Paisley's family didn't have the money. *We have fallen into genteel poverty*, she'd told them, doing Scarlett O'Hara.

"Well? . . ." Caitlin asked.

"I can't."

Caitlin's mood shifted. "I'm so sick of hearing you say that!" She jumped off the bed, unzipped her dress, yanked it over her head, and dropped it on a chair. She was wearing black lace underwear, probably French. She grabbed a fuzzy robe out of the closet, way too small, left over from some visit when she was a kid, and pulled it around her.

"You're turning into the most negative person," Caitlin fumed. "I can't believe what that *school* is doing to you!"

"It has nothing to do with the *school*. I've got responsibilities. I can't just pack up and take junior year abroad because it's a nice idea!"

"What responsibilities . . . the scholarship?"

"More than that."

"Don't tell me . . ." Caitlin sounded thoroughly disgusted. "You're tied down already and you're not even twenty!" She sat back on the bed and worked off her boots, easing them down from thigh to ankle.

"I'm not tied down," Vix said.

"Oh, please . . ." She kicked off one boot, then the other. "He needs you more than you need him. Where is he, anyway? How come he's not here tonight?"

She was hoping no one would ask because Abby had told her to invite Bru and she hadn't. She didn't want to worry about him tonight, about whether or not he was enjoying himself. She wanted to keep her reunion with Caitlin to herself. "You've never been in love," she said. "You don't understand."

"If being in love means giving up your freedom, not to mention your opportunities," Caitlin said, "then I haven't missed anything."

30

THE FOLLOWING CHRISTMAS, when she was a junior, Vix took Bru to Santa Fe. They drove out in his truck, listening to Bob Marley, Elvis Costello, James and Carly. Sometimes she worried they were acting old, settled, more tired than excited when they were together. But that would change, wouldn't it, when she was out of school? The real world couldn't be this hard.

The stories she heard at school about guys' behavior made her appreciate Bru even more. He was so sweet and loving, always concerned about her. Sometimes she wished they'd met later so it could all be new and fresh again. Those feelings. That rush. How did couples who'd been together for years manage to keep it exciting?

When they got to Santa Fe he found a cheap room in a sleazy motel on Cerrillos Road. She would stay at the house. It wasn't until they got there that she discovered her mother had accompanied the Countess to Key West. "It's the emphysema," her father said. "She can't take the high altitude anymore. She needs your mother's help getting settled."

Her father tried. He put up the old tabletop tree decorated with the gold and silver balls Tawny kept packed in a hatbox on the top shelf of the hall closet. He roasted a turkey, made mashed potatoes and creamed onions, brought an apple pie home from the restaurant. Lewis was away for the holidays, with a friend's family, planning to enlist the second he graduated from high school. But Ed invited Lanie and her family up from Albuquerque. She had two babies by then, and this was the first time Vix had seen either one of them. They had green snot dripping out of their noses and pacifiers stuck in their mouths like valves. It was a wonder they could breathe. Vix held one feverish child, then the other, trying to find some genetic connection.

"They look like *him*," Lanie said, "Jimmy." Lanie looked drained, haggard, ten years older than Vix. Vix wished they could take out the old Barbies and play on the floor. This time she'd let Lanie use Barbie's Dream House. Jimmy didn't show up for dinner, not that Lanie expected him to. He was probably at his brother's house getting stoned, she said.

At the end of the day, when Lanie got into her truck with the children and the Christmas toys, she hit on Vix for money. "I work my ass off shoveling manure while *he* sits around getting high. My life sucks." Vix felt like telling Lanie she was working her ass off, too, making every penny count, but Jesus, *she* was a student at Harvard and Lanie was existing on food stamps so she ran back into the house and dug fifty dollars out of her wallet.

"Thanks," Lanie said, pocketing the money. "Your guy is gorgeous. Marry him while you can."

Vix was surprised. "I wouldn't have expected you to recommend marriage."

"Yeah, well . . . I didn't exactly plan on winding up like this."

"Get out of it then," Vix said. "Get your life together. You could move in with Dad, go back to school. You can't just give up."

Lanie's mouth hardened. "You come back here once in three years and think you can fix everything just like that? You don't know *shit* about any of us. Tawny's gone for good, not that Dad will admit it. He's got some *cow* at work, not that he'll admit that either. You think *she's* going to put up with me and these two?" The kids were asleep, the baby in a car seat, Amber slumped against him, breathing heavily. Didn't Lanie know it was illegal to drive with an unprotected child?

"Are those bullet holes?" Vix asked, eyeing the damage to the door of the truck.

"Just some jerk at the trailer park shooting up everything in sight," Lanie told her, turning on the ignition. "Nothing personal."

Vix drove to the cemetery with her father. It was the first time she'd visited Nathan's grave since she'd left for college. She stopped at Kaune's to buy a poinsettia in a plastic pot and when they got there, she set it in front of the simple marker.

Nathan William Leonard
1970–1982
Rest in Peace

Then she asked her father for some time alone. He nodded and walked away. She kneeled at the foot of the grave.

Ed

HE CAN SEE HER HANDS moving. She's talking to Nathan. Does she still feel guilty for those summers away? He hopes not. He should tell her Nathan understood. Nathan always defended her. Took off after Tawny every time she bad mouthed Vix. How that boy loved her! He remembers taking the two of them on a camping trip in the RV. Nathan must have been six or seven. The way they'd laughed together! Vix, pushing him along a trail in his chair, uphill, then down . . . too fast . . . too fast . . . The surprise when he'd fallen. The fear in her eyes. Turned out to be only a bruised elbow. Decided not to tell Tawny. Their secret. Just the three of them.

How much does she know about Tawny and him? Did Lanie tell her he's seeing someone? Not that he wants it this way. He wants Tawny to come home. But she says it's over. They should both try to make new lives. What does that mean . . . a new life? A new life with Frankie? Frankie's okay. Makes him laugh. Long time since a woman made him laugh.

What about Vix and the boyfriend? Does she love him? He can't tell. Hard to believe she's a junior at Harvard. His daughter. A good kid, Vix. Maybe not a kid anymore. A woman. Yes. She looks like a woman now. He can feel the tears starting. Tawny hates it when he cries. Calls him weak. Maybe he is weak. So what? How come he can't talk to them . . . to his daughters? Do they know he loves them? Especially Vix. Does she know?

_____

ON THE WAY HOME her father said, "He's a nice boy." At first she thought he was talking about Nathan, until he asked, "Are you happy?"

For a minute she considered letting down her guard, telling him how uncertain she was about life and love and everything in between. Then she thought better of it, given what Lanie had told her about Tawny and him.

"So that's where you come from," Bru said on the morning they left.

"Yes, that's where I come from." As soon as she said it, she started to cry. She heard Tawny's voice warning her, *Save your tears for something important, Victoria*. But this *was* important, wasn't it? Besides, she couldn't stop. She'd be eating a burger in some joint on the highway and it would start out of nowhere, tears flooding her eyes, a lump in her throat making it impossible to swallow. Or she'd be brushing her teeth before bed in some motel and catch a glimpse of herself in the mirror, just as her face contorted and the tears began. She wept for Nathan, for Lanie, for her father, and maybe for herself. She no longer knew her family, and they certainly didn't know her.

At first Bru was sympathetic. He held her that first night, until she was able to fall asleep. But the following night, when he began to stroke her thigh and she didn't respond, he turned away, hurt. He didn't get it. He thought it had to do with him. The next time the tears began they were in the truck, just crossing into Virginia.

"Here we go again . . ." he said, pulling off at a rest stop. He jammed on the brakes. "You want anything?"

She shook her head.

He was gone for a long time. When he came back he handed her a cranapple juice and a bag of pretzels. "Whatever it is, get over it, Victoria . . . just get over it, okay?"

By the time they got to Boston and she was still at it he was angry. "I don't know you anymore."

"Maybe you never did."

"Yeah, right . . . but either way this is getting . . ." He turned away from her. "I think we need a break."

If he expected her to argue he was mistaken. She nodded her head calmly and just like that, with no discussion, no questions, no anything, they separated.

Bru

HE'S ALWAYS WAITING and worrying she's going to
end it. Always looking for signs, expecting the worst. So
he jumps the gun, says it out loud before she can. She
doesn't even cry. Nothing. That proves it, doesn't it?
Jeez . . . she cries all the way home, then he tells her
he needs a break and she just sits there like she's made of
stone. After he drops her off he's shaking so bad he has
to pull off the road, afraid he'll plow into somebody if he
doesn't.

Back on the Vineyard he has a beer with his uncle.
Unloads his problems with Victoria. His uncle keeps
nodding. *Tell me about it*, he says. *They say one thing, they
mean another. No way to understand them. I know it hurts
but there's other fish in the sea. And they'll be jumping for
you before long.*

Star comes on to him, suggests they get together. So
they do. In the storeroom of her shop, on the floor,
between cartons of chewable vitamin C and ginseng.
Her breasts are small and lopsided. She makes animal
sounds as she comes. *There are other fish in the sea*, he
keeps telling himself.

Do me again, Star says, an hour later. So he does her
again.

But when he falls asleep, he dreams only of Victoria.

31

ON JANUARY 28, the *Challenger* shuttle blew up during takeoff, killing all the astronauts aboard, including Christa McAuliffe, and that night Vix fell apart, crying uncontrollably, banging her fists against the wall. What was the point? You worked your ass off, you struggled to get someplace, and *wham!* just like that, it could all come crashing down. Nothing made sense.

She'd suppressed her feelings about Bru until that moment. But just like the shuttle, their love had come crashing down, over in a flash. Maybe the Countess was right after all. Live for the moment. There might be no tomorrow. And even if there is, nobody really gives a damn.

Her hysteria frightened Maia, who ran down the hall to find Paisley. When the truth came out, she and Paisley exchanged such looks! "You broke up with Bru and you didn't tell us?" Maia asked. "How could you keep something like that to yourself?"

But she was a master at keeping it all to herself. She'd learned at the feet of an even greater master, hadn't she? *Deny . . . deny . . . deny . . .*

When they'd returned from vacation they'd had two

weeks of reading time, two weeks to prepare for exams. She couldn't tell them about Bru then, couldn't allow herself to think about it. And if the shuttle hadn't blown up she might have made it through the semester without confronting reality. "We didn't exactly break up," she explained. "We're taking time off." That was the truth, wasn't it? They hadn't broken up. No one ever said they were breaking up.

"Whose idea . . . his or yours?" Maia asked.

"We agreed."

"Who suggested it?"

"Does it matter?"

"Just tell me, okay . . ."

"He did."

"Then he's an idiot and you're better off without him."

Maia

VICTORIA CAN BE so secretive! It doesn't make being her friend easy. But for better or worse, they are friends. And friendship is what's on her mind as she sits alone at the medical clinic waiting to be seen. She's not going to stand back and watch Victoria flush it all down the toilet because of some guy. She's not going to let her jeopardize her scholarship. They have two classes together and she happens to know Victoria hasn't been keeping up with her reading. She'll do whatever's necessary to help —if only she doesn't have cancer, because she's discovered a dark spot on her foot that she's almost sure is a melanoma. She just hopes it's not too late.

When her name is called she steps into the cubicle where a young doctor holds a magnifying glass to her foot and examines the spot. He doesn't think it's anything, he tells her, but he measures it anyway, then draws its shape on a page in her medical record. *Come back in a month*, he tells her, *sooner if you notice any change.*

You're not going to do a biopsy?

There's really nothing to biopsy at this point. He reads the concern in her face. *You don't have cancer if that's what you're thinking. So relax . . .*

How can he be so sure without a biopsy?

Are you stressed-out? he asks.

What, is he kidding? Of course she's stressed-out. She's a junior at Harvard, isn't she?

CAITLIN CALLED from L.A. on a blustery winter day. "I couldn't take another minute in London. It's been so gray, so damp. I thought I'd never feel warm again. I'm visiting Sharkey. He's so involved with whatever it is he's studying he barely has time to see me, which is just as well because you'll never guess who I ran into out here."

"I can't imagine."

"Tim Castellano."

"Tim Castellano!" She hadn't thought about him in years, not since high school. The story broke just a couple of months after the summer they'd baby-sat Max. It made the cover of *People*. Tawny brought a copy home from the supermarket. "Did you have any inkling while you were working for them, Victoria?"

"No," Vix had lied, thinking of the hardness inside his pants when she'd thrown herself over the seat and landed on his lap.

"Imagine having an affair while your wife is pregnant . . . and walking out on her the day you bring the baby home from the hospital. *Despicable*. I'll bet this ruins his career."

It didn't. He'd left TV behind for feature films, while Loren's career just fizzled.

Vix had brought the magazine to school to show Caitlin. "An eighteen-year-old model?" she'd cried. "He left Loren for some eighteen-year-old from New Zealand when he could have had me?"

"Aren't you glad he didn't?"

"I just wanted to have sex with him, Vix. I didn't want

him to leave his marriage. And I still think he'd have been a good one for my first. At least he'd have known what he was doing."

Vix thwacked her across the butt with the magazine. Caitlin said, "Someday I'm going to finish what I started with him."

And here she was, six years later, finishing what she'd started.

"I didn't have to seduce him or anything," Caitlin told her. "All I had to say was 'Remember me?' and he said, 'How could I forget, Spitfire?' So we met for a drink . . . I was wearing white, everybody wears white out here, and one thing led to another."

"So how was it?" Vix asked, angry at herself for caring.

"Actually, the first time was fantastic . . . we were both so hot we hardly had a chance to take off our clothes . . . and God, Vix, he's got an incredible Package . . . but once I'd satisfied my curiosity . . . well, we didn't have that much to say to one another. Two weeks was more than enough."

Vix looked out the window. It was still snowing. And she had a cold that wouldn't go away. She also had two papers due. So she didn't want to think about Tim Castellano's Package or how warm and sunny it must be in L.A., or why she was killing herself at school while Caitlin was running around in something white, making it with movie stars.

"It's so weird out here. There's so much insecurity. You wouldn't believe how insecure most of these people are." She took a breath. "Why are you sniffling that way? Do you have a cold?"

"Everybody here has colds."

"You should transfer to a school out here. It's eighty-something today. Then we could room together. It would be like the old days."

"I'm a junior, Caitlin. You don't transfer at the end of your junior year."

"I forgot."

"Anyway, it'll be spring soon."

"Not soon enough from the sound of your voice." Another big breath. "So, how's Bru?"

"I don't know."

"What do you mean you don't know?"

She wasn't going to tell her they were taking time off, that she'd heard from Trisha he'd already found another woman, Star, the owner of the health food store. "I mean I have two papers due and I've got a job working three nights a week so how am I supposed to find time for a social life?"

"I'll call you next week when you're in a better mood, that is, if you think you'll be in a better mood next week."

"Try me in two weeks."

"Fine. Two weeks."

Sharkey

HE DOESN'T HAVE time to worry about her. He's at the lab eighteen hours a day. Why'd she have to come to L.A. now?

How about an introduction? his lab partner asks.

I don't think so.

Come on . . . she's your sister, isn't she?

She's not available, he tells him.

She puts out vibes, man . . .

Forget about it! he says like he means it.

Okay, sure . . . no problem.

She lures him away for dinner one night, to some place on a hill with fancy prices. It's been a long time since he's been to a real restaurant. *At this rate you're going to fly through your money*, he tells her.

She finds that funny. *You worry about money, Shark?*

Let's put it this way. I don't spend twenty-five bucks on a solo pizza.

That's sweet.

Don't play cute with me, Caitlin. I'm your brother, remember?

Are you trying to tell me something?

Get a job . . . go back to school. Do something with your life.

I am doing something, Sharkey. It's just different from what you're doing.

32

Vix agreed to go home with Maia over spring break, to the white clapboard house in Morris Township with the pool and the tennis court. She found Maia's family warm and welcoming, intellectually stimulating. So how come Maia was always complaining? "They're controlling," she told Vix. "And the sibling rivalry is so intense."

She and Maia took a drive to the shore, to Maia's cousin's house. He and his friends were out on the beach, tossing around a Frisbee. She wouldn't let herself think of other games of Frisbee on other beaches. Andy was a second-year medical student at Penn, short, compact, with good shoulders and arms, blond hair, light eyes. He was funny, a gabber, the opposite of Bru in every way.

"He's going to have a good bedside manner," Maia said, "don't you think?"

Yes, Vix thought, a good bedside manner. When he grabbed her arm and led her away from the others, when he whispered, "I am insanely hot for you," she could feel something stirring inside her.

Maia said, "A doctor, Victoria. You could do worse." Then she laughed. If anyone needed a doctor in the family it was Maia. She'd begun to worry that every spot, lump, or bump meant cancer. That if her parents couldn't find their glasses or house keys they were developing Alzheimer's, that her sister or brother would behave recklessly and have sex with someone infected with that new virus.

Vix had never made love with anyone but Bru and at first she was hesitant. "Hey, you think it's any different for me?" Andy asked. "It's new every time." For once she was following her Power, not her heart, and it didn't feel that bad.

Maia

HALLELUJAH! Victoria's finally taken the plunge. Better late than never. Now maybe she'll see there are other fish in the sea. She just wishes Victoria would quit dropping lines about what a decent guy Bru is and how she drove him away. She and Paisley are constantly reminding her to stop blaming herself. It wasn't her fault.

You weren't there, were you?

You want him back? Is that it?

I don't know what I want.

Welcome to the club!

———————

IF SHE HADN'T HAD a job lined up she wouldn't have returned to the Vineyard that summer, and God knows, Maia and Paisley tried their best to get her to change plans.

"Going back is just begging for trouble," Maia said.

"I make enough in a summer on the Vineyard to get through the school year," she said, making excuses. "Plus I'm building my nest egg for after graduation."

Paisley said, "What about Bru?"

"What does Bru have to do with it?"

"Only everything," Maia said.

"He's seeing someone else," she told them for the first time. She could tell they were surprised.

"Then it's over?" Paisley asked.

"I don't know . . . maybe."

"I'd like to believe you, Victoria," Maia said, "and I hope you won't take this wrong but I've watched your on-again, off-again thing for three years and I'm, like, beginning to think you get off on it."

"She's worried about what'll happen when you see him again," Paisley added.

"Don't forget . . ." Maia reminded her, as if she needed reminding, "he disappeared when the going got tough. He dumped you when you really needed him."

"It wasn't like that," Vix said. "It was a mutual decision."

"Don't tell us," Maia said, "we were here . . . remember?"

"How could I forget?" Vix asked. "Without the two of you . . ."

"Then listen to us now," Maia said, "and get a job someplace else. There are notices posted everywhere."

But Vix didn't listen.

Abby

SHE'S THRILLED Vix is returning to the Vineyard. She'd worried at first, after the breakup with Bru, that she'd never come back. She and Lamb know this could be the last summer they'll have her with them. Next year she'll graduate and who can say what will happen? She just hopes Vix won't slip back into her romance with Bru because it's easy, because he's there. She knows how hard it is to break away . . .

33

•

IF HER GOAL was to prove to herself that it was over, that they both wanted to end it, she got her chance two days after she settled in with Lamb and Abby, when Bru came looking for her at the Dynamo office, a cramped space on the second floor of a ratty building on Beach Road. She was alone in the office, taking inventory in the supply closet, when he called, "Hello . . . anybody home?"

Please, God . . . help me live through this. Help me to be strong.

"Hey," he said, finding her as still and lifeless as one of the vacuum cleaners. He held out a bunch of peonies. She took them, her hands shaking. She was afraid to look at him, afraid if she did she'd lose it. "Hey . . ." he said again, tilting up her chin.

She tried to focus on the wall clock over his shoulder —4:15 P.M.

He waved his hand in front of her face. "Victoria?"

Okay. She could do this. She'd keep it light, as if it meant nothing, as if *he* meant nothing. "What happened to your nose?" she asked. She could see he'd had an accident. A Band-Aid covered the bridge of his nose, but it only made him more attractive, giving his face a mysterious, slightly dangerous look.

"Hockey," he said.

She nodded, reached up, touched it. A mistake.

His arms went around her. "Missed you," he whispered. "Missed you so much."

She was all over him in the truck, tugging at his shirt, undoing the zipper of his jeans. She'd never felt this kind of lust. He pulled off the road and fell onto her, pushing her panties aside, his jeans around his knees. Her head banged against the door as he pumped her but she barely noticed. The peonies crushing beneath her released their fragrance. She would never smell peonies again without reliving this moment.

She had wished for a return to the feelings of that first summer—the thrill of being with him, the rush—and now her wish had come true.

He said, "Wow . . . what have you been up to since January?"

Caitlin sent a series of postcards showing stars from old movie musicals. Judy Garland. Cyd Charisse. Jane Powell. *Where are they now?* she wrote on the back. *Are they immortal because they made movies? No answer required. Just think. To be continued.* Vix tucked them away in the bottom dresser drawer, next to the photo of Lamb's parents. She had other things on her mind.

She and Bru were daring that summer, testing themselves, testing one another. He finally asked her if there'd been anyone else during their time apart. She told him about Andy. He told her about Star. She cried even though she already knew.

When Abby and Lamb went to a wedding in Vermont she brought him to her room at their house, the first time he'd seen it. He walked around touching the shells and rocks, studying the photos of her and Caitlin. She played the tape of them singing "Dancing Queen," took off her clothes and lay on the bed beckoning to him, pretending to be a bad girl. For the first time he wasn't interested. "It's too weird, being in this room," he told her. "I feel like I'm doing something I'm not supposed to be doing."

That was the point, wasn't it?

She trained the young Dynamo cleaners, wondering if any of them were a team like she and Caitlin once were. She met with clients, organized the office, ordered supplies. She did her job so well Joanne offered to make her a partner after graduation. "Sure you work your butt off through September. But then you get to take it easy. You can marry your guy, have a couple of kids."

Vix didn't know what to say without hurting Joanne's feelings.

"So maybe it doesn't require a Harvard degree but you could always teach school during the year if that's what you want."

The problem was, she didn't know what she wanted. Except him. She wanted him.

Abby

DURING HER PARENTS' annual visit her mother says, *You look happy, Abby darling. You know that's all we want for you . . . to be happy.*

Thank you, Mother . . . I am happy.

But we don't understand why that friend of Caitlin's is still living with you. Do you think that's wise?

Wise?

Yes. Having a beautiful young girl in the house is tempting fate. You've got a good thing going. Why risk it? Remember what happened to Dory Previn when she let Mia Farrow into her life? Goodbye Andre! And don't forget Cousin Elinor!

Cousin Elinor sponsored an au pair from Norway and two years later watched as her husband and the au pair drove off into the sunset to live happily ever after, leaving Elinor with the children.

She tries to explain how different it is with Vix. *Vix is the daughter I never had, Mother. The daughter I've always dreamed of having.* Then, to assuage her mother's fears, she adds, *Besides, she's in love.*

It's serious? her mother asks and she can hear herself asking Vix the same thing.

Yes . . . I'm afraid so.

Her mother breathes a heavy sigh. *Well, I'm certainly relieved. Just make sure it stays that way.*

34

ON THE DAY Vix moved back into Leverett House to begin her senior year, Caitlin took off from LAX, on her way to Rio. "Think of it," she'd said to Vix. "Santiago, Lima, Buenos Aires . . . doesn't it sound exotic?"

By then Vix was used to the way Caitlin flitted around the world, like a bumblebee in search of the most exotic blossom. She'd lost interest in trying to dissuade her. Caitlin had her tuition money to blow on travel. She had a trust fund waiting.

"Well . . ." Abby said, "she'll always be able to find a job as an interpreter." Abby never stopped trying to come up with a positive take on the *children*. Vix didn't tell Abby Caitlin said the best way to learn a foreign language was to fuck interesting people.

She was too busy wondering and worrying about what was to come to devote any time or energy to Caitlin. And she wasn't alone. They all had *senioritis*. Though the end of their undergraduate days was in sight none of them felt ready for the real world, for life after college. Abby said, "That's why graduate school was invented." She urged Vix to take the LSAT or to think about The B-School. Some of Vix's friends were applying to graduate schools but others, like her, felt they needed to get out there. She couldn't go on as Abby's pet, as her personal charity.

She'd changed her concentration from English Literature to Social Anthropology during her junior year and had come up with what she hoped was an innovative idea for her senior thesis. *Five Minutes in Heaven*. Not the kissing game of Paisley's youth, but a video featuring disabled kids talking about their ideas of heaven. A thesis dedicated to Nathan. She would interview the kids on tape, then capture their ideas with stock footage and composites. If it was difficult to understand what they were saying, the way it would have been with Nathan, she'd use subtitles. To find the right kids she'd have to talk to twenty, maybe thirty. Somehow, she convinced Natalie Ponzo, professor of anthropology, to serve as her mentor. Maia couldn't believe her chutzpah.

She'd spent time in the editing room in the basement of Boyleston Hall last year, with a friend, Jocelyn, who was working on *her* senior thesis. From the moment she walked in and watched Jocelyn at work, she was hooked. Editing was like putting together jigsaw puzzles. You started off with a million little pieces and, if you did it right, wound up telling a coherent, interesting story.

Jocelyn was Haitian, from Brooklyn, and dreamed of making important documentaries like Fred Wiseman. But her father was pushing for law school. Was she going to waste her Harvard degree on some career that wouldn't pay chicken feathers or was she going to get out there and make him proud! "I am *not* going to law school," Jocelyn told Vix. "I'll get myself a decent day job, someplace where I have access to editing equipment, and I'll make him proud *my* way!"

Vix's parents weren't pushing for anything. Tawny had dropped out of her life, dropped out of all their lives, and her father's hopes and dreams for her, if he had any, were never articulated.

Maia thought she was lucky. "You don't have to live up to anyone's expectations but your own."

Caitlin called from Buenos Aires. "I'm studying dance."

"Dance?"

"Yes. Flamenco. I think I've found my true calling."

"Flamenco dancing?"

"Yes. I think it's important to pursue my talents at this time. I can always take academic classes but the day will come when I won't be able to dance."

The only kind of dancing she'd ever seen Caitlin do was disco. "Is this a career move?" Vix asked.

"God, Vix . . . listen to yourself! Not everything has to lead to a career. I'd rather have talent than a career."

"You mean a career based on your talent?"

"No . . . I mean just have the talent."

"But what would be the point?"

"Not everything has to have a point. Some things just are."

"That doesn't make any sense."

"Half of what I say doesn't make any sense to you."

"I'm listening. I'm trying to understand."

"No, you're not. You've already made up your mind."

"That's not fair."

"Maybe it's not . . . but that's what I'm hearing."

"Tell me about Argentina."

"I adore it here. I adore Argentine men."

"Tell me you're not going to be the next Evita."

"I'm not going to be the next Evita."

"Good."

"I suppose if I ask you to come for the summer you'll refuse?"

"Not necessarily."

"Vix . . . that would be incredible! Is it really a possibility?"

"I don't know. It all depends on jobs . . . and things . . ."

"Things being Bru?"

"Things being things."

"You'll let me know?"

"I'll let you know."

The children she interviewed were excited about sharing their ideas of heaven with her. Sometimes, in the middle of taping them, she'd find herself choking up, missing Nathan.

Heaven? I'm gonna get there real soon. I could try to let you know what it's like, if you tell me where you live. I'll call, Hey, Victoria . . . and when you look up you'll see me flying in the sky and I'll be wearing this beautiful blue dress and my hair will be so long it'll trail behind me. I might be on a horse, one of those angel horses with wings.

I think you gotta work up there. You gotta sign up for either angel or messenger or something like that. You got so many people down here to watch out for. They keep you real busy but you don't get tired. You're never tired. And no medicine either. Everyone's healthy. Strong. You know? Once a week you got to meet with God. Either him or St. Peter. You got to report on how things are going. But there's no wrong answers in heaven. There's no report cards.

Me? I'm gonna be a ballet dancer or maybe an ice princess like in the Olympics. Just twirl around all day and eat Fruit Roll-Ups.

Zillions of puppies . . . that's what they got up in heaven. The softest dogs you've ever seen. And no poop. I don't know what happens to the poop but it's not in heaven. Because heaven's clean. All those fluffy white clouds. And these zillions of puppies just jumping from cloud to cloud and you get to run and chase them all day.

Abby called Vix. "What can I do to help? Would you like something delivered to the editing room . . . something besides pizza?" Abby kept her in touch, kept them all in touch. Daniel was doing well in his second year at Yale Law, but not as well as he'd thought. Gus was finishing his master's in journalism at Columbia and had been offered a job in Albuquerque, of all places. Sharkey was turning into a brilliant scientist. And Caitlin, as she already knew, was a latter-day Zelda Fitzgerald with castanets.

"Should we start making plans for graduation?" Abby asked. "Are your parents coming? Can we throw a party or do you and Bru have other plans?"

She couldn't begin to think about graduation. She was consumed by her thesis. She discovered creative energies she didn't even know she had. She'd fall into bed exhausted after midnight and be up at six to start again. She had to keep up with her regular courses, too. Just because it was senior year she wasn't off the hook. This was Harvard, after all. And a Harvard degree stood for something. Just ask any graduate.

Bru said, "I'll be glad when it's done. I don't like anything that keeps us apart." He asked her to talk sexy to him over the phone. "Tell me what you want me to do to you. Tell me what you'd do to me." So she told him.

Natalie Ponzo talked up *Five Minutes in Heaven*. It was suggested she send a copy to WGBH. She had an interview with the producers of *Nova* who offered a summer internship but not a real job. She thanked them and sent a copy to Jocelyn, who was working at an industrial film production house in New York. Jocelyn showed the tape around but cautioned Vix against taking a job with her company. It was a job leading nowhere, she'd discovered. She had to waitress weekends to make ends meet. She'd already given notice. As of June 15 she was out of there to work nights as a word processor while she waited to hear from NYU film school, which meant more student loans, which she'd be paying back for the rest of her life, but hey . . . so was everybody else she knew.

Vix signed up for job interviews on campus. By the time she met Dinah Renko she'd had plenty of practice. She had her anecdotes down. They all liked the story of how she'd learned to swim at fourteen, were mildly interested in her work on the Mondale–Ferraro campaign. *Good hair can take you far.* And since they all loved Santa Fe there were plenty of questions about quality of life— *How about raising kids? Public school or private? Was the sky always so blue? Were drugs a problem? What about job opportunities?* Their questions had nothing to do with job opportunities for Vix. She was amazed that these people, who seemed to her to have it made, were already looking for a way out.

Dinah worked at Squire-Oates, a large PR firm in New York. "I liked your video," she told Vix. "That's really all that matters. The Harvard education doesn't hurt. It means you're intelligent. You'll have ideas. The rest of your résumé is very nice, but to tell the truth, it doesn't interest me."

Dinah was in her forties, with blunt-cut silver hair, a gray pants suit, and red heels that caught Vix's attention. Vix wore her usual black pants and white shirt. Maia, who'd bought a suit for interviews, told Vix *she* looked like a waitress. "At least wear a scarf, something to give you some style!" So Vix bought a silk scarf in the Square, an Hermès knockoff, and Maia taught her how to drape it. "Wear those silver earrings and your Santa Fe bracelet."

Dinah twirled a strand of hair around her finger as she spoke. "We're a very large corporation, Victoria, with offices around the world. There are opportunities for a hardworking, talented young woman like you. You won't be answering phones or filing. I can promise you that. This is not your typical entry-level job. You'll be working with captains of industry, editing from the start."

Vix nodded as Dinah spoke, making mental notes. *Captains of Industry. Editing from the start. Plays with her hair.*

"You'll get a decent, competitive salary and good benefits. You'll find an apartment share. You'll enjoy the city. And we'll be there for you, nurturing your career, moving you up as soon as you're ready." She checked her watch. "I've got to catch the 5:30 shuttle. Can you make quick decisions? Because I'd like a yes or no right now."

Actually, Vix didn't have a clue. She asked if she could give her an answer the following day.

Dinah sighed. "There are others who want this job. I won't even say how many. That's how tight the market is."

"I'll take it," Vix said. After, she couldn't believe she'd done it.

Paisley

SHE AND MAIA take Victoria to dinner to celebrate her job. She's the first of them to know what she's doing next year. When Maia asks, *What does Bru think?* Victoria knocks over her glass of red wine. It spills on the white cloth and onto Victoria's lap. In the commotion that follows, the question never gets answered.

She assumes that means Victoria hasn't told Bru yet. But she's sure he'll follow her anywhere. She's decided Victoria is impossibly lucky. Ever since she spent Labor Day weekend on the Vineyard and had the chance to get to know Bru, she's developed a teensy crush on him herself. Obviously, she's careful to keep these feelings to herself. She would never act on them except in her fantasies and fantasies don't count.

Or maybe what it's really about is seeing her friend adored by a great guy. Either way, Victoria has it made.

_____

BRU CAME TO SEE VIX the first weekend in May, during a freak spring storm that began as wet snow, turned into a serious thunderstorm, and knocked out half the power in Cambridge. Not that they cared. They were in bed most of the time. Bru pinned her wrists above her head and watched her face as he drove into her. It was fierce, possessive sex and it made her uneasy. Not that it didn't turn her on. Put her near Bru and like a knee-jerk response, her juices ran, her Power lit up. Her attraction to him never wavered.

When the rain ended they ventured out to walk along the muddy banks of the Charles. Vix longed for sunshine. She tied her new silk scarf around her neck and zipped her jacket. She'd been waiting for Bru to ask to see _Five Minutes in Heaven_. So far, he hadn't. She would offer to show it to him later, after dinner, then break the news about her job.

Suddenly he stopped and blocked her path, his hands on her shoulders. She couldn't tell from his expression what he was thinking. He took a small jeweler's box out of his pocket and handed it to her. "We don't have to get married right away," he said.

Married?

"We can wait a year if you want . . . but I need to know at the end of my wait you're going to be there for me. You're going to be my wife, have my kids . . ."

She opened the box and choked up as she looked at the tiny diamond set in gold, sparkling on blue velvet. Do you marry someone because the sex is good? Do you marry someone because you know, deep down, he's a decent person, even if you can't talk about the same books? She thought about the couples she knew—her parents, Lamb and Abby, even Loren and Tim Castellano. What was it that made them choose one another? How do you ever know it's right? "Come with me to New York," she said, urgently.

"Why would we go to New York?"

"I've been offered a job there."

"So tell them no."

"What about Boston?" she asked, grabbing at straws. "I could probably get a job in Boston."

"How many times do I have to tell you," Bru said, "I hate cities. They make me claustrophobic. I'm an islander . . . you know that."

"I just need some time to find out . . ."

"I put in indoor plumbing. I got a phone!"

She looked back at the ring. She sensed if they broke up now it wouldn't be like last time.

"If you can't say yes to marriage and island life that's it. I mean it. I've waited four fucking years for you. You're almost twenty-two. What's your problem?"

"I need vitamins?" she asked, trying to lighten it up.

She could see the disappointment in his eyes turn to anger. He grabbed the jewelry box out of her hand and for a minute she thought he might hurl it into the river. But no, he shoved it back in his pocket, too practical to give in to his emotions. They were a lot alike, weren't they? Two people who had trouble sharing their thoughts. Two people who kept everything inside. Had she mistaken his silence for depth? His wounded look for sensitivity? She didn't know. She didn't know anything except she wasn't ready. She couldn't promise him the rest of her life. She had no idea where she was going.

Her eyes filled. Her throat felt tight. Was she making the biggest mistake of her life? "Bru . . . please, let's not . . ." She tried to embrace him.

He pushed her aside. "I'm not enough for you anymore. That's it, isn't it?" He spit out the words. "The *island's* not enough . . . now that you're almost a *Harvard* graduate."

"You don't get it, do you?" she said. "It has nothing to do with Harvard . . ."

He let out an angry laugh. "Let me be the first to break the news, Victoria. *You're* the one who doesn't get it."

PART FOUR

*Didn't We Almost
Have It All
1987–1990*

35

SHE'D FINALLY ARRIVED. This was life after college, life in the real world. The world of *first, last, and security*. It gave her a heady feeling. She and Maia came to the city together, in June, and Paisley, who had an entry-level job at ABC, caught up with them a few weeks later. Maia took them both to Loehmann's. "Put yourselves in my hands," she said, gathering jackets, pants, and tops. "Trust me. No colors!" she scolded, when she caught Vix holding up a pink sweater. "Only neutrals. Sophisticated. Professional."

"But . . ." Vix began.

"Trust," Maia told her.

"This is worse than shopping with my mother," Paisley joked. Vix laughed with her, though she couldn't remember ever having shopped for clothes with Tawny.

Maia bought herself a pinstripe suit. Very investment banker. To go with her job on Wall Street as a trainee at Drexel Burnham. She was testing the waters before committing to an MBA. When the stock market crashed on October 19, the worst crash in history, with the Dow Jones average tumbling five hundred points in a single day, Maia became one of the first casualties. That night she sat glued to the tube, watching every financial show, looking for clues to the day's events. But they offered none. Her Wall Street friends from Harvard were totally freaked. Even seasoned pros were in a daze. Surprisingly, no bodies flew out of tall buildings. Instead, most of them picked themselves up and went back to work. Except for Maia. Axed on the very day she wore her pinstripe suit for the first time. Vix and Paisley took her to see *Fatal Attraction* to distract her, maybe not the best choice, considering, but boiled rabbit jokes were making the rounds.

By the end of the week Maia developed an assortment of symptoms, convincing herself she had ovarian cancer, like Gilda Radner. When the tests proved negative she called for applications to law school and signed up for an LSAT review course. "A pinstripe suit will never go out of style," she told Paisley and Vix. "I just don't know about big shoulders." A week later she found a part-time job filling in as an assistant to a real estate entrepreneur.

In early November Caitlin came to town, stopping in New York on her way back from Buenos Aires. She came directly from the airport to the apartment. She'd never met Maia and Paisley, who referred to her as Vix's childhood friend, but she dismissed them as quickly as she did the furnishings. "Cute . . . very post-college-working-girl." She wore jeans and a big sweater, no makeup. She'd let her hair grow long. She looked fabulous. Flamenco dancing must have agreed with her. She asked Vix to spend the weekend at Lamb's pied-à-terre at the Carlyle and while Vix threw her things together

Paisley, the gracious southern hostess, offered Caitlin wine and cheese, but Caitlin declined. "Maybe some other time?"

"So, you didn't like Buenos Aires?" Maia said.

"I liked it fine. But it's time to move on."

"Where will you go next?" Paisley asked.

"To Madrid, I think."

"What will you do there?"

"What I always do . . . study, gather experience, fuck interesting people."

"How lucky you are," Maia said, with a hint of sarcasm.

"You think so?"

"You're living out everyone's fantasy."

"Not everyone's."

In the taxi, on their way to the Carlyle, Caitlin gave Vix a flat package wrapped in red tissue paper. Vix opened it carefully and pulled out a gorgeous antique silk piano shawl, printed with poppies and edged in black fringe.

"For your graduation," Caitlin said, kissing Vix first on one cheek, then the other. "I always forget how much I miss you when we're apart. You look tired. You're not getting enough sex, are you?"

Vix laughed. "Maybe I look tired from too much."

"No," Caitlin said. "Not enough. I can always tell. Are you seeing anyone?"

"I've only been in the city a few months."

"A few months can be a long time. It used to feel like a long time when we were kids. Sometimes I wish we were twelve again. Don't you?"

"No. I wouldn't want to go through all that twice."

At the Carlyle Caitlin collapsed on the sofa in the living room. "Do you realize I left Buenos Aires twenty-two hours ago and I haven't really slept or had a proper meal since?" She picked up the phone and ordered dinner for two—shrimp and scallops over linguine, an arugula and radicchio salad, lemon tarts for dessert. While they waited she opened a bottle of chardonnay and poured them each a glass. "I want to hear everything about your work."

But when Vix began to talk Caitlin's eyes glazed over and Vix could tell she wasn't really that interested. Or maybe she was as genuinely tired as she claimed because halfway through dinner she put down her plate, stretched out on the sofa, and fell asleep. Vix covered Caitlin with a blanket, finished her meal, and carried the plates of uneaten food to the tiny kitchen, where she set them in the empty fridge.

Then she turned out the lights and sat in the darkness watching Caitlin sleep, the beautiful face relaxed, the long, lithe body curled up like a cat. Later, on her way to the bedroom, she touched Caitlin's hair, touched her cool cheek, the way she'd dreamed of touching her when they were children.

The next day Caitlin slept till noon. Vix had already finished the *Times* crossword puzzle and one of the lemon tarts left over from dinner.

"Thanks for last night," Caitlin said when she awoke.

"I didn't do anything."

"Yes, you did. You let me sleep." She wandered into the kitchen and opened the fridge. "Oh good. You saved everything." She came back with a plateful of cold linguine. "So now I want to hear all about your life," she said, slurping up a mouthful, "starting with Bru's proposal."

"There's not that much to tell."

"But he gave you a ring and you said *no*?" Caitlin prompted.

"I said I wasn't ready."

"It's supposed to be guys who aren't ready . . . guys who can't commit."

"I guess I'm an exception to the rule."

"You surprise me. I always thought you'd wind up married to him with a houseful of kids by the time you were thirty . . . leading an incredibly boring, ordinary life."

"How could I? I signed the NBO pact, remember?"

Caitlin laughed. "NBO or die! So you're *really* over him?"

"Yes, totally!" She was pleased at how sure of herself she sounded, considering that she'd called him just weeks ago, on a night she'd felt so blue, so alone, she could hardly bear it. Her hands had trembled and her mouth had gone dry when he'd answered. She should have hung up right away. Instead, haunted by the idea that he thought Harvard had turned her into an elitist, she'd said, "Just so you know . . . I hate snobs!" She regretted it the second the words were out of her mouth.

"Are you saying you've changed your mind?" he asked.

When she didn't respond he said, "Victoria?"

"I'm sorry," she whispered.

"Do me a favor . . . don't call again."

By the time she said, "I won't," he'd hung up the phone.

———————

That night Caitlin danced for her decked out in full flamenco—red and black dress cut down to reveal the tops of her breasts, a slit up to her crotch, her hair pulled back, a flower tucked behind her ear—heels and castanets clicking. A fiery, seductive dance that ended with her body on the floor . . . hands outstretched to her audience of one. When the music stopped Caitlin waited for her to make the next move. Finally, Vix cleared her throat and said, "I think we should go out . . ."

"You're sure?"

"I'm sure."

"So that was Caitlin," Maia said when Vix got back from the Carlyle on Sunday afternoon. She and Paisley were painting the kitchen cabinets a deep blue. "It doesn't take a shrink to see she's jealous of us . . . of Paisley and me. She doesn't want anyone in your life to be more important than her."

"You saw all that in ten minutes?" Vix asked, tossing her overnight bag on her bed.

"I saw it the second she walked in. And the way she turned up her nose at the wine Paisley offered . . ."

"Caitlin's complicated," Vix said, changing into a T-shirt and sweatpants.

"We're all complicated," Maia said. "And we've all had friends like her."

"I don't think so," Vix said, coming into the kitchen where she picked up a paintbrush, dipped it into the tray of blue paint, and got to work. "Oh, please . . ." Maia said. "There's a Caitlin in every junior high. You have to get over her and get on with your life."

"I am getting on with my life."

Paisley

SHE HAS TO SAY, she admires Victoria for her loyalty to the Phantom Friend, as well as for having the guts to tell Bru she wasn't ready. They never talk about him. The subject is off limits. Victoria says it's easier that way. She realizes *her* crush on him was just a momentary thing. She's way past imagining herself on a desert island with him, or any other island. Besides, there's this guy who's been pitching a sitcom to her boss . . .

36

THE PLACE THEY SHARED in Chelsea had just one bathroom, a tiny kitchen, and eight hundred square feet of open space. "Think of it as a loft," the rental agent had said, "in a very *now* neighborhood."

The week they'd moved in they constructed individual sleeping areas by hanging Indian print fabrics on rods suspended from the ceiling, making it look as if they were patients in some eclectic hospital ward. As far as privacy went, forget it. But with the threat of AIDS, with everyone talking about Safe Sex, they weren't exactly whooping it up.

Of the three of them only Paisley slept around, refusing to waste her youth worrying about some disease she wasn't going to get, because the men in her life were Ivy League types, from good families.

"At least insist they use condoms," Maia lectured regularly. She'd become so cautious she swabbed the toilet seat with alcohol before sitting on it, convinced Paisley was going to bring home herpes, or the papilloma wart virus, or trich at the very least. "You don't know who's bi, you don't know who's doing what with whom . . ."

Every Tuesday night they ate supper in front of the tube, watching *thirtysomething*. Was this where their lives were heading?

Vix's job at Squire-Oates had turned out different than she'd expected. *Working with Captains of Industry* translated into editing videotapes of corporate executives during an intensive three-day course in communication, each course geared to that specific individual's needs so he or she, but mostly he, could face a press conference with confidence when grilled about the latest mishap, lawsuit, merger, whatever, at the corporation.

It was up to Vix to catch their flaws on tape. Did he touch his balls, stroke his chin, do that thing with his jaw? Were his hands flying out of control as if he might take off at any moment? Was his speech clear and concise or did he stumble, mumble . . . and how about those long *aaahhhs*, as if he had a tongue depressor lodged in his throat while he was trying to come up with the answer to a tough question? Did she fiddle with her jewelry, lick her lips, constantly flick her hair away from her face?

In just three days, with endless practice in front of the agency's team of specialists, most of these Captains of Industry learned to face the camera and come off as trustworthy, believable individuals. It amazed Vix. She wondered why Dinah didn't take the course herself.

Dinah was as determined and ambitious as any of them, yet often couldn't make decisions. She'd sometimes drop a folder on Vix's desk. "Victoria, I'm giving you this one," she'd say, twisting a strand of hair around her finger or, if she was in a real bind, sucking on the ends. "Don't disappoint me."

Squire-Oates had an impressive client list and Vix found she was good at coming up with strategies for their campaigns to promote policies, personalities, and products. She decided she was more of an idea person than a technical one and looked forward to the day when Dinah, recognizing this, would come through on her promise to nurture her career.

In the meantime Dinah took full credit for Vix's suggestions. Vix wasn't in a position to complain. Unemployment was not on her agenda. Sometimes, when Vix started thinking about it, she'd get scared, not sure she was ambitious enough, determined enough, to make it in this city. Sometimes she felt old and tired. She hated it when Dinah referred to her as a *puppy*, reminding her of how young she was, of how she had her whole life ahead of her.

As a kid, Vix had had some warped idea that *grownup* meant having a job and living on your own. It meant no one could tell you what to eat, or what to wear, or how to behave. It meant it was okay to have sex with guys. What a joke! When she first came to New York she decided being *grownup* had to do with responsibilities, but then she'd think about her sister and change her mind. Lanie was hardly grownup although God knows she had responsibilities.

Lanie considered Vix a big success. She referred to Vix as her *rich* older sister. She'd constructed a fantasy about life in the Big Apple that was more 90210 than

10003. She was convinced Vix lived in a fabulous apartment, got expensive haircuts, and wore clothes right out of the pages of *Cosmo*. To Lanie, with her two little kids and the same useless husband, Vix's life seemed like Cinderella's after the ball—even without the Prince. Lanie didn't get that Vix was struggling, too. It was just a different kind of struggle, at a different level.

From what Vix had seen, having children didn't necessarily make you grownup. Besides, what about people who chose never to have them? She'd always felt uncertain about having kids because of Nathan. Not that she'd necessarily have a child with a physical disability but she knew what it was like to live with that kind of burden, the sacrifice it required, the strength, the love. Bru wanted a houseful of kids. Caitlin swore she would never have them. "Not everyone has to be a mother," she'd say. "A person can have a happy and fulfilling life without children."

A postcard from Caitlin dated December 2, 1987, Seattle.

Forget Madrid. This is it! I've finally found my place. It's young, it's cool . . . and I don't just mean the weather. Start packing.

Abby

SHE TRIES TO KEEP UP with all of them, sending addresses and phone numbers around the world so they can keep in touch with each other. She wishes Daniel and Vix would get together. Maybe someday . . . In the meantime she gives Vix's phone number to sons of her friends.

Lamb teases her, saying she should open a matchmaking service. Actually, not a bad idea. She enjoys helping people find happiness. But at the moment her plate is full. She's taken over management of the Somers Foundation. And none too soon. She's reorganizing from scratch. She never dreamed this was where life would take her.

Gus

HE DECIDES AGAINST the job offer in Albuquerque. He likes being around water too much. Blame it on all those summers on the Vineyard. He's lucky to get a second offer and jumps at the chance to write for the *Oregonian*. Aside from all that chauvinistic crap about keeping outsiders out, the people in Portland are friendly and the women are fresh, outdoorsy types.

When he's sent to Seattle in March to get a story on Microsoft he calls Caitlin and arranges to meet her for a drink. Abby's sent him her phone number. She's the chronicler of their lives. Caitlin arrives with two guys in tow. James and Donny.

Can you believe I once tried to seduce this guy, she tells them, pressing her thigh up against his. She and James and Donny fall all over themselves laughing, as if the idea of her seducing *him* is a sick joke. He's sorry he called. He doesn't need this.

So how's the Cough Drop? he asks to change the subject.

You mean you haven't heard?

Heard what?

She eloped with Bru. Just last week.

No way . . .

Does that surprise you?

Yeah, it surprised him.

Only joking, darling Gus! she tells him, taking his hand. And she dissolves into laughter again.

He gets out of there as soon as he can. Doesn't tell anyone he saw her.

37

ANOTHER PRESIDENTIAL election but this time Vix and Paisley were less than thrilled with the candidates. "At least *Barbara* will be better than *Nancy*," Paisley said, as if the election were over and the votes counted. "She's got a sense of humor. And she wears the same pearls as my grandmother."

Maia found their political discussions hilarious.

"I don't see how you can defend the Republican party after what happened to you," Paisley told her.

"Please," Maia said, "if your guys had been in office we'd be in the middle of a serious depression."

When the phone rang Vix couldn't find it. "Check in the bathroom," Paisley called. "Next to the toilet."

It was Caitlin. "Vix . . . where are you?"

"In the bathroom, actually."

"I mean where are you, as in, when are you coming? I've found the perfect place for us to live. It's furnished in antique wicker and there's a small garden. Roses, Vix . . . all year round. But you have to give me a date. They won't hold it for long."

What was she talking about?

"Vix . . ."

"Wait a minute. I'm losing you." She walked with the phone back to the kitchen. "I never said I was moving to Seattle . . . did I?"

"No . . ." she began. "But you'd mentioned you were disappointed with your job, so I assumed . . ." She paused. "I must have misunderstood."

"Besides," Vix said, "you never stay in one place long enough . . ." Why was she making excuses?

"It will be a year in November."

"Well, I'd love to come for a visit."

"Great. How about next week?"

Vix laughed. "I can't take off whenever I want. Maybe next summer. If you're still there. I need to save up some money first."

"I'll send you a ticket."

"No . . . don't."

"Same old Vix."

But she wasn't the same old Vix. She wasn't fourteen anymore, or even seventeen. She'd graduated from Harvard, survived a year in the city on her own, a year of working for Dinah Renko.

It was true she'd grown bored at Squire-Oates. Last week she'd tried speaking to Dinah about her job, but Dinah hadn't been in a listening mood. "Your generation hasn't learned to pay its dues, Victoria," she'd said. "Just because you have a Harvard degree doesn't mean you can run the company."

"I don't want to run the company. I just want to try something besides editing the Captains of Industry. It's been a year. You told me when I first interviewed there would be opportunities."

Dinah had gained twenty pounds since they'd first met, but it showed only in her face and upper body. She'd taken to wearing short skirts with tunics and Vix wondered how she kept from toppling over in the three-inch red heels she favored to show off her legs, her best feature. She had two young children, both in private school, and a husband who'd lost his job in publishing and was now at home trying to write a novel. Once, when she'd brought the kids to work, she'd dumped them on Vix. "I'm sure you can find a way to amuse them," she'd said. They'd wrecked the place in an hour.

"This job is an opportunity!" Dinah's voice rose. "Working with *me* is an opportunity! But not if you're without patience."

She was not without patience but by now she knew Dinah was never going to set her free. And moving to Seattle wasn't the answer.

The next morning on her way to work Vix stopped to listen to the Bag Lady on the corner of Fifty-sixth and Sixth as she sang her version of "Lullaby of Broadway," substituting *Timbuktu* for *ballyhoo*. When Vix dropped a few coins into her cup, the Bag Lady looked directly at her and nodded. For the first time Vix saw the person inside the beggar. She worried that whatever had happened to this Bag Lady could happen to her.

She began to make discreet inquiries. Three weeks later she accepted an offer from Marstello, a boutique PR firm with an eclectic list of clients, and the next day when she passed the Bag Lady, she dropped a dollar bill into her outstretched cup. The Bag Lady responded with "You've Got a Friend."

Dinah was furious. "I discovered you. Why didn't you come to me if you were unhappy?"

"I did come to you."

"Really . . . when was that?"

"Not very long ago."

"I don't remember."

Had she made so little impression?

"You owe me an explanation," Dinah said, chewing on the ends of her hair.

Fine, Vix thought. Here's your explanation. "This job isn't taking me in the right direction. And I've been offered one where I'll be working directly with clients."

"You're going to another PR firm?"

"Yes."

"Which one?"

Vix paused. Should she tell Dinah?

"I'll find out anyway," Dinah said.

"Marstello."

Dinah laughed. "Marstello! You'll be lucky if your paycheck doesn't bounce."

"I'm sorry, Dinah. I've done my best here. My decision has nothing to do with you personally."

Dinah shouted, "I want you out by five!"

"But what about . . ."

"By five, you ungrateful little bitch!" She picked up an Empire State paperweight and Vix ducked. This was the professional world?

"Vix . . . I have the most exciting news! Did I wake you? Sorry."

It was after midnight on a rainy October night. Caitlin never could keep the time difference straight, no matter how many times she reminded her. And hanging up, just to teach her a lesson as Maia had suggested more than once, seemed harsh. Maia was now a law student at Columbia. *Do you know what happens to the sleep deprived?*

"I'm going into business," Caitlin said. "A restaurant. I feel I've finally found my calling. And my partners are fantastic. James and Donny? I think I've mentioned them to you. They're a couple. Anyway, it's going to be down by the water. Lots of glass, clean, spare. We've hired a fabulous architect. And we're bringing in one of the finest chefs in the city. But here's the best . . . we're calling it *Eurotrash*. After me. Don't you love it? We're hoping to open in June. It sounds so far away, but really, it's not. So start calling the airlines to get the best deal. I'm going to work the front. I'll wear all black, only black, very chic . . . very elegant. Of course if you'd made the move *you'd* be doing our PR. But that's beside the point now. So what do you think?"

She sounded so happy and excited Vix had to wish her well. "And guess what else? I've sworn off sex. James and Donny are helping me. They make me happier than any straight man ever could. I was an addict, you know? Like some guy following his pointer through life. But now I'm free."

Vix hadn't exactly sworn off sex but it had been a long time since Bru. She dutifully went out on blind dates with sons of Abby's friends, not that she could remember one from the other they were all so alike. And one night she'd gone to a downtown party with Jocelyn and had wound up in the bathroom with a scruffy, sexy filmmaker who'd kissed her breasts while she gave him a hand job. They hadn't exchanged names or numbers and when she thought about it the next day she was glad. Too dangerous. A heartbreaker. Instead, she satisfied herself with fantasy lovers—sometimes reliving the moment in the truck with Bru and the peonies. And once, but only once, playing out the night of Caitlin's flamenco dance and how it might have ended.

Paisley was conducting a flirtation with an older man at ABC and Maia . . . Maia worried every time she met a new guy about how it would end, how bad she'd feel when it did, how long it would take her to get over him, whether it was even worth the trouble in the first place. She had no time or energy for bad relationships. Celibacy was the key to making Law Review.

Paisley said, "What's the point of thinking about how it's going to end when it's just beginning?"

"Ask Victoria," Maia told her.

But Paisley didn't ask. Instead she said, "Some people never get over their first loves. They spend their whole lives trying to recapture the thrill. Sometimes, after fifty years they get back together. They meet at some reunion or other and realize they were meant to be together."

"Do you have anyone in mind?" Vix asked. "Or are you talking in the abstract?"

"Abstract," Paisley said. "Strictly abstract. Though it's not a bad concept for a show. I may just write a treatment and pitch it to my boss."

As they were planning their holidays, wrapping Christmas gifts while Paisley's holiday cookies baked in the oven, Vix heard a familiar voice on the tube and looked up to see one of the Captains of Industry, an international expert in the field of aviation, commenting on a disaster. She shushed the others and moved closer. *PanAm . . . Lockerbie, Scotland . . . carrying home Americans . . . many of them students . . .* Vix motioned for Paisley and Maia. Together they listened to the grim news, as the Captain of Industry spoke with representatives of the airline. He came across as sincere, honest, and caring. Vix remembered him. She remembered the ones who had the most trouble.

Ed

HE'S WATCHING THE NEWS when she calls. As soon as he hears her voice his stomach sours. She doesn't call more than once a month and he's expecting her to wait until Christmas. Does she have bad news? Does she know something about Lewis? He's not sure where Lewis is. Germany, he thinks. But no reason to believe he'd be on Pan Am when he can fly military. And Tawny? Hell, she could be anywhere, anywhere the Countess is, but the Countess isn't traveling anymore, is she? No. He doesn't think so.

Vix reassures him. *Everything's fine,* she says. *I was going to wait until Christmas but I thought I might have trouble getting through.* He knows she's been watching the news. Same as him. He knows his girl. They don't talk for long. He's never been one for long conversations. *Everything's about the same here,* he tells her. *No news is good news, as your mother used to say.* He doesn't say he misses her. Doesn't say he hopes she'll come to visit soon. *How are things up your way?* he asks. She tells him her job is interesting. *Can't ask for more than that,* he says, *can you?*

When he hangs up, Frankie asks who was on the phone. He tells her it was Vix. She says, What does it take to get that girl to come for a visit?

38

ABBY INTRODUCED VIX to the School Volunteer Program the same way she introduced her to eligible young men. Vix signed up and every Wednesday night from six to eight she tutored a sixteen-year-old dropout, D'Nisha Cross, who was trying to get her GED.

"Cool name, huh?" D'Nisha said at their first meeting. "Sound like a movie star or a rapper, don't it?"

"Very cool," Vix agreed.

When D'Nisha came to Vix's place she checked it out, circling around a couple of times. "You could blade in here," she told Vix. For a minute Vix felt guilty to be sharing eight hundred square feet with two friends while D'Nisha lived in the projects with who knows how many relatives. She had to remind herself it was okay, unfair maybe, but okay.

"You read all these books?" D'Nisha asked, running her hand across a shelf of paperbacks.

"Not all, but a lot."

"I like to read but not the stuff they gave us in school."

"Starting tonight you can choose whatever you want."

"Cool." She browsed for a minute. "You married?"

"No."

"Got a boyfriend?"

"No."

"A computer?"

"At work."

"I gotta learn computer. You learn computer you get a job."

Vix made a note to pick up some computer intro books.

"You got luck?" D'Nisha asked.

Was this some code word? A new drug? "What do you mean by *luck*?" Vix said, cautiously.

"Shit . . ." D'Nisha looked at her as if she were hopeless, a person who just didn't get it. "You know . . . good things happen when you got it? Nothin' happens when you don't."

"Oh, *that* luck."

"You know another kind?"

"Not really."

"So?"

"Sometimes I have it," Vix told her, "but not always. How about you?"

"Not yet. But I keep waitin'."

Luck. Luck had changed her life, hadn't it? Sometimes, when she couldn't sleep she played the What If game. What if Caitlin hadn't chosen her for her summer sister? What if Abby and Lamb hadn't taken a personal interest? What if Nathan hadn't died or she hadn't gone to Harvard or she'd married Bru? What would her life be like? Would she be happy, fulfilled?

She was a great believer in luck. Every week she bought a lottery ticket from the newsstand near her office because, as the guy in the commercial said, *Hey . . . you never know . . .* She even signed up for a junket to Atlantic City in early April just to see what all the hoopla was about. Gus had taught her to play poker the summer she was seventeen, the last summer they'd shared the house with the Chicago Boys. He'd been impressed with her stone-cold expression. *You don't give away a thing, do you, Cough Drop?*

Never, she'd told him.

Sometimes she dreamed about how it would feel if her ship came in. About how she would spend all that money. But she wasn't as certain now as she'd been at fourteen.

She withdrew a hundred dollars from the ATM near her office in preparation for her trip. But she didn't take her checkbook or credit cards. That way there'd be no danger of blowing more than she could afford, not that she could afford even a hundred, given her salary and expenses, but just this once couldn't hurt.

Maia and Paisley were heading out to the Hamptons to look for a summer share. They'd wanted her to join them but Vix said, "Not this weekend."

"She's probably got a hot date lined up and doesn't want us to know," Maia joked.

"Something like that," she told them.

For added luck, she wrapped her piano shawl over her raincoat. She felt exotic when she wore it, like a flamenco dancer. And if she didn't exactly find *luck* in Atlantic City, she found Luke. She wouldn't tell Maia and Paisley they met at the craps table. No one ever had to know the truth unless she and Luke wound up together. Then Maia would say, *Can you believe Vix met Luke at a casino in Atlantic City? At the craps table?*

No, they wouldn't believe it. She kept her impulsive side to herself. She'd once overheard Maia telling a friend at school, *Victoria is the least spontaneous person in our entire class, but I'd trust her with my life.*

Actually, she didn't really *meet* Luke at the craps table. She watched him. He was hot, on a roll, with a stack of chips in front of him that doubled and tripled every time he threw the dice. He was boyish, flush with excitement. She didn't know it was a twenty-dollar table until she tried to place a bet. Embarrassed, she quickly retrieved her dollar chips. She hung around to watch anyway, as the crowd cheered Luke on, betting with him. He looked up once, caught her eye, and smiled.

At the end of the day, as she was playing a slot machine, he came up behind her, dropped a quarter into the slot, covered her hand with his, and pulled the handle. Three cherries, clanging bells, and twenty . . . thirty . . . fifty dollars' worth of quarters came spilling out. He caught them in a cup as she stood with her hands over her mouth, fighting the urge to jump up and down and shriek. "Some days you just can't lose," he said.

He was slight, just her height, charming, with bedroom eyes. "Have dinner with me," he said. When she didn't answer right away he pulled out his wallet, fished out his driver's license with its photo ID, held it up for her to see. "Luke Garden," he told her. "New York

City. Thirty-one, single, respectable, straight, Cornell '80, sports management. I just won *big*!"

So she had dinner. She told him her name was D'Nisha Cross. She told him she worked at ABC, in development. Two things borrowed, nothing blue.

"Stay," he said after dinner. "I've got a suite. Two bedrooms, two bathrooms. You get to sleep wherever you want. Really. Here . . ." He pushed a key at her. "Check it out."

So she checked it out. While he filled the Jacuzzi tub, turned on the music, and turned down the lights, she wrapped the piano shawl around her naked body like a strapless gown. When the scene was set he slowly unraveled it, letting it fall to the floor.

The next morning he was gone. She found him in the casino, playing blackjack. She took the next bus back to New York and never said a word to anyone. If she were Paisley, she'd write his name on her list. But she didn't need to write down names. For her there was still only one that counted. Only one she'd loved.

A postcard from Caitlin, dated April 4, 1989, Seattle.

Ran into some bad luck. Donny sick. Plans for restaurant postponed. Will call when I can.

Abby

SHE TELLS LAMB they should get on the first plane to
Seattle and see what's going on for themselves. But
Lamb says they have to allow Caitlin, and all the grown
children, to work out their own lives. To solve their own
problems. How else are they going to learn to make
their way in the world?

This friend of hers, Donny, who's in hospice care, has
the disease. Not that Caitlin's said anything, but she can
read between the lines. She admires Caitlin for wanting
to be there for her friend but she can't help worrying.
She's been reading everything she can find on the subject and it's horrifying, even if it's not contagious in the
usual way. And really, how can they be sure Caitlin
hasn't been intimate with someone . . .

Another postcard arrives asking them to respect her
time with Donny. Please don't leave messages on her
machine. She can't return their calls right now. And tell
Vix, will you, that she's not out of touch, she's just . . .
preoccupied.

VIX WAS WORKING on three accounts at Marstello—a former Miss America starting her own line of cosmetics, a political consultant who had written a memoir, and an off-off-Broadway theater company they were representing pro bono. She'd become friendly with Earl, the writer/producer/director and sometimes hung out at the theater in the evening, watching rehearsals. Earl was ruthless in his revisions. He never threw the rejected scenes into a wastebasket like a normal person. He was paranoid enough to think someone might find his discarded work and plagiarize it so he bought a mini shredder, a cheapie on sale at Staples. He could feed it just a page at a time. Watching him, Vix sometimes wondered what would happen if you could do that with real life. *Revise and shred.*

She dropped a few notes to Caitlin, saying she was thinking of her and hoping it was going okay with Donny. Earl had already lost two of his closest friends and was sure his own days were numbered. She didn't share that with Caitlin. She tried not to think of it herself.

She brought in her first major client, a cutting-edge fashion designer. When Vix asked how she had heard of *her*, the designer said, "Caitlin Somers."

"You know Caitlin?"

"We met in Milan. I was an apprentice at Gucci. Caitlin did some modeling for us. We got to be friendly. I ran into her in Seattle. She told me to look you up now that I've got my own shop . . . says you're the best. You are, aren't you?"

Gus

CAITLIN CALLS HIM on June 5, screaming, *Goddamn it, Gus, you're a reporter, aren't you? Why aren't you doing something about this massacre?*

The massacre's in China, he reminds her, *but even if it weren't, what do you think I can do?*

I'm not talking about Tiananmen Square, you fucking idiot! I'm talking about here. People are dying. Does that mean anything to you?

Okay . . . let's start again, he says.

What's the point? She slams down the phone.

What was that all about? Should he call someone? Abby and Lamb? No. No need to upset them. Maybe Vix? But what would he say?

39

PAISLEY DRAGGED HER to a fall fundraiser at the public library, where they filled in at the ABC corporate table. Paisley was becoming known on the benefit circuit and told Vix and Maia it was a great way to network, not to mention meet the right men. Vix gave in and bought a dress on sale at Bloomingdale's. Black lace top. Elegant yet sexy, the salesperson told her.

Will approached her on the grand staircase where she'd stopped to watch the dancing below. "Great cheekbones," he said.

"A gift from a Cherokee ancestor," she told him. She'd been waiting a long time to try that line.

"A drop of Cherokee blood means the tribe can claim you forever, but not before I claim you for the night." He extended his hand. "C. Willard Trenholm. But my friends call me Will."

"Victoria Leonard."

"Glad to meet you, Victoria." He guided her down the stairs and out onto the dance floor. He was tall, maybe six five, and even in heels she came up only to his chest. He knew how to fox-trot, waltz, and lindy hop, all to music played by Peter Duchin himself. *If her family could see her now!*

She heard Bru's voice chiding her but she pushed it away and concentrated on her feet, trying to avoid being trampled or, worse yet, stepping on Will, since she had no idea how to dance that way.

Later Paisley approached to say she'd met someone and was leaving with him. "Take a cab home, Victoria . . . okay? I mean it, no subways tonight."

Vix nodded, then returned to the dance floor with Will. She didn't have to worry about getting home. He took her to the Rainbow Room for a nightcap and to admire the view. In the cab on the way back to her place, they made out like teenagers. When the taxi pulled up in front of her building, Will leaned forward and told the driver to go around the block again.

She saw him three times that week. And the weekend after that. He sent flowers to her at home and Godiva chocolates to her office.

"A person could get used to this," Maia sang.

Vix began to flirt with the idea of being a rich girl, of never having to worry about money again. *You were wrong when you told me I wouldn't fit in* . . . she'd say to Tawny.

Money was Will's favorite subject, sex his second. He chased her around his family's Park Avenue duplex, playing hide-and-seek in the gallery, which was lined with suits of armor, like a museum. In the forest green library he unbuttoned her shirt and admired her breasts. "Beautiful," he said. "Are they implants?" She assured him they were the real thing. "I thought so," he said, "but you hardly ever get the real thing these days."

He invited her to the ballet. She'd never been and borrowed a crushed velvet suit from Paisley. The following week it was Shakespeare at the Public, followed by dinner at Chanterelle.

Maia began to call her The Heiress.

"She wouldn't be inheriting," Paisley said, setting the record straight. "She'd be acquiring."

"Either way . . ." Maia said.

That night the three of them sat around the coffee table, eating Chinese food from the cartons, while they watched *Don't Look Now* on the VCR. As Julie Christie and Donald Sutherland chased one another around Venice, Maia said, "I hope Vix will invite us to Venice . . . to her palazzo on the Grand Canal."

"Mmm . . ." Paisley shoveled in chicken with cashews. "I've always wanted to see Venice."

"How do you feel about Cincinnati?" Vix asked. "Because that's where the business is based. That's where the patriarch has his palazzo."

Will had his own place in the East Sixties with a view of the Russian Consulate. "I think of you every night, Victoria," he said, breathing heavily, when he finally took her there. His hand was under her skirt. "Have you been thinking of me? Have you?"

Well, yes . . .

Will had a king-size bed, a gray comforter, down pillows. When he kneeled over her sporting a hot pink condom she thought, a penis dressed as Malibu Barbie, and she tried not to giggle. Maybe her mother was right. Maybe the rich *were* different.

She was flattered by his attention and curious about his world but she couldn't say she was in love with him.

She found him arrogant and, at times, even boring. They spent a long rainy weekend at an expensive inn in the Berkshires. While he read *Forbes*, *Barrons*, the *Financial Times*, Vix found herself fantasizing about Bru.

At Sunday brunch Will said, "Tell me about your family, Victoria. Aside from the fact that you're from Santa Fe I don't know anything about you."

"What you see is what you get, Will."

"But what does your family *do* there?"

"My father manages a restaurant and my mother is the amanuensis to the Countess de Lowenhoff." She was glad to finally have the chance to use Abby's description of her mother's job.

"Restaurant . . ." he said, raising his eyebrows. "Amanuensis. How charming. What about your grandparents?"

"There are no grandparents." She smiled at him. "Are you checking out my ancestry, Will?"

"I'm interested in everything about you, Victoria."

"Well . . . my sister's on welfare and my brother enlisted on his eighteenth birthday. I went all through school on scholarships. I owe my benefactors everything. They invested in my future so I could hold my own with snobs like you."

Will laughed, then applauded. "Brilliant!" He leaned over and kissed her. "You should write novels, Victoria. With your imagination and flair . . ."

What was she doing with him?

On the drive back to the city she decided to end it. "I've enjoyed our time together, Will . . . but I don't think we should continue to see each other."

She waited for his reaction, then realized he hadn't

heard a word she'd said. She leaned forward and snapped off the CD player.

"What?" he asked.

"It's over, Will."

"No, it's not. He does 'Say You Say Me' next."

"I'm not talking about Lionel Ritchie, I'm talking about us."

"What about us?"

"It's over . . . we're over. *Fini, finis, finito.*"

"But we're just getting started," Will argued.

"That should make it easier."

"Give me one good reason to end it now."

"We have nothing in common."

He took her hand and pressed it to the front of his pants. "We have this."

She shook her head.

"Oh, come on, Victoria . . . just one more time . . . so you'll have something to remember me by."

She hadn't expected him to let go so easily and was angry at herself for feeling disappointed.

"Feel how hot he is for you. He's been such a good boy, waiting patiently all day."

"Sorry, Will. Send him my regards . . . I mean, my regrets." She opened the door at the next red light, grabbed her bag, and jumped out of his car.

"Really Victoria . . . you're hopeless," Paisley said. "Not that I'm pushing marriage. I'm all for making a life on your own first, but if it falls out of a tree and hits you on the head, you can't just walk away from it, especially when it comes with that kind of financial security. I mean, do you know how few straight, stable, single guys there are in this city . . . not to mention *husband* material? You could count them on one hand. *One hand.*"

"Your southern roots are showing, Pais," Maia said.

"Maybe," Paisley said. "Or maybe it's that a person never gets over her first love."

"Not that old song again," Vix said.

Her life was full. It was interesting. A person didn't necessarily have to be in love. She signed up for a yoga course, took on another student through the School Volunteer Program, vowed not to waste her introductory membership at Crunch. She met Jocelyn for lunch a couple of times and confessed she'd never experienced the creative high of *Five Minutes in Heaven* in the real workplace. They talked about doing a documentary together, forming their own production company. "You have to keep chasing your dreams," Jocelyn said.

A postcard from Caitlin, dated December 20, 1989, Zacatecas, Mexico.

I've seen death and it's ugly. Ugly and frightening.

No mention of James or Donny. Vix called the Seattle number, was told it was disconnected at the customer's request. She called Abby, trying not to show her concern, and told her she'd misplaced Caitlin's number.

Abby said, "She's in Mexico, Vix. At a monastery. You can't call. None of us can."

New Year's Eve. They decided to stay at home—Maia, Paisley, and Vix—to celebrate together. They ordered in, rented *Annie Hall*, and Vix laughed, then cried, remembering the night Lamb had taken Caitlin and her to see it. And after, how they'd begged to ride the Flying Horses but instead had found Von in the alley with some girl's hand wrapped around his Package.

By ten, friends began to drop in—Jocelyn, Earl, Debra. Each of them brought a few of their friends. They sent out for more food. Abby and Lamb called from Mexico City to wish Vix a happy New Year. They were on their way to the monastery, hoping to see Caitlin. "Send her my love," Vix said. "Wish her a happy New Year for me." Daniel and Gus phoned from Chicago, where Gus was visiting his family. They sounded smashed. So what? It was New Year's Eve. They'd thought of her, just as she'd thought of them. Old friends. Coming of age together. The end of one decade, the beginning of another.

40

On a Wednesday morning in late March, just after Vix stepped out of the shower, the phone rang. It was the woman named Frankie calling from Santa Fe. Vix's father had had chest pains during the night. He was in the hospital. They didn't know yet how serious it might be. Could she come right away? She called Angela, her boss, at home, explained the situation, threw some things into a bag, and headed for the airport.

The news in Santa Fe was better than she'd expected. Her father had had a severe angina attack, but no real heart damage. By the time she got there they'd done angioplasty to remove the blockage. He was asleep. Frankie, an ample woman in sweats, with rusty hair, freckled skin, and fringed moccasins, gave Vix a hug. "Thanks for coming, sweetheart. We're mighty lucky."

Vix excused herself to use the public phone in the hall where she called Tawny. "I'm in Santa Fe," she told her. "Dad's sick . . . it's his heart." For a minute Tawny didn't respond and Vix thought they'd been disconnected. "Hello . . ." she said. "Are you still there?"

"I'm here," Tawny said quietly. "Does it look serious?"

"How can it not be serious? I just told you, it's his heart!"

"Get hold of yourself, Victoria. They can do a lot these days. There are procedures . . ."

"He's already had the *procedure*."

"That's good."

"Are you coming? That's all I want to know."

"I'm not married to him anymore. He's not my responsibility."

"I didn't know the divorce was final."

"It's final enough."

"Well, nobody told me."

"How can I tell you if you never call?"

"I have a phone, too, you know, but I haven't had any calls from Key West lately." She waited for Tawny to say something. Anything. When she didn't, Vix said, "Is that it, then? That's all you have to say about the man you were married to for . . ." She tried to remember how many years it had been.

"Send your father my wishes for a speedy recovery, Victoria."

"Send them yourself!" She slammed the receiver down, then looked around, chagrined, as the other people in the waiting room quickly looked away. After all, they had their own problems. She had no idea how to get in touch with Lewis so she tried Lanie's number next. Amber answered. "Mommy's in the bathroom with Ryan. He's got diarrhea. Who's this?"

"Aunt Victoria, from New York."

"Mom . . ." Amber shouted into the phone, "it's *Anti-Vix*!" She pronounced it as if it were some right-wing political group. "Mommy says hang on. She's coming."

"Well, this is a surprise," Lanie said.

"I'm in Santa Fe. At the hospital. Dad has a heart problem but he should be okay."

"They called you before me?"

"Let's not argue about it, okay? Can you come up?"

"Yeah . . . I suppose."

"Good."

"You think he'll last the night?"

"I certainly hope so!"

"Then I'll come tomorrow."

When Lanie got there Ed was sitting up eating apple-sauce. His color had improved. The doctor had checked him earlier. He could go home in a day or two with a new diet, an exercise plan, and beta-blockers. Frankie fussed with his pillows, offered water. Amber and Ryan were fascinated by the equipment monitoring Ed's heart until they discovered the buttons to raise and lower the hospital bed. Lanie grabbed each of them by an arm and dragged them into the hall. You could hear her scolding, telling them to behave or she'd let them have it.

Vix offered to watch the kids while Lanie visited with Ed. She took them down to the coffee shop where they ordered chocolate ice cream with strawberry syrup, whipped cream, and sprinkles. Amber asked Vix for a pony and if not a pony something from F.A.O. Schwarz, which she pronounced *Fa-oh*.

"How do you know about F.A.O. Schwarz?" Vix asked.

"From the movie *Big*. We have the tape. I've seen it a hundred million times."

"Oh, right . . ."

"Mommy says you're rich. So how come you won't buy us ponies?"

"Actually, I'm not rich."

"How come?"

"I just don't make that much money."

"Mommy says you spend it all on yourself, when you could be helping us."

"Mommy's wrong." She had to remind herself Amber was just six years old and Ryan, not even five.

"Grandpa spends it on the Cow," Ryan said.

"What cow?" Vix asked.

"The one sitting in Grandpa's room," Amber said, answering for him.

"Frankie? You mean Frankie?" Vix said.

"Uh-huh." Ryan smiled.

"It's not nice to call her a cow," Vix said.

"But it's funny," Ryan told her. Now he was laughing, his face a mess of chocolate and strawberry.

"Frankie's a good friend to your grandpa," Vix said.

"Frankie's a good friend to herself," Amber said.

Vix couldn't believe the lines Lanie was feeding her kids.

"My mom works three jobs," Amber said proudly. "She takes care of horses, she cleans houses, and she pumps gas. Plus she takes care of us. How many jobs do you have?"

"Only one at the moment."

"My dad doesn't have a job," Ryan said. "But he doesn't yell at us like Mom."

"Will you take me to New York?" Amber asked.

"Maybe someday," Vix said. "When you're older." *A lot older* . . .

Ed came home from the hospital the next day and the day after that he urged Frankie to go back to work.

"You're absolutely sure, Chick Pea?" she asked.

"Go on now," Ed told her. "I've got my own private nurse."

Frankie looked at Vix for confirmation. Vix said, "It's okay . . . really."

When they were finally alone, her father said, "Big surprise, eh? Thought the old heart would just keep ticking, you know?"

"Well, now it will."

"Till the next time."

"The next time won't be for twenty years, at least."

"Twenty years. How old will you be then?"

"Forty-four, almost forty-five." She couldn't imagine herself middle-aged.

"Think you'll be married by then, have some kids?"

"I don't know. Maybe."

"Or maybe you're going to be one of those career women."

"Every woman's a career woman these days, Dad." She sat beside him, took his hand. "One of my roommates is in law school and the other one is climbing up the ABC ladder so fast she'll probably be running the network by the time she hits thirty."

He smiled at her. "You're a good girl, Vix. Always were. I told Frankie, 'Vix is dependable. She'll come if you need her.' "

Vix swallowed hard.

"How's Caitlin? You see her lately?"

She shook her head. "Not lately."

"Too bad. Got to keep in touch with your old friends. Old friends know you best."

She nodded.

"You call Tawny?"

"Yes."

"How'd she take it?"

"She hopes you get better soon. She sends her love."

"Love, huh? That's a good one." He laughed. And Vix laughed with him.

Vix was grocery shopping at Kaune's, stocking up on heart healthy foods for him, when she wheeled her cart into the fresh produce aisle and found Phoebe, selecting avocados. "I'm thinking of a chicken and guacamole salad," Phoebe said, as if she and Vix were in the middle of a conversation. "What do you think?"

"High in cholesterol. Avocados, that is." Vix tried to remember the last time she'd seen Phoebe, but couldn't. Phoebe looked fantastic. She could have passed for Caitlin's big sister. Vix wondered if she had staples in her scalp.

"I suppose you know Caitlin's on the Vineyard," Phoebe said.

Vix dropped the honeydew melon she was holding. It split open, spilling its runny guts all over the floor.

Phoebe went right on talking, as if she hadn't even noticed. "She says she needs to get back to basics. She's going to raise sheep and spin wool and live a simple life.

She thinks she's Rumpelstiltskin," Phoebe said. "Or maybe it's Rapunzel. I always confuse the two."

"Rapunzel's the one with the hair," Vix heard herself saying, as a guy with a mop appeared and began to clean up the mess.

Phoebe sniffed a box of strawberries. "Mmm . . . sweet. Want some?"

"My father's allergic to strawberries."

"Too bad. How's he doing?"

"Pretty well, considering."

"Send him my best."

"I will."

As she began to push her cart away Phoebe turned. "Vix . . . give Caitlin a call."

Phoebe

SHE HADN'T MEANT to take Vix by surprise. That look
on her face. The way she'd dropped the melon. *Gads!*
She was sure Vix would have known. After all, the two of
them were inseparable, weren't they? She couldn't begin
to guess what game Caity was playing this time. Not
that Caity tells *her* anything. Never has. Not really.
She's missed that part of the mother-daughter relationship. She has the feeling Vix has, too. Ah well . . .
maybe they'll do a better job with their daughters. The
idea of Caity having a daughter makes her laugh, until
she realizes that would make *her* a grandmother! Now
there's an experience she can do without for another ten
years, at least.

"I'M TRYING TO give my life meaning," Caitlin said when Vix called. "Does that make any sense to you?" When Vix didn't answer right away Caitlin added, "Why am I asking you? Your life has always had meaning."

"You sure you're not confusing *meaning* with *struggle*?"

"How do I know? Do you think by trying not to be ordinary I've become neurotic?"

"Are you seeing a shrink . . . is that what this is about?"

"Of course I'm seeing a shrink. Do you know anyone who isn't . . . besides you?"

"I can't afford therapy."

"I'm sure Abby would help."

"Is that a jab?"

"Does it feel like one?"

"Yes." After a long pause Vix said, "I'm sorry about your friend."

"Friends."

"Both of them?"

"I'd rather not discuss it. My shrink is helping me understand that my involvement was inappropriate. In my quest for family I mistook them for . . . Oh, what's the difference? Remember when John Lennon was killed? Remember how Lamb fell apart?"

"Not really."

"Well, he did. Flying me in from New Mexico so I could keep the midnight vigil with him. Also inappropriate, in case you're wondering."

"Are you sure your shrink is . . . qualified?"

"Can anyone ever be sure? It depends on the results, doesn't it?"

"I guess . . ." Another long pause then Vix said, "I thought you were in Mexico, at a monastery. Why didn't you let me know you were on the Vineyard?"

"You sound angry. Are you angry?"

"Why would I be angry?"

"You tell me. I mean, last I heard you had no interest in living on the Vineyard."

"Neither did you . . . you haven't set foot on it since you were . . ."

"Seventeen," Caitlin said.

Vix couldn't ask any of the questions running through her head. *Have you seen him? Is he going with anyone? Does he ask about me?* "So . . . have you seen Von?"

Caitlin laughed. She knew damn well what Vix was really asking. "Of course. Von and his ridiculous wife. And Bru and Trisha and everyone else. I haven't turned into a hermit. I'm just taking a break . . . a reality check kind of thing." She paused, then said, "I'm sorry about your father."

"He should be okay."

"I'm glad."

"He's got a . . . friend," Vix told her. "Frankie. She calls him *Chick Pea.*"

"Oh God . . ." They both laughed. "I miss you, Vix."

"I miss you, too. Come to New York for a week-end."

"You come up here."

"I don't think so. Not now."

"Maybe over the summer?"

"Maybe."

41

THE NEXT TIME they talked it was late June. Caitlin called Vix at the office. "You have to come up." She was using her breathy princess voice, the one she'd picked up in Europe, halfway between Jackie O's and Princess Di's. "I'm getting married at Lamb's house."

"Married?"

"Yes. And you have to be my Maid of Honor. It's only appropriate, don't you think?"

"I guess that depends on who you're marrying."

"Bru," Caitlin answered, and suddenly she sounded like herself again. "I'm marrying Bru. I thought you knew."

Vix forced herself to swallow, to breathe, but she felt clammy and weak anyway. She grabbed the cold can of diet Coke from the corner of her desk and held it against her forehead, then moved it to her neck, as she jotted down the date and time of the wedding. She doodled all around it while Caitlin chatted, until the whole page was filled with arrows, crescent moons, and triangles, as if she were back in sixth grade.

"Vix?" Caitlin said. "Are you still there? Do we have a bad connection or what?"

"No, it's okay."

"So you'll come?"

"Yes." The second she hung up she made a mad dash for the women's room where she puked her guts out in the stall. She had to call Caitlin back, tell her there was no way she could do this. What could Caitlin be thinking? What was *she* thinking when she agreed?

When she came out her boss, Angela, was leaning over the sink taking out her contacts. Vix splashed her face with cold water and rinsed out her mouth. "Victoria . . ." Angela began, squinting at her. "You look terrible. You're not coming down with that bug, are you?"

"I don't know . . . maybe."

"Go home," Angela said, "before you infect the whole office."

She staggered home in the record heat. Her Bag Lady was singing, *I am woman, hear me roar* . . . She stuck her paper cup in Vix's face but Vix brushed it away and the coins scattered on the sidewalk. "Bitch . . ." she called after Vix.

"I give you money every day," Vix shouted, "so watch who you're calling a bitch!" The Bag Lady gave her the finger as someone else stopped to help retrieve her coins.

Hours later, Maia and Paisley found Vix sitting on the floor of the apartment. She was surrounded by photo albums and piles of loose pictures, wearing only a tank top and Calvin briefs. The fan was turned to high but it pointed away from her to keep the photos from blowing. Pat Benatar was singing on the CD. *Heartbreaker . . . love taker . . .*

"What?" Maia asked.

"She's marrying Bru," Vix said.

"Who's marrying Bru?"

"Caitlin."

"Jesus!"

"She wants me to be her Maid of Honor."

Paisley and Maia looked at one another. "She can't be serious," Maia said.

"She's serious," Vix told them.

Paisley said, "I think I'll send out for Thai." She searched for the phone, finding it in the basket where they ripened their bananas.

When the food arrived they sat around the coffee table, all three of them stripped down to their underwear with their hair pinned up. "Can I speak frankly?" Maia asked, munching on a spring roll.

"Please . . ." Paisley said.

But Maia was waiting to hear from Vix. "Go ahead," Vix told her, knowing what was coming.

"It's time for you to get over him, Victoria. Once and for all."

"I thought I was supposed to get over *her*."

"Him, her . . . get over the whole mess."

Vix dug her chopsticks into the pad Thai.

Maia took this as permission to continue. "And for God's sake, call her up and tell her you're not coming to the wedding. You have other plans. You're . . . I don't know . . . going to Hawaii with some gorgeous guy. And the next time she decides to get married and wants you for her Maid of Honor she should give you more notice."

Vix kept on eating, sampling the curried vegetables, then the pineapple shrimp.

"You're not thirteen anymore," Maia said, growing frustrated. "She has no power over you. And I just don't see the point in all . . . this." She pointed to the albums, the loose photos. "In surrounding yourself with these . . . memories."

Paisley touched Maia's arm. "Look . . ." she said, "being a member of the wedding party could be therapeutic for Victoria. It could offer closure . . . you know?"

"What closure?" Maia asked. "It'll just mean more photo ops, more heartache." She shook her head at Vix.

Maia

SHE'S ALWAYS KNOWN Victoria's fascination with the NBO girl would come to no good. From the day Victoria moved into their room at Weld South and set out those photos she knew. *Go ahead and laugh*, she tells Paisley when they discuss it. *I knew!*

She disagrees with Paisley completely. Victoria should not go to this wedding. And really, what kind of guy marries his longtime girlfriend's best friend? She'll do everything in her power to keep Victoria from going to the Vineyard, short of tying her up and sitting on her, which, come to think of it, might not be a bad idea.

Paisley

SHE ADMITS, it's a shocker. But it's not the first time in the history of the world something like this has happened. It probably happens more often than they know. Only not to their friends. She disagrees with Maia one hundred percent. Victoria *needs* to be at this wedding. *Needs* to experience it. That's the only way she'll ever be free of them. Not that Victoria is listening to a word either she or Maia have to say on the subject. Her mind is already made up, was probably made up at the moment Caitlin asked her to come.

_____

FOUR WEEKS LATER Caitlin, her hair flying in the wind, met Vix at the tiny Vineyard airport. Vix spotted Caitlin from her window as soon as they landed but felt glued to her seat.

"Going on to Nantucket with us?" the flight attendant asked and suddenly Vix realized she was the only passenger still on the plane. Embarrassed, she grabbed her bag and hustled down the steps onto the tarmac. Caitlin found her in the crowd and waved frantically. Vix headed toward her, shaking her head because Caitlin was wearing a T-shirt that said *simplify, simplify, simplify*. She was barefoot, as usual, and Vix was betting her feet would be as dirty as they were that first summer.

Caitlin held her at arm's length for a minute. "God, Vix . . ." she said, "you look so . . . grownup!" They both laughed, then Caitlin hugged her. She smelled of seawater, suntan lotion, and something else. Vix closed her eyes, breathing in the familiar scent, and for a moment it was as if they'd never been apart. They were still Vixen and Cassandra, summer sisters forever. The rest was a mistake, a crazy joke.

PART FIVE

Steal the Night
1990–1995

42

THEY SAY WHEN you're about to die your whole life passes before your eyes like a movie run in slow motion. That night, at Caitlin's prenuptial dinner at The Black Dog, Vix feels her whole life passing before her and wonders if maybe this is it. If this is how it's all going to end, standing in Caitlin's shadow, celebrating her marriage to Bru.

Maia and Paisley are wrong. Caitlin isn't someone to get over. She's someone to come to terms with, the way you have to come to terms with your parents, your siblings. You can't deny they ever happened. You can't deny you ever loved them, love them still, even if loving them causes you pain.

A commemorative T-shirt is handed out to every guest entering the party, featuring a screened picture of the bride and groom looking over their shoulders, each of them smiling broadly, a shared towel covering their naked backsides. The caption reads:

Caitlin and Bru—July 31, 1990

Nice of them to choose Vix's twenty-fifth birthday for their wedding date. "That way you'll never forget our anniversary," Caitlin told her. As if . . .

Earlier that day, Abby stopped by her room at the B&B where she and Lamb have put up some of their guests. "Can I come in?" she asked, knocking on Vix's door. Vix threw on her robe. When she opened the door Abby hugged her. "Oh, Vix . . . I hope this isn't too hard for you."

"I've been through worse," Vix said.

Abby walked around the room straightening the sea-shell picture on the wall, touching the lamp, picking up the flashlight from the bedside table. "Do you think she knows what she's doing?"

"I don't know," Vix said.

Abby clicked the flashlight on and off a couple of times. "Will he be enough for her? Will the island be enough? Or is she just playing some game?"

"I don't know that either."

Abby dropped the flashlight on the bed and took Vix's hand. "How about you . . . will you be all right tonight?"

"I'll be fine."

"And tomorrow . . . at the wedding?"

Vix nodded. "Don't worry."

Abby kissed her. "That's my girl."

Abby

WHAT CAN SHE DO? You have to be happy for your children even when you don't understand their decisions. Lamb is as surprised as she is, but pleased. Of all the choices Caitlin might have made over the years, this one doesn't seem so bad to him. And it's close to home. After the tragedy of losing her friends, after the monastery, this feels like a positive step. Besides, he reminds her, Vix and Bru broke up years ago. He's sure Vix has given them her blessing.

———————

PHOEBE SPOTS VIX across the room and waves her over. She introduces Vix to her current boyfriend, Philippe, who's French, older, dignified. "Tacky, *n'est-ce pas?*" she asks, pulling the T-shirt over her head. She bends over, letting her hair hang to the floor, before quickly straightening up and flipping it back. Then she belts the T-shirt over her long denim skirt. With her Santa Fe silver Phoebe still looks stylish.

Vix isn't thrilled about wearing the T-shirt either since she's carefully chosen a dress with an eye-catching neckline. Looking good tonight is important to her. But she can't be a spoilsport. Dorset, Lamb's sister, is the only one who refuses to don the shirt. No one argues with her.

Bru's extended family greets Vix—the uncles, the aunts, all those cousins, including Von with a very pregnant Patti and two little girls, one of whom is wailing.

"What do you say, Vix?" Von asks. "Wasn't sure you'd show."

"Please . . . I'm the Maid of Honor." She tries to keep it light. No bad feelings on her part. After all, she's the one who'd said no. She's the one who wasn't ready. And that's exactly what she'll tell anyone who asks, as if saying it will make it easier to take.

"So, how's it going in the Big Apple?" Von says.

"It's lively . . ." She starts to say more, then thinks better of it. Why try to justify her decision now, especially to Von?

"More lively than here, I'll bet," Patti says.

"Bitch, bitch, bitch . . ." Von gives Patti a look of

such contempt it makes Vix cringe. Patti shoves the screaming toddler at Von and heads for the women's room. Vix follows.

"You just don't know," Patti says. "He's always like that . . . pissed off at me for living." She goes into the single stall while Vix applies lip gloss and brushes her hair.

"Everybody goes crazy on this island," Patti continues, from inside. " 'Just take me to Boston a couple of times during the winter,' I beg him. You think he cares? But let somebody give him tickets to a Bruins game and he's outta here in a flash. Now you see him, now you don't." The toilet flushes and Patti steps out, adjusting the T-shirt over her maternity dress. "That's all they care about in winter anyway. Every night it's hockey, hockey, hockey . . . then it's a couple of beers with the guys and God knows what else . . ."

Patti washes her hands and fluffs out her hair. Vix remembers the first time they saw her with Von, at the Ag Fair. She and Caitlin were fourteen, Patti was probably a couple of years older, punk, pierced, and painted, with a purple streak running through her hair. Von introduced her as his main squeeze.

"Does he give you fish heads?" Caitlin had asked.

"He gives me better than that," Patti told her, sliding one of her legs between Von's, kissing him open-mouthed.

Caitlin applauded. "I didn't know they were doing live sex at the fair this year."

The guys laughed. Guys always laughed when Caitlin talked tough.

———————

Patti's hair is natural now. "He thinks he's God's gift to women." She's still going on, ranting about Von. "He can't stand that *she's* marrying Bru. He says, 'Jeez . . . all that money and a great piece of ass, too. Now that girl could give blow jobs!' As if I haven't been sucking his dick since I'm sixteen!"

Vix pretends to be studying her reflection in the mirror. She doesn't want to hear this. She has her own problems tonight.

"They're all the same, aren't they?" Patti asks. "You think it'll be any different with Bru just because he's marrying up? Ha! He'll be out playing hockey and chasing pussy with the rest of them. You were smart to go somewhere else, to make a life for yourself." Patti's face contorts and she begins to cry silently, her shoulders shaking.

Vix pats her back. "You going to be okay?"

Patti nods. She fishes a tissue out of her pocket. "I just need a minute . . ."

"I'll see you outside," Vix tells her.

Von is waiting, one little girl in his arms, the other hanging on to his leg. "I'll bet she gave you an earful."

"Nothing I haven't heard before," Vix says.

"Look, it was always a mistake. But I never thought it'd get this bad . . . you know?"

She couldn't believe it when Bru had told her Von and Patti were married. *Married!* That Patti was pregnant. He'd called her at school with the news when she was just starting her sophomore year.

"You look great," Von says, coming on to her. "Very

sexy . . . but then you always were, weren't you?" He's
in her face, whispering into her ear. His free hand rests
on the back of her neck. The toddler pulls at his hair.
"How about that birthday party on Chappy?" he says. "I
think about that a lot . . ."

Vix wriggles away and sees that Bru and Caitlin have
arrived. The Bride and Groom. The Happy Couple. Bru
is looking directly at her. Damn! He looks good. She's
been hoping he'd turned flabby, that she'll feel nothing,
nothing but relief that she's not the one marrying him
tomorrow. But the old physical reflexes kick in, her
knees go weak, her palms grow clammy. *The moment of
truth, Victoria. Don't blow it!* They make eye contact. He
gives her his soulful look, that look that could melt her
insides. *You're my girl, Victoria. You'll always be my girl.*
She has no idea what he's really thinking. Maybe it's
more like, *Get a look at Victoria! Jeez . . . has she gained
weight or is it just that stupid T-shirt?*

She grabs a glass of champagne as it's passed on a
tray, holds it up as if to toast him, then gulps it down.
He smiles as she ducks out of Von's reach. *There, it's over
. . . they've acknowledged one another and she's survived.*

She makes her way across the room to Sharkey. She
hasn't seen him since Lamb's fiftieth. There's a woman
at his side with a small child clinging to her back like a
koala. He introduces her to Vix as Wren, and the child
as her daughter, Natasha. Wren has a hair wrap and
wears a long Indian print skirt. Is this a romantic relationship? Does Sharkey have a woman in his life? *You
might as well marry into it, Victoria. What about the
brother?* She feels like laughing, either that or crying, but

she's her mother's daughter. She doesn't wash her linen in public.

Sharkey hugs Vix carefully, bending his body so that nothing of importance touches her and vice versa. "Are you okay?" he asks, and she understands that his question has nothing to do with her health.

"I'm fine, really . . ." she tells him, helping herself to a second glass of champagne.

"Good. That's good." He moved back east after he got his Ph.D. and is a post doc in the artificial intelligence program at M.I.T. "Daniel and Gus are here," he says, nodding in their direction.

Vix follows his gaze and there they are. The Chicago Boys together again. She's Alice, fallen down the rabbit hole. Her whole history is connected to the guests at this party. Daniel is tall and slim, with thinning hair, impeccably dressed in Polo Sport, and wearing that same bored expression as the day she met him. He practices law now, with his father's firm in Chicago. Vix knows that Abby has some unspoken wish for the two of them to wind up together. She wonders if Daniel knows it, too.

Gus is a big man with a thick neck, broad shoulders, dark hair. Vix hasn't seen him since the summer she walked out on Caitlin, eight years ago. She wades through the sea of T-shirts, Caitlin's and Bru's faces smiling at her from all directions, and takes The Chicago Boys by surprise.

"*Cough Drop*!" Gus gives her a tight hug. Unlike Sharkey, he has no fear of pressing his body close to hers or of kissing her too close to her mouth. "Good to see you." And for once, she's glad to see him. The summer sister and the summer brother. Daniel holds her by the shoulders and plants a cool kiss near her ear. "How are you, Vix?"

It's driving her crazy, all these condolences. She can't stand the idea of them thinking she's been betrayed. It's important to set the record straight, to let everyone know once and for all that whatever she and Bru had, it's officially over, it's been over for a long time. He's free to marry whomever, even Caitlin. Okay, so it's awkward. But look . . . is she falling apart? No, goddamn it! Can't they see she's fine? That she's one hundred percent!

"So . . ." Gus says, "is your boyfriend here?"

"My boyfriend?" She pauses, thinking she should have brought someone. Why didn't she? Earl would have come with her. He'd have found enough material here for at least two new plays. But she says, "No . . . he couldn't make it. What about your girlfriend?"

"What girlfriend?" Gus asks. "I'm still trying to get over you. You were my first love."

This time she laughs for real.

"You don't believe me? Ask the Baumer if it's not true."

Daniel gives her his haughty look. "God help us . . . it's true."

"Well, Gus . . . here's to what might have been," Vix says, downing a third glass of champagne. This one is a mistake. She knows it the minute she sets the empty glass on the tray. It goes straight to her head, making her dizzy and slightly nauseous. The Chicago Boys escort her outside, where the three of them sit on a log on the beach.

Daniel

VIX IS LOOKING GOOD. Lost that baby fat. You can see her cheekbones now. Not his type though. He prefers cool blondes. Sleek. The last one told him, *You're just too intense for me, Daniel. I need someone, you know, with less intensity.*

He's working on it but given his genes he doesn't expect to wind up anywhere near loose. Not like Gus with his easygoing humor. Women find him irresistible. Don't mind his unkempt look. Maybe they dream about making him over, about buying him clothes. You never can tell with women.

Look at Ab . . . Who'd have guessed his mother had it in her? Drives his father nuts that she's done so well for herself. Not just the part about Lamb and the money. The other stuff, the philanthropy. She sits on the boards of four major organizations. Lamb's turned out to be a decent guy. Bought Ab's folks a place on Longboat Key. Grandma's the queen of the condo set.

He's not sure about working at his father's firm. Since his father divorced the Babe he's been having some kind of personal crisis. Gets depressed. Doctor had him on Prozac for a while. Maybe it's time for *him* to move on, relocate even. Miami's hot, in more ways than one.

AFTER A MINUTE Vix slides down in the sand, resting her head against the log. Her eyes close. She floats in and out as Gus and Daniel reminisce, their voices coming from far away, though she can feel their bodies right next to her.

"She never could resist those island guys," Gus says.

He's got it wrong, she thinks. *It was only Bru she couldn't resist.*

"There we were, horny as hell," he continues, "and she goes and boffs the one with the ponytail."

Oh, Caitlin . . . he's talking about Caitlin.

"She's still gorgeous," Daniel says.

"But jaded now," Gus tells him.

"You think?" Daniel asks.

"You can see it in her eyes."

They're talking right through her, as if she's not there, as if she's invisible. Maybe she's dead and just doesn't know it.

"So this one time," Gus is saying, "I'm walking by her room and she pulls me in and shuts the door. 'Gus . . . would you do my back?' she says, and she hands me a bottle of suntan lotion. She's wearing that yellow suit—remember that yellow suit?—and she pulls down the straps . . . hell, she pulls the whole suit down to her waist. I'm nineteen or something . . . a kid with hormones."

Vix isn't sure if she's going to throw up or not. She tries opening her eyes but that makes everything spin so she quickly shuts them.

The Chicago Boys must remember her then because

she can feel them looking down at her, making sure it's safe to continue. Gus says, "The Cough Drop is totally out of it."

Daniel says, "If you tell me you made it with Caitlin and kept it to yourself all these years . . ."

"Not even close," Gus says. "I got to cup those perfect little tits in my hands for about two seconds, then she says, 'I want you to use it while I watch.' 'Use what?' I ask her. She says, 'The whole package . . .'"

"The package?" Daniel asks.

"The *package*," Gus tells him. Vix imagines him jiggling his balls to show Daniel what he means, because the two of them began to laugh.

Vix wants to laugh, too. Wants to laugh about how Cassandra counted Vixen's pubic hairs. *Sixteen. You're so lucky!* But she feels herself on the verge of tears instead.

"I always thought she'd make something of her life," Daniel says. "Something important."

A bell clangs announcing dinner, and Gus shakes Vix. "Okay, Cough Drop . . . time to get up." He helps her to her feet. "How're you feeling? You going to survive?"

She's wobbly but she makes it down to the water, where she pulls off the stupid T-shirt, wets it, then holds it to her face and neck. "Now that's more like it," Gus says, eyeing her dress, still a big kid with hormones.

"And just for the record," she tells him, "I was the one with the yellow bathing suit."

She's sandwiched between Daniel and Gus at dinner. When Gus catches Phoebe's boyfriend giving Vix a sleepy-eyed once-over, he turns to Daniel. "Cough Drop attracts guys like a magnet."

Caitlin was the magnet. She was just a particle in her magnetic field.

After dinner they're asked to gather on the beach for a display of fireworks honoring the bride and groom. Daniel covers her shoulders with his linen jacket. She leans back against Gus, who, she thinks, sniffs her hair as the sky lights up, taking her back to other fireworks on other beaches. *You're not scared of me, are you? No, I'm scared of these feelings.*

When the party breaks up, Caitlin offers to drive her back to the B&B. "Aren't you going home with Bru?" Vix asks.

"Not tonight. It's bad luck for the bride and groom to spend the night before the wedding together."

Vix never heard that one but she gets into Caitlin's white Jeep. The top is down and as they head out of town the wind whips their hair. "This isn't too hard for you, is it?" Caitlin asks. "I mean, seeing us together?"

Vix is grateful for the darkness and the champagne.

"It was over between the two of you so long ago . . ."

Vix would like to be generous, to reassure Caitlin, but she can't find the right words, so she says nothing.

"I hate it when you clam up that way!" Caitlin shouts. The Jeep swerves. Vix shuts her eyes and hangs on, sure Caitlin is going to kill them. But no, she just makes a sudden decision to pull into the Tashmoo Overlook where she cuts the engine and rests her head on the wheel. "Oh, God . . ." she cries. "I don't even know if I want to marry him."

Vix stiffens.

"That shocks you, I suppose?" Caitlin says. "You've never done a single thing you've regretted, have you?"

At that moment Vix feels such a rush of . . . what? She's not sure. She's not sure if she hates Caitlin or herself, or maybe Bru, for creating this situation in the first place.

"Oh, hell . . ." Caitlin wipes her nose with the back of her hand. "It'll be a good party, anyway." She turns the key in the ignition and revs up the engine, then drives to the B&B where she drops off Vix. "Sleep tight . . ." she calls, blowing Vix a kiss.

"You, too."

43

SHE KNOWS she won't be able to sleep. She tries to read but she can't concentrate so she grabs her sweater and the flashlight and heads back outside. The wind is picking up. She shines her flashlight along the wooded road leading down to the beach. She doesn't see the figure stepping out of the shadows until he grabs her. She's paralyzed by fear. She can't scream, can't run. *So this is how it's all going to end. Talk about screwing up the wedding party!*

He spins her around . . . but wait . . . it's not a madman, at least not the kind she had in mind. It's Bru. "We have to talk," he says. She shakes him off and walks faster. He strides alongside her. "I don't know how any of this happened. I don't know what I'm doing with her. What we're doing together."

She stops and aims the flashlight at his face. "You two should have a really happy marriage!"

"Look, Victoria, it's a mistake . . . I admit it . . . okay?"

"Spare me," Vix says, holding up her other hand. He reaches for it and pulls her to him, making her gulp for air. She's seventeen again, swimming for her life . . .

but this time she's being sucked under . . . this time she's drowning. She drops the flashlight to the ground.

He begins to kiss her. Soft little kisses at the sides of her lips, then hungry deep kisses. He takes her hand and leads her quickly, quickly down the road to his truck and without a word they head up island to his cabin.

She awakens to the sound of the foghorn just before dawn, her heart pounding, her head throbbing. She grabs what she can find of her clothes from the pile on the floor, tiptoes barefoot to the door, and quietly, so as not to wake him, lets herself out. She steps into her shoes, drops her dress over her head, then she's running . . . running through clumps of beach plum and bayberry that scratch her legs . . . running . . . running, until she comes to the main road, where she hitches a ride with the first car to come along, two women on their way to the early morning ferry.

Maybe she should keep going, just get on the ferry, get off this island. But they'd worry about her. Abby would say, *Look, her bed wasn't slept in. Something terrible has happened . . . I know it.* They'd call the police who would find her underwear in Bru's truck or his bed or wherever she left it and accuse him of something even worse than the truth. The wedding would be postponed.

"Is this close enough?" the driver asks at the sign pointing to the B&B.

"Yes, thanks." As Vix is walking the mile back she runs into Philippe—*shit*—who's out for an early morning jog. Does he notice she's still in last night's clothes?

"Ah, Veek-toria . . . enjoying an early morning walk?"

"Yes," she tells him, picking up her pace. "I always walk before breakfast."

He eyes her up and down and she knows that he knows she didn't sleep in her room. But he doesn't have a clue about where she spent the night or with whom.

44

By TEN THE SUN has burned through and as Vix dozes in the worn wicker rocker on the porch of Lamb's house she breathes deeply, catching the scent of the stargazer lilies from Abby's garden. She pictures herself walking down the aisle an hour from now, wearing the straw hat that's resting on her lap, the gauzy ivory dress skimming her ankles. She'll be carrying sunflowers. She's been instructed to smile. After all, she's Caitlin's Maid of Honor. Or is it Made of Honor? She winces at her own bad joke. She can't help wishing the same fairy godmother who let her be Caitlin's friend in the first place would swoop down and rescue her now, carrying her away from this island, this island of memories—all the best and worst of her life.

She hears Caitlin calling to her from far away. "Vix . . . get your ass up here! A Maid of Honor's got responsibilities, you know." Caitlin laughs and an echo of laughter follows.

Phoebe shakes her gently. "Vix . . ." When she opens her eyes Phoebe asks, "Hard night?"

Vix fans her face with the straw hat. Philippe has probably told Phoebe that he saw her early this morning, that she'd pulled an all-nighter. She prays none of them will ever know the truth.

Abby has finally redone Caitlin's room. The walls have been whitewashed, the old twin beds have been replaced with an antique iron bedstead piled high with lace-trimmed pillows. Books line the shelves where broken toys once sat. Their beach stone collection, sorted by color—lavender, tortoise, gray—is stored in glass canisters. A blowup of a black-and-white photo hangs on the wall, taken that first summer when she and Caitlin were twelve, arms around one another, looking into each other's eyes, as if they're sharing a delicious secret.

Caitlin waltzes across the room holding out the ivory satin skirt of her wedding dress. She's exquisite, as radiant as if she just stepped off the cover of *Bride's* magazine. "It's my grandmother's gown," she tells Vix. "I took you to see her grave once . . . remember?"

"I remember."

"Dorset sent it to me. It fit perfectly. Didn't even need alteration. I wonder if Grandmother Somers will notice? Probably not. She doesn't see that well. She's ninety-something." She stops in front of the mirror. Her face is flushed. "I can't imagine living that long, can you?"

Vix can't imagine anything beyond today and she's having trouble with that. She lifts the veil from its nest of tissue paper but before she can set it on Caitlin's head, Caitlin catches her by the arm. "Wait . . ." She turns away from the mirror to face Vix. "About last night . . ." she begins.

Oh God . . . she knows . . . he's told her! Maybe she should confess now, get it out of the way, beg her forgiveness . . .

"What I said in the Jeep?" Caitlin continues, as if she's asking a question. "When I told you I wasn't sure about marrying Bru?"

Vix feels dizzy.

"I never finished what I was trying to say, what I needed to say . . ."

"You don't have to explain," Vix tells her, hoping she won't. "Everyone gets last-minute jitters."

"No, it's not about last-minute jitters," Caitlin says. "It's about Bru and me . . ."

Vix holds her breath. She's never regretted anything the way she regrets last night. If only she could take it back.

"I always wanted what you had," Caitlin says.

"You're the one who had everything."

"That's not the way I saw it. You were the daughter Abby always wanted. You were worthy of the Somers Foundation scholarships. You even had breasts. So I had to prove I was sexier. I had to prove I could have any guy I wanted . . . even Bru."

"Well, now you've got him."

"I don't mean now, although there's something quaint about marrying your first lover."

Vix is thoroughly confused. "Aren't you forgetting the ski instructor . . . in Italy . . . junior year?"

Caitlin shakes her head. "I invented him for you."

"You invented the ski instructor?"

"So you'd think I was first."

Vix is having trouble digesting this. "You mean you lied?"

"Couldn't we just say I was imaginative?"

"Imaginative?"

"Okay . . . so I lied."

"What about Von? Did you make him up, too?" *And what about the other hundred or so she's heard about over the years?*

"Oh, Von . . . we never actually, you know, consummated our affair. He wouldn't wear a condom. You can see where that got him. Anyway, he liked all the other stuff better."

They stand there looking at one another until Caitlin says, "You mean you never knew . . . you never guessed?"

Vix feels as if she can't breathe. She grasps the bed rail.

Caitlin's voice goes whispery. "After Nathan . . . after the funeral, when I came back to the Vineyard . . ."

Vix turns away. *No!* She refuses to believe this. She looks out the window as the flower girls line up by size, each one carrying a bunch of daisies.

"You asked me to explain to him," Caitlin says. "You asked me to tell him why you couldn't come back." She comes up behind Vix and lays a hand on her arm. "It just happened. It didn't mean anything. Really."

Vix doesn't move. Caitlin grabs hold of her, forces her to listen. "I admit I was jealous because he loved you so much . . . but even more, because *you* loved *him*. I wanted to prove to you that he was just like all the others, following his pointer through life."

"Bru was never like that." She can't believe she's standing here defending him after last night. She's going to tell Caitlin the truth. Right now. She's going to even the score.

But Caitlin hasn't finished. "Why do you think I stayed away?" she asks. "Haven't you ever wondered about that?"

You think you know someone really well and then you find out . . .

"It never happened again," Caitlin adds. "We never even saw each other again until a couple of months ago when I came back."

Vix catches a glimpse of herself in the mirror and is shocked that her face shows nothing, *nothing*.

The photographer knocks. "One for the road," she says, pushing open the bedroom door with her foot. She asks Vix to lean over Caitlin's shoulder while they both look into the mirror. "That's it . . ." she says, guiding them, "a little closer, so that your faces are almost touching. Yes!"

Vix places the headband with the attached veil on Caitlin's head, centers it just so, fluffs it out so that bits of lace and seed pearls frame Caitlin's lovely face. The photographer snaps that one, too.

Before they leave the house Caitlin leads Vix over to a table in the living room where Abby has displayed the wedding gifts. "Look at this," she says, holding up a porcelain figurine of a girl in a tutu, standing atop a horse. The card reads:

Darling girl, if all else fails, join the circus!

Vix begins to laugh. Caitlin joins her. They hold on to one another, convulsed, until Phoebe separates them. "Time to get going," she tells Caitlin, "if you're sure you want to go through with this."

At the church, Grandmother Somers asks loudly, "Which one is she marrying?" Dorset points to Bru. "Oh, he's quite handsome, isn't he? Who are his parents? What do they do?"

Sharkey escorts Phoebe down the aisle. She's relaxed, smiling. Daniel escorts Abby, who looks tense, although she's trying to hide it. The two women sit next to one another. Vix can't look at Bru. She prays he won't say anything . . . ever. How can *he* be sure Vix will keep their secret?

Caitlin sails down the aisle on Lamb's arm. He looks so proud, so loving, tears come to Vix's eyes. Caitlin smiles directly at her. She has a feeling that Caitlin is about to pull something but she doesn't know what. She half expects her to shove her island-grown bouquet of cosmos, bellflowers, and daisies in Vix's face and say, *You marry him. You two deserve each other!*

Bru

HE WAS CRAZY last night. Out of his fucking mind. What was he doing? Trying to get out of it? But here comes Caitlin on Lamb's arm, drifting down the aisle like some kind of angel. Smiling right at him. Shit! What's he supposed to do?

He remembers the night she came to him with a message from Victoria, just after Nathan died. Beautiful Caitlin at seventeen, looking so sad, so sad . . . He'd taken her in his arms to stop her tears. Hadn't meant to kiss her. But the way she'd looked at him, her lips parted and moist. Hadn't meant to make love to her. And jeez . . . she'd been a virgin . . . had bled all over the place. A real surprise after all those stories Von told him. A mistake, he'd told her, after. Did she understand? Because it was never going to happen again. She understood. And she'd stayed away from the island, away from him . . . until now. It suddenly occurs to him he was not only Victoria's first lover, but Caitlin's. Maybe that's his problem. He loves them both. He's glad he doesn't have to choose. Glad they've done it for him.

———————

CAITLIN AND BRU face the young minister who plays hockey with the guys on Mondays and Thursdays. She promises to love, cherish, and respect Joseph Brudegher until death do them part and he promises the same to her. They slip matching rings on one another's fingers. The minister pronounces them husband and wife. They kiss and the guests applaud while the smallest flower girl lifts her dress and scratches her backside.

A tent is set up on the lawn of the house, with tables to seat one hundred fifty. Vix's heels sink into the soft ground as she marches in with the other attendants and takes her place at the head table. The guests dance to the music of the Martha's Vineyard Swing Band on a wooden floor that slopes downhill. Vix drinks only designer water but feels light-headed anyway. *Fini, finis, finito* . . . Maybe Paisley was right when she told Maia this could offer closure. They'll all be grownup now, won't they?

She dances once with Bru, who says, "About last night . . ."

"Forget last night," she tells him. "Last night never happened." Her knees don't go weak. Her stomach doesn't do flips. Last night was the end and they both know it. She can sense his relief.

"She's beautiful, isn't she?" Bru asks as they both watch Caitlin waltzing with Lamb. "I can't believe she's my . . ."

"Wife," Vix says, finishing the sentence for him. The

music ends but they don't break apart. She thinks abou
asking him if it's true, if he and Caitlin really . . . Bu
what's the point? For all she knows Caitlin made it up
like the ski instructor. For all she knows there was no
woman in Paris who cut up Caitlin's panties, no Tin
Castellano in L.A., no married man who got her preg
nant in London. It hardly matters anymore.

Gus comes up beside her, slips his arm around her
waist. "I think this one is mine, Cough Drop."

Trisha and Arthur sail by dipping and twirling. None
of the younger people know how to dance to this music
but they follow the older generation's lead and pretend
they're dancing anyway. "So," Gus says, "the beautiful
princess marries the prince and lives happily ever after
on a magical island. True or false?"

"True," she tells him.

"Suppose he turns into a frog. Then what?"

"Suppose *she* does?"

Gus laughs and pulls her closer.

The rowdy cousins cheer when the band switches to
rock. Abby hands out earplugs to anyone in need. The
little children chase each other up and down the lawn.
Von has too much to drink and rambles on toasting the
bride and groom. Lamb comes to his rescue but Patti
leaves in a huff anyway, taking the two little girls with
her. Dorset moves in for the kill. She's been eyeing him
ever since the party last night.

Late in the afternoon, after the cake has been sliced,
after the requisite pictures of bride feeding groom and
groom feeding bride, the cousins carry Bru down to the
pond and throw him in. When one of them picks up
Caitlin and slings her over his shoulder she pounds on

his back and cries, "Not in my wedding dress, asshole . . . it's an antique!" He puts her down and she
steps out of it, leaving it on the grassy bank above the
pond. They throw her off the dock wearing just her long
ivory slip. Bru catches her in the water. They kiss. He
wades out of the pond with her in his arms, as if he's
carrying her over the threshold. The photographer captures the moment.

"You're next, Victoria," another of the cousins says,
sweeping her up and tossing her in from the end of the
dock. Then they all jump in, one after the other, the
cousins, their wives and girlfriends, most of the young
guests and some of the not so young, all in their finery.
But not Sharkey, who has taken Wren out in the dinghy,
and not Daniel or Gus, who wait for Vix to emerge.
"You can't stay in all day," Gus calls, laughing.

She feels awkward and self-conscious, like an unwill-
ing contestant in a wet T-shirt contest. When she finally
comes out, her arms folded across her chest, Gus wraps
a beach towel around her. "You always were on the shy
side, Cough Drop."

"Are you going to keep calling me *Cough Drop*?"

"What should I call you?"

"How about Vix?"

"Vix . . ." he says, trying it out.

Upstairs, Caitlin hands her a pair of shorts and a T-shirt
so she can get out of her wet clothes. Caitlin has already
changed into jeans. She's zipping up her backpack, pre-
paring to leave for her honeymoon, a camping trip to
Maine. "Thanks, Vix . . . for being here with me." She

looks up at the photo of the two of them at twelve "Who says a picture isn't worth a hundred words?"

"Thousand," Vix says. "I think it's a thousand words."

Caitlin laughs. "We were a great team, weren't we?"

"Yes."

Caitlin hugs her. "I'll always love you. Promise you'll always love me?"

"You know I will." And it's true, Vix thinks, no matter what, she'll always love Caitlin.

Caitlin hoists on her backpack. "Did you ask Bru . . . about that summer?"

"Yes," she lies.

Caitlin nods. "Did he tell you the truth?"

"Yes." Another lie.

She nods again. "I figured he would."

45

THE FOLLOWING MAY Caitlin gives birth to a baby girl. They name her Somers Mayhew Brudegher but they call her Maizie. Vix drives up for the naming ceremony with Gus, who's moved to New York to write for *Newsweek*. They've been seeing each other since the wedding, going to movies, sharing late dinners, blading on Sundays in the park. They're friends, but neither one has been willing to risk spoiling things by changing the relationship.

One night, coming out of a movie in the Village, they're caught in a downpour. There's not a taxi in sight. They're closer to his place on Tenth Street than hers on Twenty-sixth so they run for it. They're drenched by then so he hands her a towel, a sweatshirt, jogging pants. She takes off her clothes in the bathroom, and is about to pull on the sweatshirt when she spies a robe hanging on the back of the door. She wishes it were silk instead of flannel as she pulls it on, tying the belt around her waist and rolling up the sleeves. She runs a comb through her wet hair, then rummages around in her purse for that sample of Obsession she's been saving. She dabs some between her breasts, behind her ears and knees, which are beginning to shake. She hears John Coltrane playing on the CD.

Gus has changed into a T-shirt and jeans. At first he's not sure what she has in mind. She can see his confusion and smiles. His eyes go to the opening of the robe. He turns away. "Don't do this unless you're sure, Vix."

"I could say the same to you."

"I've never been so sure about anything in my whole life."

The attraction between them is so strong she's sure there will actually be sparks when he touches her.

A year later they gather on the Vineyard for Maizie's first birthday. Caitlin is distant, distracted. Bru is careful and protective. When Maizie cries, Abby is the one who picks her up and comforts her.

The next day Vix flies to Florida with Gus, to see Tawny. They haven't seen each other in years. But Tawny has called, asking her to come. There's someone she wants Vix to meet. And Vix has news for her, too.

In Key West Tawny watches shopping channels. She says she likes to dream she has the money to buy everything she sees, though she knows most of it is junk and she wouldn't want it even if she could have it. Everyone has fantasies, Vix supposes. Tawny seems relaxed, even happy. She lives in Old Town, in a tiny yellow conch house with a jacaranda tree shading the veranda. She can walk to the ocean every day if she wants to. The *someone* she wants Vix to meet is Myles, a beefy, suntanned man in a captain's hat. Vix isn't sure if Myles is his first name or last. "He's retired navy," Tawny says proudly. "With a good pension." She shows Vix a photo of him in full uniform. "He was dashing, wasn't he? Of course this was taken a while ago but you can still see it."

Vix knows it's important for her to agree with Tawny. So she says, "Yes . . . I can still see it."

Myles spends his days tooling around in a small wooden boat. Tawny still works for the Countess, who lives a block away in a pink eyebrow house on Francis Street. She's tethered to an oxygen tank. She can hardly take half a dozen steps without it. Tawny supervises the round-the-clock caregivers. The Countess is partial to handsome young men. And they adore her.

Tawny tells Vix the Countess is leaving most of her money to animal rights, but there will be a small trust set up for her. "I won't be rich but I don't need much living down here and I intend to stay, even after the Countess . . . is no longer with us. This way your father can have his savings for himself and Frankie. So if all goes well, you won't have to worry about taking care of us when we're old. At least we can do that much for you."

Vix is stunned. She'd assumed Tawny had just written them off.

Tawny

THERE, SHE'S DONE IT. She's been practicing for a week and she's finally told Victoria she's a good daughter and deserves only the best. Well, maybe not in so many words but she's sure Victoria got the message. Nice young man. She hopes they'll be happy. Just don't expect anything from her. She's already given everything she has.

———————

TAWNY LIKES GUS. Everybody does. Vix feels incredibly lucky. True, he can make her crazy sometimes but his sense of humor saves them every time. He knows just how to make her laugh. She feels comfortable, yet deliciously sexy with him. They're not afraid to play. Once he suggested she straddle him in the bathtub. *Bite my neck . . .* he'd whispered, *pull my hair . . .* Another time, while they were driving on a country road, she'd smelled peonies and felt so horny she'd unzipped his fly and reached inside his pants. He'd pulled off the road and they'd made love in the car, with the passenger door thrown open and her head hanging down. When she's nestled in his arms she knows the others were just practice. This is for real. There's no way she'll ever be bored with him. She won't let him grow bored with her.

When she takes him to meet the Countess they're greeted by one old dog who sniffs Gus but doesn't even bother with Vix. The Countess pats her bed and tells Gus, "Sit here and let me look at you." He sits beside her. She holds his hands and gazes into his eyes. Finally, she nods and says, "Love's a hard game to play, my darlings. Play it well."

"Stevie Nicks," Vix says.

"Who?" the Countess asks.

"It's the title of a song I used to like."

"Stevie knew what he was talking about."

Vix doesn't tell the Countess Stevie is a *she*. She kisses the Countess on her cheek. The skin feels paper-thin against her lips.

They've decided to marry in September, the best

month on the Vineyard. It will be a small wedding at
Abby's and Lamb's, just family—her father and Frankie,
Gus's parents, his brother and sister-in-law, his sister
and her boyfriend—and a few close friends. Maia and
Paisley joke that maybe one or the other will fall for
Daniel. Vix tells them not to count on it.

They'll be married in the garden by a judge from
Boston, the same one who married Abby and Lamb fifteen years ago.

A week after Maizie's first birthday, about the same time
Vix and Gus are returning from Key West, Caitlin takes
the ferry to Woods Hole, drives to Cambridge with
Maizie, and asks Abby and Lamb to watch her for the
day while she does some shopping. She calls at six to ask
if they can keep Maizie overnight. She's run into an old
friend and they'd like to have dinner together. She
doesn't add that dinner will be on a plane en route to
Paris. But when she next calls that's where she is. She
promises to return in a week, two at the most. Two
weeks turns into two months, two months into two
years.

Bru

HE SHOULD HAVE seen it coming. Maybe he just didn't want to. Maybe that was it. That would be like him. Ignore all the signs. But something was wrong from the start. As soon as the wedding was over she changed. He figured it was the pregnancy. Too soon, maybe. And sick every day. But he knew she'd love being a mother. *Babies*. That's what they all wanted. His cousins complained that once there was a baby around forget it . . . no more sex.

Problem was, she was never like other women. Didn't take to motherhood. Something unnatural about that. And the sex thing . . . she still wanted it. Even more than before. Every day, sometimes twice a day. But taking care of a baby at night wiped him out. Not that she noticed. *Honey, fuck me . . . fuck me, hard. Hurt me, honey . . .*

What did that mean? It wasn't right. They were married. She was a mother. He didn't like it when she talked that way. Especially the *hurt me* part. He'd never wanted to hurt her. Never wanted to hurt any woman.

What do you want? he'd asked her.

It's not what I want, it's what I need.

What . . . what do you need?

A lot of loving.

I don't give you a lot of loving?

She smiled at him, a come-on. *You do, honey . . . you give me a lot of loving.*

Then what? What are you asking for?

Everything.

You've got everything.

She gave him a sad smile.

You need vitamins, he told her. *Vitamins with minerals.*

She laughed.

He didn't care. *And you need to get out of the house more. A job maybe . . .*

I have a job. I'm your wife. I'm Maizie's mother.

Trisha

SHE SHOULD HAVE spent more time with Caitlin after Maizie was born but she was so busy building her dream house with Arthur. Lamb was right. As soon as he'd set her free her life turned around. Of course, if Lamb had chosen her over Phoebe way back when, if *she'd* had his children, none of this would have happened. But what's the point in going on about that now?

Bru looks dazed. The way he looked in church on his wedding day. But did he have to start up with Star again . . . and so soon? As if Caitlin hadn't happened, as if Maizie hadn't?

It's all getting to be too much for her . . . Lamb and his family. But Maizie is so sweet. She'd love to have a baby with Arthur. Is it too late? Maybe they can adopt. Suppose Caitlin had left Maizie with them?

———————

EVERYONE ASSUMES VIX knows more than she's saying, that Caitlin still confides in her. She can tell they don't really believe it when she swears she doesn't have a clue. She's in shock like the rest of them. But at least they know Caitlin is more or less okay. Lamb hired a detective who tracked her down in Barcelona. She signed divorce papers so Bru is free to marry Star, who's seven months pregnant. He didn't waste any time. Vix hates him for that.

How ironic that Caitlin chose to leave her baby with Abby. Or maybe it's what she always wanted for herself —to live with Lamb and Abby, to have a real sense of family—but out of some kind of loyalty to Phoebe she felt she couldn't.

Whenever they visit the Vineyard she and Gus stay in Caitlin's room. Across the hall, in the room the Chicago Boys once shared, is the nursery, where Maizie sleeps clutching a pink pig.

Phoebe

FRANKLY, SHE CAN'T BELIEVE IT. Not that she'd expected the marriage to work. She'd always known it was just another of Caity's games. But Maizie. For God's sake! Even *she* didn't abandon her children. And leaving her with Lamb and Abby. What kind of statement was that?

Oh, please . . . don't tell her Caity wasn't well loved! Don't give her simplistic explanations. While *she* might not have been the most nurturing parent in the history of the universe, she was *there*, for crissakes! And Caity knew Lamb adored her. No, it's something else. Some flaw. She wishes she could put her finger on it. Vix must know but she's not talking.

She'll try to see Caity this summer. She's already changed her plans to include Barcelona. Barcelona of all places. Why not Venice or Paris?

Lamb

HE LIVES WITH A terrible feeling in his gut twenty-four hours a day. He gobbles Maalox tablets by the handful. He cries at the drop of a hat. He can't understand what's happened.

Abby is careful not to blame him, not to blame anyone. Phoebe calls it wanderlust. *Some people are born with it*, she tells him. Whatever it is, he's not sure he can bear it.

She refused to see him in Barcelona. Sent a messenger to his hotel with the name and address of a lawyer in New York instead. *Refused to see him! His precious daughter.* How can he help her if she won't let him? He'll forgive her anything. He just wants her to come home. *Come home, Caitlin, and be a mother to your baby!*

Sharkey

What did they expect?

Abby

SHE THINKS OF Grandmother Somers in her forties, taking in Dorset and Lamb. *She's* past fifty, menopausal, but feels young, younger than she has in years. And more relaxed. Maybe it's the hormones. Maybe it's Maizie.

It's as if she and Lamb have changed places. He's the anxious one now, carrying around a baby monitor, checking on Maizie three or four times during the night. Sometimes she'll find him standing over Maizie's crib, watching her breathe, tears streaming down his face.

He's listening to the Beatles again, for the first time since John Lennon was killed. She tries to reassure him. Maizie will be fine. She'll grow up strong and confident, surrounded by loving adults, with cousins and step-siblings for company. They'll set limits, guide her, teach her to be responsible. But the way he looks at her when she talks about Maizie's future breaks her heart.

She dreads the day Caitlin comes waltzing back into their lives, expecting to take Maizie away with her. Even though Caitlin has signed the papers relinquishing all rights—giving her and Lamb physical custody, while they share legal custody with Bru—she knows biological mothers have an edge in court. But *she* won't give up Maizie easily!

Well, Abby . . . her own mother says, *you've finally got your little girl.*

46

JUST BEFORE HER thirtieth birthday Vix receives an airline ticket in the mail, a ticket to Milan with train connections to Venice, along with a note:

Celebrate the Big Three-O With Me!

Vix is beside herself. Gus asks, "Do you want to see her?"

She's almost six months pregnant with their first child. She can't decide what to do. Can she ever forgive Caitlin for leaving Maizie? "I don't know," she says. "Maybe. I think so. Yes."

"If the doctor says it's okay," he says, kissing her neck, "it's okay with me. I'm not worried you won't come back."

In Venice, Caitlin meets her at the train station. Caitlin is all in white, her hair tucked inside a wide-brimmed straw hat. She's wearing huge designer shades and is carrying a second hat for Vix, who's boiling in a blue denim maternity dress. The conductor helps her off the train with her bag. "God, Vix . . ." Caitlin says, hugging her, "you look so . . ." Vix expects her to say *grownup* but instead she says, *pregnant*. They both laugh.

Caitlin plunks the straw hat on Vix's head and carries her bag to a waiting boat that whisks them to the Gritti Palace, on the Grand Canal.

Their room, overlooking the canal, is huge and the bed linens are actually made of linen. They have two bathrooms, one for each of them. The floor is stone and helps to keep the room cool. Everything is clean, spare, yet unbelievably luxurious. It could be years before she and Gus can afford such a trip, if ever. She gets pangs thinking of him in New York, going to work every day, while she is here in the most romantic city in the world.

Caitlin's Italian sounds like the real thing. Everyone she speaks to responds not as if she's some American tourist but as if she's a native, a northern Italian blonde. Forget bare dirty feet, forget the Dingleberry Award. This Caitlin is elegant. Heads turn to follow her.

She sets up rules. "I get to ask questions, you don't." Vix nods. If that's the way she wants it. Besides, she's always learned more by just listening. Caitlin wants to hear about her life, about her marriage, her work. Vix waits for her to ask about Maizie.

They venture out only in the morning and again at night. She discovers the Italians love pregnant women. No one can do enough for her, including Caitlin, who acts as her private tour guide. They take gondolas the way Paisley takes cabs in New York. They do the cathedrals, the ancient Jewish sector, the Peggy Guggenheim museum, where Caitlin snaps a photo of Vix atop the statue of a well-hung donkey. Caitlin even takes her across the canal by private boat to swim at the Hotel Cipriani, where she knows the manager. At night they meander down narrow cobblestone alleyways to tiny restaurants that should be impossible to find, where they eat freshly prepared fish and delicious pastas.

In the afternoons they close the old wooden shutters in their room and take a long siesta. One day Vix awakens to find Caitlin sitting beside her. "What?" she asks.

Caitlin smiles. "You." She rests her hand on Vix's belly. "This."

"I love being pregnant," Vix says.

"Tell me about Maizie," Caitlin says softly.

"She's wonderful . . . sweet, bright . . ."

"Does she look like me?"

"She's lovely, if that's what you mean. I brought pictures . . ."

Vix reaches for her bag but before she can open it, Caitlin says, "Not yet. I can't do this yet . . . okay?"

Vix mouths her answer without saying it. *Okay*.

On the final morning of Vix's visit, Caitlin says, "I'd like to see those pictures now." They're having breakfast in their room, with the shutters thrown open so they can watch the boats gliding gracefully along the canal.

Vix hands the photos of Maizie to Caitlin and watches as she carefully studies each one. "Is she sad?" Caitlin asks. "She looks sad in this picture."

"Sad? No. She's quiet, sensitive, but I wouldn't describe her as sad. She loves to hear stories about you."

"What do you tell her?"

"About us . . . when we were young. I take her to the Flying Horses. She calls her favorite horse Mudhead."

Caitlin looks away for a minute. "Is she okay with Abby and Lamb?"

"Abby's a . . ." She's about to say that Abby is a good mother, a loving mother, but that would imply Caitlin wasn't, so she stops herself.

"I always thought Abby would be a good mother if she weren't so intense."

"She's more relaxed with Maizie."

Caitlin nods. "What about Bru?"

"He spends time with her, especially in summer."

"That's not what I mean."

"Married to Star, from the health food store. He always had a thing for vitamins."

They laugh for a minute then Caitlin grows serious again. "Do they have . . ."

"A boy and she's pregnant again."

Caitlin sips her cappuccino. This can't be easy for her but Vix reminds herself *she's* the one who left.

"What about you . . ." Caitlin asks. "Are you happy?"

Vix holds her belly. She thinks about how lucky she is to have Gus, the baby that's coming. Her life is filled with friendship and love. She gets teary and homesick thinking of all of them. "Yes, I'm happy," she tells Caitlin.

"No regrets?"

"Regrets?"

"About Bru . . ."

Bru? It's funny, because when she sees him now he's more like an old friend than a lover. They talk about Maizie, about the building bust of the late eighties and

early nineties. Business is picking up again since the
President vacationed on the Vineyard two summers in a
row. The islanders gripe about the influx of the rich and
famous, but the rich and famous are good for the local
economy.

"No regrets about Bru," she tells Caitlin. But she
does have regrets. She regrets that Nathan's life was cut
short, that she and Lanie and Lewis aren't close. Most of
all, she regrets that Caitlin couldn't confide in her,
couldn't ask for her support, because she understands
now that Caitlin must have been deeply troubled to walk
out on Bru, to leave Maizie. So she says, "I have regrets
about you."

"Me?" Caitlin says.

"That you couldn't come to me when you were
struggling," Vix tells her, "when you were in pain."

"You think I was struggling? You think I was in
pain?"

Vix nods.

"Why can't you see me for what I am?" Caitlin asks.
"A self-centered bitch who doesn't give a flying fuck
about anybody but herself, who takes off when the going
gets tough, who lies and cheats to get what she
wants . . . who lies to her best friend just to stay ahead
of the game."

"No," Vix tells her, "that's not who you are."

"I did Maizie the best favor I could by leaving."

Vix shakes her head.

"Aren't you going to ask me how I could do it . . .
how I could abandon my own child? Aren't you going to
tell me what a fuckup I am?"

"I don't have to," Vix says softly.

Caitlin's face crumples and she begins to cry. "I'm useless, worse than Phoebe ever was."

Vix holds her, strokes her hair, tries to comfort her.

"How can you care about me after all I've done to you?"

"To me? I don't think that's the issue . . ."

"But it is. I used you. I took everything I could from you."

"I never saw it that way. I was grateful just to be your friend."

"Then you're a fool," Caitlin says. She fishes a tissue from the pocket of her linen dress and blows her nose. "I'm thinking of marrying again."

Vix is caught off guard.

"His family is from Tuscany. They own vineyards." She laughs. "Isn't that fitting? But they have business in Milan, too. Actually, that's where I met Antonio. He's handsome, thirty-seven, never married. He's perfect except he's a mama's boy. But then, all Italian men are. He wants bambini, of course. He doesn't know about Maizie. But how long can I keep her a secret?"

Vix can't imagine keeping Maizie a secret. Someday Maizie is going to want to know Caitlin. She's going to come looking for her.

"I'm going to decide this afternoon," Caitlin says, "after I put you on the train to Milan. I'm going out in my sailboat to think it through. I've always been able to think more clearly on the water. And by the time you get back to New York, I'll have made my decision. I'll call you and say yes or no . . . just that much."

Vix waits for the message on her answering machine. She waits for Caitlin to say *yes* or *no*. But there are no messages.

Epilogue

A YEAR LATER they gather on the Vineyard to dedicate a wildflower meadow overlooking the sea to Caitlin. It's magic hour, just before sunset, when the light is so extraordinary it makes Vix believe in the possibility of heaven. They're a small group—Abby and Lamb with Maizie; Sharkey with Wren, who's pregnant, and her little girl, Natasha; Bru and Star and their babies; Von and Patti and their trio; Trisha and Arthur.

Daniel, who has flown in from Chicago, is staying with Gus and Vix in the little house they've rented for the week in West Tisbury. She and Gus have been talking about moving to the island full time if only they can figure out a way to support themselves doing what they want.

Daniel is still single, still waiting for the perfect woman to show up. Abby has asked him to please turn off his cellular phone during the dedication.

Phoebe sent regrets. She'd be out of the country. Dorset can't make it either, but promises to think of them from her home in Mendocino, where she moved following Grandmother's death, just shy of her ninety-ninth birthday.

Abby starts off by reading from Shelley. Wren, who is so shy she makes Sharkey seem gregarious, surprises all of them by singing the Beatles' "Yesterday," in a clear, beautiful soprano. Sharkey loses it halfway through the song. Lamb embraces him, his own face streaked with tears, the two men comforting one another.

Didn't she know how much she was loved? Didn't she care? Vix wonders if somewhere in Tuscany a handsome man who also loved her is grieving. Or was he another of Caitlin's fantasies?

Vix planned on reading the essay she'd written for her college application—*Caitlin Somers, the Most Influential Person in My Life*—but realizes at the last minute she can't, so Gus reads it for her while Vix holds their baby, Nate, who tries to shove the turquoise beads Vix wears around her neck into his mouth.

Maizie, who is five, skips up and down in a floral pinafore, scattering rose petals into the wind. She says she remembers Caitlin but Vix doesn't think that's possible. What she remembers are the stories Vix has told her, the stories Maizie calls *Caitlin Summers*, and the albums of photos she and Vix pore over whenever she visits. Caitlin is just a fantasy figure to Maizie, someone to dream about, someone from another time and place. She doesn't really understand what they're doing here, except that it's some kind of party, a party for Caitlin, her birth mother. Vix doesn't understand either. She's tried to make sense of it but she can't. No one can explain what happened that day. There was no storm in the area. Winds were moderate. They found her boat two days later, drifting, but there was no sign of trouble. There isn't any evidence she was lost at sea, except for the little boat and her plan to go sailing. There's no way Vix or anyone else will ever know the truth. The truth is with Caitlin, wherever she is.

Sometimes Vix hears Caitlin reminding her, *No matter how many guys come and go we'll always be together*. She hears her infectious laugh or that seductive voice, whispering, *I'll always love you. Promise you'll always love me?*

Two days later Vix rides her bike out to the wildflower meadow by herself. She kneels at the stone, which they have all been careful to call *commemorative* rather than *memorial*. She runs her fingers over the engraved letters.

In Celebration of Caitlin Somers
August 1996

Alone on the bluff, with the sound of waves crashing below, Vix unleashes her anger. "Damn you for leaving! For not caring enough about us!" She shouts and screams at Caitlin, going on and on about friendship and love, refusing to believe either that Caitlin is gone forever or that she, who was so terrified of disappearing, has orchestrated her own disappearance. Could she possibly be so cruel?

Vix blames herself, too. How could she have missed Caitlin's desperation? She was the last one to see her. Surely she could have done something. She dissolves into tears. She cries the way she did when she left Caitlin the morning after her seventeenth birthday. She cries the way she did driving back from Santa Fe with Bru, great gut-wrenching sobs, until there's nothing left. Finally, she lies beside the stone and sleeps.

When she awakens she's thirsty. Her breasts are full, her nipples are beginning to leak. She has to get back for Nate's feeding. She reaches into her bag and pulls out a pure white beach stone. She places it atop Caitlin's stone. "The next time I see you *I* get to ask the questions," she tells her. Then she laughs. She laughs thinking of Caitlin listening to her, blathering about friendship and love.

Sometimes Vix thinks when the Big Four-O comes along she'll get an envelope from some exotic place and inside will be an airline ticket and a note—*Come celebrate with me.* Gus will say, "Go . . . don't worry about the kids." So she'll go. Caitlin will meet her at the airport, her hair flying in the wind. After they hug Vix will hold Caitlin at arm's length for a minute. *God, Caitlin*, she'll say, *You look so . . . grownup.*

And Caitlin will laugh and answer, *It's about time, don't you think?*

© MARION ETTLINGER

JUDY BLUME's twenty-two books, including the *New York Times* bestsellers *Wifey* and *Smart Women*, have sold over sixty-five million copies worldwide and have been translated into twenty languages. She spends summers on Martha's Vineyard with her family.

In the summer of 1977, Victoria Leonard's world change
forever—when Caitlin Somers chose her as a friend. Dazzling
reckless Caitlin welcomed Vix into the heart of her sprawling
eccentric family, opening doors to a world of unimaginabl
privilege, sweeping her away to vacations on Martha's Vine
yard, a magical, wind-blown island where two friend
became summer sisters. . . .

SUMMER SISTERS

Now, years later, Vix is working in New York City. Caitlin i
getting married on the Vineyard. And the early magic of thei
long, complicated friendship has faded. But Caitlin has begged
Vix to come to her wedding, to be her maid of honor. And Vix
knows that she will go—for the friend whose casual betrayal
she remembers all too well. Because Vix wants to understand
what happened during that last shattering summer. And, after
all these years, she needs to know why her best friend—
her summer sister—still has the power to break her heart. . . .

US $7.50 / $10.99 CAN

ISBN 0-440-22643-0

A Main
Selection
of the
Literary Guild

22643

0 71009 00750 5

S

COVER PRINTED IN USA